Releasing Kate
novel

D. KELLY

Copyright © 2014 D. Kelly

Editing by - Tiffany Tillman

Cover design by - Regina Wamba of www.maeidesign.com

    This book is a work of fiction. Any references to historical events, real people, or real places are used fictitiously. Other names, characters, places, and events are products of the author's imagination, and any resemblance to actual events or places or persons living or dead is entirely coincidental.

    All rights reserved, including the right to reproduce this book or portions thereof in any form whatsoever. For information contact Dee Kelly www.dkellyauthor.com

    This book contains mature subject matter and is not appropriate for minors. Please note this novel contains profanity, sexual situations and alcohol consumption.

Dee Kelly

P.O. Box 630185

Simi Valley, CA. 93063

Books by D. Kelly

The Acceptance Series –

Breaking Kate – Book One

Catching Kate – A novella Book 1.5

Releasing Kate – Book Two

Coming Soon –

Loving Kate – Book Three of The Acceptance Series, March 2015

Just an Illusion – Spring 2015

Dedication

This book is dedicated to my street team, D's Divine Divas. Without the strength, love, and support of these amazing women, I don't know where I would be. They are my pickle pimping, margarita loving, sombrero wearing, Friday night story telling crew. They are not only my friends, but have become family, and I love them more than they could possibly know. We are going to take Vegas by storm next November and I can't wait! I love you girls and I hope I do you proud. Thank you for all your love and support.

Releasing Kate

"Ever has it been that love knows not its own depth until the hour of separation."
— Khalil Gibran

Prologue

Connor – Six weeks after the engagement party

"Don't, Connor, just DON'T! Kate is my best friend—my fucking sister—but she is out of her ever loving, god damn mind! What the hell was she thinking tonight? She just crossed the most uncrossable line, and of course there was no reasoning with her because she was so damn drunk."

As she walks toward me, I can see exactly when her anger slowly begins to dissipate into sadness. This happens whenever she gets worked up over Kate and her situation, which has been a lot lately. "I know, Jess, but put yourself in her shoes for a minute. How would you be acting if the two loves of your life were playing tug of war with you? I'll be the first to admit her tequila habit is an issue, but after what she thought she saw tonight, can you blame her?"

"Yes I can because she's smart enough not to drink herself to the point of oblivion. Her actions have a trickledown effect and we're *all* going to have to deal with the consequences."

She's so stubborn.

"She did what I told her to, she let loose, she was having a good time; she *almost* looked like our Kate again. With all the chaos in her life right now, that's a *good* thing."

"Why are you defending her?"

"I'm not defending her, but before we judge her, we need to assume she knows what she was doing. I'm not sure she was *that* drunk, either, but our girl is heartbroken with a capital H. All else aside, we just have to be there for her when she finally succumbs to the pain and falls. Unfortunately, that's going to happen sooner rather than later, but maybe that's a good thing. Once she breaks and lets it all out, only then will she begin to heal."

Taking her hand in mine, I pull her into a tight embrace. She clings to me in desperation, as if I'm her anchor. Her mood is one of sadness and longing. During the last few weeks, we haven't had a whole lot of time for ourselves. Instead, we've been managing our friends, trying to keep them sane and from inflicting bodily harm on each other. All of it is putting a strain on our relationship. We haven't had much alone time and forgot our sex-a-thons. I make a mental note to find a way to change that real soon.

"Go upstairs and take a nice, relaxing bath. I'll wait up for Kate and talk her off the ledge when she gets home, *if* she gets home. Besides, you're way too worked up to talk to her gently and I don't think she can handle more than a gentle discussion, not after tonight."

Jess sobs into my chest, clutching on to my shirt extra tight as her tears begin to fall. I brush them aside tenderly with my fingers and tilt her head up so I can kiss the rest away. It kills me when she cries, and she's been crying a lot lately.

"I just... I just... damn, Connor, I just love her so fucking much, you know? She was happy. For the first time in years she was my Kate again. There was light in her eyes, happiness in her laugh, and so much love in her heart. I'm losing her slowly this time and it's worse than before. She's self-destructing right in front of our eyes and none of us are going to come out of this unscathed."

She's right. After tonight, the boundaries of our friendships are going to be put to the test.

"I'm exhausted and my feet hurt, so I'm going to take you up on your offer to deal with her. I'm the last person she'll want to see, anyway. Just don't stay up too late, okay? I have a feeling her bed isn't going to be slept in." She places the whisper of a kiss on my lips, and instead of those fuck me heels she had on all night being wrapped around my neck, they're now in her hands as she drags herself up the stairs.

When did our happy group become the biggest episode of *Dawson's Creek* ever written? Yes, I went there, don't judge. April made us watch the whole damn series with her when she had her tonsils out. However, in our version of the creek I would be the straight version of Jack. I guess that makes Kate our resident Joey, Mike would be Dawson, and Daniel would be

Pacey. On the show, where Pacey clearly violated every rule known to man by stealing his best friend's girl, it's the flipside over here. In our creek, Dawson, aka Mike, is clearly in the wrong. He gave up any and all rights to Kate when he stormed out of her life four years ago, never to return. Daniel is devastated but determined, and Jake has taken Mike's side in all of it which makes things difficult. I'm trying to stay neutral. I love them, but my priority is Kate. In their defense, they are trying to be amicable, but how they're going about it leaves a bad taste in my mouth. It doesn't always work, though, and things can get tense between them. Thankfully, it's typically not when Kate's around. Thank god for that because that is *the* last thing she needs to worry about. They need to work that shit out themselves and leave her out of it. This isn't on Kate's shoulders—it shouldn't be—this whole mess is between them. While Kate is being the strong one, the moral one, the one standing up for family, and for friendship, they're being pig-headed assholes in the midst of the biggest pissing match I have ever seen. They're all hurting and will likely continue to do so until after the baby comes, and then who knows what will happen.

I can see it in Kate's eyes, though; she's in love with them both. After hearing about her past with Mike and knowing how her fairytale with Daniel started, I can see why. After what they've been doing the past few weeks it's just making those feelings stronger. I wouldn't want to be in her shoes; it's an impossible decision. I know who she belongs with, who her heart leans to. I can hear it when she speaks, see it in her expressions. But tonight she took the path unchosen—the one that might lead her to temporary bliss—but it's going to leave a trail of destruction in its wake. She essentially opened Pandora's Box. Let's just pray when it's all said and done that hope still remains in the bottom of the box.

The sound of keys jiggling in the lock awakens me from a broken sleep. When I look at my watch, I see it's almost five thirty in the morning. There's a blanket over me that wasn't there before. Jess must have come down and covered me; I can't believe I didn't notice. I'd give anything to be wrapped in her arms right now, but tonight, well actually morning now, I *know* Kate's going to need me more. I'm sure Jess knows it, too, which is why she didn't wake me.

Kate opens the door and immediately locks it behind her.

Good girl.

As she turns around, she lets her shoes fall from her hands and drop to the floor. She leans against the door and slides down to the floor. Her cheeks are stained with tears, with endless more falling as she hugs her knees and buries her head into them. My heart breaks for her because I know her bottom has finally fallen out. Taking the blanket with me, I cross the room, dropping to the floor beside her. I proceed to cover her with the blanket and wrap her in my embrace.

"Connor, oh god what have I done?" Her words are expelled between massive sobs that show no signs of slowing down. I can empathize with her, but I've never been in this situation. All I know is whatever I say, it needs to be said carefully, so I don't make things worse. I wish Jess was here, but ever since Kate found out about the message Jess kept from her a few years ago things have been tense between them to say the least.

"It's going to be okay, baby girl. Whatever happens next, you just need to trust it will *all* be okay."

She continues to sob while I rub her back, trying to calm her down. Using my free hand, I pull her hair away from her face.

"You don't know what I did tonight, Connor. I can't take it back, no matter how hard I try, I can't take it back. They're going to hate me and I deserve it." I've got a good idea what she did tonight. You'd have to be a fool not to know, but I don't say anything. She needs comforting, not scolding.

"No they won't, Katie Grace, they won't hate you. No one could ever hate you. They're going to be pissed. *Really, really,* pissed. But *you* didn't do anything wrong. You're not in a relationship with them. *Either* of them. They'll get over it. At one time or another we've all done something we shouldn't have, something in our lives we've regretted along the way. It happens and we learn from it. That's why they're called mistakes and no one can keep us from making them, because if they did we would never learn the lesson we're supposed to gain from them."

Her sobs are beginning to slow and she's even wiping her tears away from her bloodshot eyes. This is a good sign, something I can work with.

"I don't regret it *at all* but I was *so* mad, Connor. I've never felt that kind of anger and pain before and I finally understood."

"Understood what?" I'm officially lost now.

"Why Mike did what he did, why he left me all those years ago. And in that instant, tonight, when I let all of that anger consume me, I couldn't blame him anymore. Because I get it now."

I let out a low whistle and try to wrap my head around this piece of information.

"So what now?"

She sits up against me, shoulder to shoulder, and leans her head against mine.

"Now, I deal with the fallout. I'm not going any further down this rabbit hole. Mike did it for years and look where it got him. I did it for one night; I'm not equipped for this. I can't cover pain with pleasure; it just hurts more in the end."

"You just went about it wrong, baby girl. Mike's rabbit hole was filled with nothing but strangers. Yours was a little too close to heart. Not that I'm encouraging your delinquent behavior, but next time try the stranger route. If you want, I can try and find Aimee and Julie for you."

Ouch, she socked me, hard. Too soon to joke, I guess.

"Not funny," she replies with a pout.

I place a kiss on top of her head. "No, I suppose not. I just wanted to lighten things up a bit."

"Next time, tell me a dirty joke. I don't want to think about the two of them with the two of *them*."

She shudders next to me. "I still can't believe those assholes kept that a secret all this time. But you're not enjoying this conversation at all so let's change the subject. What's your plan?"

Sighing, she replies, "Well, I'm sure since I snuck out I'm going to have some shit to deal with tomorrow aside from the stuff I already have to deal with."

"Umm, yeah, about that, I guess now is as good of time as any to tell you. He was there tonight. He went to talk to you, and he wanted to clear things up. He saw you, Kate. He knows. And he was devastated."

"Well I saw him, too. Earlier, remember?"

"Sometimes, looks can be deceiving. I tried to tell you I didn't think he would do that. Not now, not with everything going on. If you would have talked to him you might have had a different opinion."

Rage flashes in her eyes and she scrambles to her feet.

"So you're on his side now? Whatever, Connor, I don't need this, not from you and *most definitely* not right now."

Damn she's pissed.

She spins around and starts to run away but I'm faster than she is. Reaching out, I grab her around the waist, pulling her into me.

"Stop it. I know you're hurt and you're reeling from more than just what happened tonight. *Even* if you won't admit it to yourself. I'm not on anyone's side here but yours. Haven't you realized by now? That I'm in this for the long haul with you? I'm being honest with you because that's what *you* deserve. You reacted to what you saw, or *thought* you saw tonight. You're human and it happens, but now it's caused a domino effect. Things have been falling down around you in rapid succession for weeks; it was only a matter of time before you snapped. All you can do now is OWN it, ACCEPT it, EMBRACE it, and MOVE ON from it. You made a choice and now they can all either live with it or get the fuck off."

She relaxes into me and her tears hit my hands as they fall.

"I just don't know what to do anymore. I don't know how to be me without them. *Either* of them."

After gently kissing the top of her head, I spin her around and wipe away her tears. I hate that we've missed out on so many years of our lifelong friendship.

"I don't know, either, but I'll be here with you until you figure it out, I promise."

Chapter One – Kate

Six weeks earlier

Everyone's downstairs; I heard Daniel and Mike begin to argue, but as quickly as it started, it stopped. I'm sure Connor and Jess squashed it. I'm not immune to this situation. I know I'm withdrawn and likely came off cold when I told them what occurred last night. But it was the only way I could get through the conversation without collapsing on the floor and crying my soul right out of my body. Sounds dramatic, right? That's because it is, but it's also the truth. Maybe this is karma paying me back. I've always had empathy for people, but I've never understood those who say they're in love with two people and don't know how to choose one. I've always considered their situation a self-made mess because the truth of the matter is that if you loved the first person with all your heart and soul you would have never been able to fall in love with the second. Now I realize that what I previously thought was black and white has a *really* wide margin for grey.

I am in love with Daniel—head over heels, catch my breath, heart skipping a beat, butterflies in my stomach, would throw myself in front of a train to save him kind of love. Daniel is everything I ever hoped to find in the man I want to spend my life with. I've envisioned our life already—our home, our kids, our family, our happily ever after. Daniel is the epitome of the definition of one true love and soul mate.

Then there's Mike, my Michael, the boy who made my world work when it crumbled at my fingertips. I don't have any memories from the time I was seven years old until I was nineteen that don't include him. He was the one who walked me to school every day and got me home safe and sound every night. He's the boy who kissed me for the first time so gently as well as being the first one to kiss me breathless. Our love was all-encompassing and strengthened by our lifelong friendship. He would do anything for me then…or now…I can still see it in his eyes. And I would do anything for him, even after everything we've been through. We shared a child, and even if she wasn't meant for this lifetime, it is an unbreakable bond that holds us together. I've missed him so much. I should be happy having him back in my life, but not under these circumstances.

My time with Michael has passed, and although I have a never-ending amount of love *for* him, I'm not in love *with* him. Unfortunately, I can see those lines being easily blurred because of our past. I guess that is where those shades of grey come into play. If this was only about love I would get my happily ever after with Daniel. Everyone deserves to be made love to and fucked by a man who can give it in equal doses all while covering you in a love so strong you'll never want to let go. I can't imagine finding anyone else I connect with on that level…ever again.

Michael was my great love and Daniel is my true love. Now, if and when I ever find love again, I'm going to have to settle for less. What's left? Comfortable love? Companionable love? Damn sure *not* forever love. I'll never again believe in forever love. I thought I had forever love with both of them, but now I know all we'll ever be is friends. Friends, god it sounds like such a fucking joke right now. My mind tells me I'm being smart, that this is the best decision for us all. Eventually, we'll all be good friends and more than that; we'll be family. That's what's important in this life: family, the ones we're given and the ones we make. Michael and Daniel are family, and no matter how much I hate not being with Daniel I'll get over it. I won't be responsible for the loss of their friendship by picking one over the other. In the beginning, it will be rough for them, but eventually they'll move past it and their friendship *and* brotherhood will remain intact. I only wish I could say the same for my heart.

Once we know who the father of Vanessa's baby is maybe we can find a new reality. At that point, I'm sure whoever the father is will be in Vanessa's life. How could he not be?

They both want a family someday so I'm sure they'll try for the sake of the baby. At that point, I can reconsider my decision, but for now, all I can do is take this day by day and see what happens.

There's a light knock on my door and it opens before I answer. I check my reflection in the mirror before turning around. I look tired; the bags under my eyes are horrendous. It really doesn't even matter what I look like. At this point, the day is going to get worse before it can ever have a chance of getting better. There's nothing like breaking up with the love of your life and then taking your ex to meet his dead daughter, the one you couldn't save, to start off your day.

"Kate. Did you hear me? I said the car is here and waiting for you." Connor's looking at me with concern. He's grasping a bouquet of gardenias in his hand, tentatively holding them out to me. I take them from him gratefully. I don't ever see Lila Hope without taking her gardenias.

"Sorry, Connor, I was lost in my thoughts. Thanks for letting me know and for the flowers. How did you know?"

"Jess asked me last night if I could pick them up. She told me you always take them to the cemetery so Lila can always recognize your scent." I nod with understanding.

"I know it's silly because she's not really there, but if her soul can somehow connect to the smell…I don't know, it just makes me feel better."

He pulls me into a comforting hug. "It's not silly, it's motherly. Are you sure you can do this alone? I can follow you guys in case it gets to be too much."

I love him. He's going to make someone such a great husband someday. "No, this is something I have to do alone, just Mike and I, but thank you for offering. I really do appreciate it."

"Anything for you, Kate, you know that. After today you're going to be starting a whole new chapter in your life. Keep an open mind for things yet to come. Once they cool down a bit, this might blow over."

Giving him a sad smile, I reply, "I think that's pretty wishful thinking, Connor, but I love you for trying to give me hope where there isn't any."

"There's always hope, Kate, don't ever forget that."

"I can't believe in hope right now. I did that when Mike left and look where it got me."

After grabbing my purse off of my bed, and with flowers in hand, I head downstairs, mentally preparing myself for the heartbreak ahead. Thankfully, Jess has Mike outside in the car already. Daniel is sitting at the table with his head in his hands.

He looks how I feel… like shit. He tries to talk to me, but I just can't right now.

"Kate, I just…"

"Daniel, I can't. Not now, okay? I'm sorry I couldn't be what you needed." I move to take off the ring; the one I swore would never come off of my hand. His eyes widen in horror and he raises his hands.

"No, Kate, don't take it off…please not now. Let's talk about this." Tears are welling up in his eyes and I know this is hurting him as much as it is me. Taking his hand in mine, I place the ring in his palm, closing his fingers over it, and I miss it immediately. Not only the ring itself, but his love and the security that come with it.

"I'm sorry, Daniel, but I can't keep it. We'll talk tonight, I promise. I said I'll text you on my way home and I will, but wearing this ring any longer isn't right. You deserve so much more than I can give you." The first tear falls from his eyes and I rush outside to the car before breaking down completely. I never, *ever*, wanted to be the cause of Daniel's pain.

Jess hugs me tight before I get into the car. "I'm here if you need me, Katie Grace." I nod to acknowledge her and get into the car. I place the flowers and my purse between Mike and me in the backseat of the town car and let the driver know we're ready to go. Thankfully, we ride in silence for a little while before Mike decides to talk to me.

"Katherine…"

"It's Kate!" I snap at him and he's taken aback. That was completely uncalled for and I feel like such a bitch.

"Sorry…Kate."

"No, Michael… Mike, I'm sorry. I shouldn't have snapped at you, especially when I just did the same thing. Guess we've got a lot of catching up to do, don't we?" Even though we're talking, I can't make eye contact with him. This is going to be so much harder than I could have ever imagined. The cemetery Lila Hope is in is an hour and a half away from my house. This is going to be a long ride.

"Yes, I guess we do." He sighs loudly and runs his hand through his hair, that's his sign he's stressed out. I'm acutely aware that a small piece of me wants to hug him and take care of him like he took care of me for so many years.

"I know sorry doesn't even begin to cover what I did to you, but I'm hoping you can accept my apology. Kate. I… I let my mom and Tom convince me of things I later came to realize couldn't be true. At least not about you. I've still never come to a conclusion about your dad."

He has no clue what's been going on. Not only do I have to tell him about Lila Hope, I have to tell him about Tom Beringer and what he did to us. I close my eyes and silently count to ten, running my fingers across the place where Daniel's ring used to be.

"Kate, where's your ring?" Great time for him to choose to be extra observant. I finally look up at him and *really* look at him. The tenderness in his eyes is unexpected; he really cares that my ring is gone. I hope it's not because he thinks I want him back.

"I gave it back to Daniel before I left. It's not fair to him for me to give him false hope about where we stand by wearing his ring." A few tears fall from my eyes and I quickly wipe them away.

"I'm sorry, Kate. Sorry you're hurting, sorry I left you in the first place, and I'm so sorry I've been *such* an asshole for so long. But I'm not sorry that I'm here with you, I'm not sorry I wrote you that letter, and I'm *not* sorry you broke up with Daniel. I know I don't have much ground to stand on, but I'm *going* to fight for you, Kate. I want you back. I'm a different man now and I want us to get to know each other again. I know we've both changed and we can't pick up where we left off. I'm okay with that. Don't answer me now, Kate, just know I'm here and I'm not going *anywhere* ever again. I want to be friends again. *I miss you* and I've *never* stopped loving you, not for a second."

Those tears I had wiped away are now falling faster than I can control. When I reach for my purse to grab some tissues, Mike grabs my hand, pulls it to his mouth and kisses it. I don't even know how to begin to describe the feeling that washes over me when he does it. It makes me feel at home but also like we're in another time and place. Gently, I pull my hand away and finally find those tissues I was looking for. I was hoping to not tell him about Lila Hope until we were closer to the cemetery. Now I've got that chance by telling him about Tom.

"I know you're sorry, Mike, I can tell, but I just can't think about it right now. We've got time to address those demons later. I missed you, too, even though I didn't want to. There's so much to talk about but first we need to talk about your mom, Tom, my dad, and what happened on Friday."

I've definitely got his attention, so I repeat the conversations I had with my dad and his mom to him verbatim. I watch him go through all the emotions I went through: anger, disbelief, pain, sadness and acceptance. I pass him a few tissues when we get to the part about Grant and hold his hand while he cries. Every part of me wants to comfort him, but this is the only way I can allow myself to let him in right now.

Time passes faster than I would have liked, and before I even get the opportunity to explain where we're going or what happened after he left, we pull into the cemetery.

Chapter Two – Mike

I figured merging my old life into my new one might be problematic. Never could I have imagined how difficult it was actually going to be. I feel like such an asshole, especially now. Daniel and I have *never* fought over a girl, not even once. We've shared them easily enough but there's no sharing Kate and we both know it. Kate knows it, too, which is why she's drawing the line and putting her heart back in its protective armor. Can't say that I blame her at all; this situation is quite the mess.

Hearing about all the things I've missed out on is difficult. What's even more difficult is I've known her long enough to know she's keeping something from me. Something big and I'm not sure what could be bigger than what Tom did to us all. I cried when she told me about my dad. Tears of anger, sadness, and frustration fell, and with them came the feelings of guilt and regret. I knew she was innocent in it all. Instead of pushing things aside, I should have fought my way back home to her sooner. Kate is my home, wherever she is, that's where my heart belongs.

As the car slows, it dawns on me we're at the cemetery where my dad is buried, where Lila is buried. Why is Kate bringing me to see our parents? Is she looking for closure since I refused to let her come to my dad's funeral? If I could take it back I would...Hell, if I could take it *all* back I would. When I look over at Kate, her eyes are filled with sorrow and tears are starting to fall. She's struggling for words and reaches out and grasps my hand.

"I knew this day would come and I've thought about how to explain to you all you need to know. I've just never been able to figure out a way that would make this any less painful for either of us."

The pain she's feeling is palpable and fuck if I'm not going to do whatever I can to right her world again. "Will you please come with me, Mike?" She doesn't even have to ask. I would go with her anywhere. I nod my head, suddenly not able to find my words. I've got a sinking feeling my world is about to change.

We step out of the car into a secluded area of the cemetery. My dad is buried right around here. This area had just opened when he passed away, it's beautiful. There are giant oak trees shading the area and a creek that runs along the backside of the road. There are now two benches here as well, one on each side of the tree, that weren't here before.

"You wanted to come with me to see my dad? I'm so sorry, Kate; I never should have done what I did." She cuts me off, still holding my hand and leading me to my dad. "No, Mike, this has nothing to do with Grant."

I don't understand. It seems like this has everything to do with him.

"Michael..." Her voice is pained and filled with sadness.

Her eyes are pleading with mine, but for what I don't know. All I know is that in all the years I've known her, I've never seen the sorrow on her face that I see now. I have a sickening feeling I'm the reason she feels it.

"I don't know where to start or how to do this."

She begins sobbing and I pull her in for a hug but she quickly pulls away, wiping her tears from her face. I want to comfort her, but I also want to give her the space she needs. As she leads the way, I follow a few steps behind. Every few seconds, she glances over her shoulder to be sure I'm still following.

When she stops, I watch her place a kiss into her palm and touch the headstone in front of her. She lets her hand linger there for longer than I would expect and then places the flowers gingerly along the bottom. It's a very loving and intimate moment that stops me in my tracks, allowing her the privacy I think she needs. After a brief moment passes, she motions me forward. As I reach her, I glance down at the headstone.

Lila Hope Matthews

January 2011

'The angels caught you before you could fall. You are forever loved as you fly amongst them, gracing us with your blinding light. You are loved, always."

I look up at Kate only to see she's crying again. Then I look back down and read it again, and again, and again.

This can't be happening.

"Ours?" I choke out.

"Yes," she whispers.

As I fall to my knees, a howl escapes me. My eyes are clouded with tears that are falling uncontrollably. This can't be. All I e*ver* wanted was a baby with Kate, a family, *our* family. A little girl. I had a little girl...*had*...I *had* a little girl.

"NO." I scream through my tears as a pain unlike anything I've ever felt before takes a permanent hold on my soul.

"No, no, no, no, no," the words come out in wails. Kate drops to her knees and hugs me. I can't bring myself to look at her, but I let her hold me in her loving embrace. The sorrow on her face was because we lost a child. It's a sorrow no one should *ever* experience. It's not natural; parents shouldn't outlive their children. There's a natural order to things and this isn't it.

"I'm so sorry, Michael. I tried so hard to get her here. I tried so hard to take care of her, but she was taken from me anyway. I'm so, so, sorry."

Both of us are crying uncontrollably as I pull her onto my lap and hold her in my arms. I don't think I could get closer to her if I tried and yet we still aren't close enough. We're trying to comfort each other, to ease each other's pain, but I don't think this kind of pain can ever get easier. We sit in silence for a long time and finally when my tears start to slow, I reach up and wipe hers away. Her scent is enveloping me in a cocoon of love and I don't even give kissing her a second thought. Our kiss is slow and sorrowful and beautiful and makes me long for more. She opens to me briefly and when I taste her, my heart floods with the love I never thought we'd find again. I've missed her so much.

She pulls away, shaking her head. "This isn't... we can't... not here... not now." I rest my head against hers. "I know. I'm sorry. Can you please tell me what happened?" Nodding, she points to the bench. I help her up and we sit.

"We tried to get in touch with you, but you had disappeared. I knew you would call or text or something eventually. I had my phone on all the time. Even in class. I knew you were hurt, and running scared, but I also knew you better than anyone and I knew *us*. I always knew you would come back...it was just a matter of time."

I continue watching her with a newfound intensity and more than a lifetime's worth of regret.

"I didn't find out I was pregnant for a while. I was a mess when you left. I didn't eat, I wasn't sleeping, I couldn't focus in my classes... When I *could* eat, I threw up almost immediately. I was a mess—I was stressed and heartbroken. Then one day, I passed out right in front of Jess and she was terrified something was happening to me like my mom. She took me to the hospital and that's when I found out."

"How long after I left?"

"A few months... October."

October

The message I left her was in October. Jess told me to come back. Jess told me she was in the hospital.

What have I done?

"As it turned out, I was suffering extreme dehydration and depression and I was three months pregnant. They admitted me to the hospital and assigned me a counselor. I knew I wanted the baby with all my heart, but I needed help to understand it was all going to be okay. The counselor was great. She worked with me, and every day after that I did a little bit better than I did the day before."

She closes her eyes and releases a sigh.

"I still held on to hope that you would come back. I talked to her every single day, making sure to let her know how much she was loved by the *both* of us. How excited I was to meet her and how when you stopped grieving you were going to be so happy to meet her."

She has no idea how happy I would have been.

"How did you get pregnant? You were always so careful."

She laughs, but it sounds hollow "Antibiotics decrease the pills' effectiveness."

"The Bahamas?" I ask, but I already know the answer.

"Yup, our island paradise. It makes sense. Beauty created in beautiful surroundings."

I wished her pregnant for so long. I grasp her hand in mine and squeeze it.

"If I had known, Kate, I would have been here. You know that, right? All I ever wanted was a family with you. I'm so sorry," I tell her, hanging my head in shame.

"I…I didn't know. I didn't realize, you only mentioned it twice."

"Yeah, and you freaked out so I let it go. I knew it would happen eventually but I would dream about it, hope for it, and when it finally did I missed it all."

She opens her purse and pulls out a small frame and hands it to me. It's an ultrasound, a 3D one and I can see her face. *Oh my god, I can see my baby girl's face.* It's the most amazing thing I've ever seen in my life. Tears are falling from my eyes onto the glass of the frame and I quickly wipe them off with a tissue. When I hand the frame back to her she shakes her head.

"That one is yours; I've been waiting for a long time to give it to you."

"Thank you."

She nods. "Since you weren't around, I kept a journal. It's at the house. It's not much because it's only about three months' worth of entries. I'll give it to you later; it's an accounting of her growth and mine. How it felt when she kicked. Little things like that. You weren't here, but I knew you were coming back, and we would be an 'us' again. I didn't want you to miss anything. It was my way of sharing her and the experience with you even though you weren't there."

"You should hate me," I reply sadly

"I did, or at least I *thought* I did, but I was just hurt. I went through a lot, and I was broken. Jess and I went from planning our classes around each other so one of us could always be with the baby to planning a funeral in the span of three months. I've never felt the kind of pain I felt back then. I was hoping you would come back because I was absolutely lost without you. My heart was broken and then when I lost Lila Hope, I never thought I would be whole again."

"So what happened?"

"We were heading up to see Maryanne for the weekend and we were in a car accident. It was just an unfortunate chain of events—a car blew a tire and it all spun out of control from there. It wasn't a big accident, pretty slow speed, actually. We ended up hitting the center divider but with just enough speed for the airbags to deploy. The airbag hit my abdomen just the right way and caused a placental abruption. I hemorrhaged and needed a blood transfusion. Eventually they got control of the bleeding and I should still be able to have kids, but Lila Hope was gone before they could even get her out."

I lose it all over again and am overcome with the need to be as close as I can to my little girl. Before I know it, I'm sitting at the base of her headstone.

"It was just a random, freak accident?"

"Yes. Jess blamed herself for a long time because she was driving, but I knew it wasn't her fault and that helped me heal. By convincing Jess it was just an accident, I was also able to convince myself that was the truth."

Now I know why Jess got rid of her Audi; she would have never been able to get in it again after that. Poor Jess. I know how she thinks and I'm sure she carries a big burden of guilt over all of this.

"How far along were you?"

"Twenty six weeks, so about six and a half months."

"I wasn't here for her *or* for you. Kate, how could I have missed it? I missed my own daughter's funeral. God... I missed her... funeral. I missed it, I missed it all. I didn't get to say goodbye. She didn't *know* I *loved* her. I would have loved her so much. She would have been my whole world, you both would have. God, Kate, I'm *so* sorry. I know it's not enough, it will *never* be enough, but I'm so *fucking* sorry."

My heart is officially shattered, so much so I don't understand how I'm even still alive. Yet I'm still here and I'm still breathing while my little girl is in a box underneath me. Kate's sitting with me now, holding my hand like she'll never let it go. Suddenly, I realize this is just the beginning of my pain, but for her this is closure. I don't even know how to begin processing that fact.

"She knew, Michael. I *promise* you, she knew. I told her every day how much we both loved her. No one even really knew I was even pregnant. I mean, it was noticeable, but aside from the doctors, only Jess, Maryanne and Marc knew what was going on. Even our parents only found out last week."

My jaw clenches when she says his name. *Marc*. I'm even angrier with myself because he was here and I wasn't.

"I buried her with your bracelet. She needed to know your love would catch her, too."

Just when I thought it wasn't possible to cry anymore, the floodgates open and I cry until my stomach is heaving and the tears have run dry. Kate is patient and calm; she's the pillar of strength while sitting with me and holding my hand. She's my rock and I don't deserve her comfort. But I'm weak and I continue to let her comfort me because I need her right now more than I've ever needed anyone before.

"Daniel and Connor know. Daniel wanted to come up here with me but I just couldn't let him meet her before you. It just didn't seem right."

My eyes lock onto hers and I see the sincerity radiating from them.

"Thank you," I reply quietly

She nods. "Your dad and I have had plenty of talks. Well, of course I talk and he listens, but I like to think I knew him well enough to know his advice."

She rises and holds her hand out to me, which I take eagerly, and she leads me directly behind Lila Hope's headstone. I immediately know she had those benches put here.

"Since Lila and Grant passed so close to each other, I was able to get them back to back. Your mom owns the two plots adjacent to Grant but I bought the rest of this area. I guess not too many people buy ten plots in an underdeveloped part of a cemetery. They gave me a good price; I just couldn't imagine my little girl not being surrounded by her family. There was no room left by my mom since she was buried so long ago but this worked out better in the long run."

It's comforting to know my dad is so close to Lila Hope.

"Thank you, Kate."

"For what?" she asks, surprised

"For being the mother my little girl needed, for being a strong enough woman to get through it and then strong enough to walk me through it, too. If I would have known…"

"It's okay, Mike, I know you would have been here if you were in the right head space. We have a lot to talk about and catch up on, but can this be enough for today?" she asks wearily.

We've been here for hours and I know she still has to go talk to Daniel.

"Of course, let's get you home."

We ride back in complete silence, both of us lost in our own thoughts. It doesn't escape my notice that she's been holding my hand the entire two hour ride home. Hopefully, that is a good sign for things to come.

Chapter Three – Kate

I texted Daniel on our way back from the cemetery but haven't looked at my phone since. I just want to be somewhere else—anywhere else—but right here, right now. I thought taking Mike to see Lila Hope would give me a sense of closure and in a way it has. However, I never imagined all the emotions the trip would evoke in me. My heart is absolutely breaking for him, for us, and for what we lost. I've been holding his hand since we got in the car and I don't know if I can let it go. All I want to do is take him inside and curl up with him and never let him go. I know we're grieving, but his kiss made my heart soar in a way it hasn't in a very long time.

Am I still in love with him?

I don't know, I don't think so, but every part of my being wants to comfort him. I can't imagine letting him drive home to deal with this all alone. As the car pulls up to the curb, he squeezes my hand tighter. Daniel is here; it's likely he never even left. After exiting the car in silence, I reach back behind me and give Mike my hand. I want him to know I'm here for him and he doesn't have to go through this alone. As we walk inside, still hand in hand, I don't miss the flash of anger in Daniel's eyes, but it's gone as quick as it came. He knows I have to be here for Mike right now; I'm all he's got.

Jess practically rips Mike away from me and hugs him tightly, whispering in his ear. Connor is next, followed by Daniel. I don't know why that surprises me, but it does. It's just another reason why I love him; his ability to put others' needs above his own. For that exact reason, he should understand why I'm doing this.

"I'm so sorry, man," Daniel says to Mike. Mike is clutching on to him in that way guys do when they're emotional and Daniel is clutching right back. Watching them together just reinforces all the reasons why I can't pick between them, even though it doesn't ease the pain in my heart.

"I know you are and so am I." They aren't just talking about Lila Hope anymore, and even if this doesn't solve anything, it's a start.

Jess pulls me to the side for a private conversation. "I'm not going to ask if you're okay because I can tell you're not, but you should know that Daniel stayed here all day. He's a mess, Kate."

I just nod my head at her because I'm exhausted and it's all I can do right now.

"Look, we're going to take Mike to Connor's house so you and Daniel can have some privacy. Text me when he leaves and we'll come back."

"Jess, can you give Mike my number, please? And don't let him drive right now, okay? Let him ride with you guys. He's not in the frame of mind to be behind the wheel."

"Sure, we can do that. How did it go?" she asks

"Besides burying Lila Hope, that was the hardest thing I've ever done in my life."

"I'm so sorry, Kate; you shouldn't have to go through this again."

Connor pops his head in, "Are my girls okay?" he asks and we nod in unison.

"Well, in that case, are you ready to get going? It's a little *tense* out here."

"Yup, let's go. Call me if you need anything, Kate, and I'll be back here as fast as I can."

I step into the bathroom as they leave and splash my face with water. I'm a mess but I know Daniel doesn't even care. Trying to get the nerve together to go and speak with him is harder than I thought it would be. It's just the two of us now, and as much as I want to find my comfort in him, I need my space to start getting over him.

There's a light rap on the door. I've been in here way too long avoiding reality. It's not my usual style, but this is so hard.

"Kate, can you please come out and talk to me?"

I swing open the door and he immediately pulls me into his arms—my home, my comfort zone, the only place I thought I would ever want to be. I don't want to feel conflicted like this. I want him with every fiber of my being and yet, I want Mike, too. It's so much better this way, being forced to push them both away. I don't want to have to choose between them. They both mean too much to me. Even so, there's nothing better than the feeling of being wrapped in Daniel's arms. When he kisses me on the forehead, I want to melt into him. Instead, it's my cue to pull away.

"Talk to me, Kate." His voice is pained

"It was awful, Daniel, just so awful. It broke him, like it broke me. But in a way, it was almost worse, so much worse. I was on the outside looking in and yet I felt every shatter of his heart encompassed in my own."

"I'm sorry you guys had to go through that. I wish… I wish things were different and I could help Mike get through this. That we could separate our feelings for you from our friendship, but I just don't see that happening."

I sigh softly; it's a relief knowing that he sees it, too.

"I'm glad you understand, maybe that will help make this easier."

He looks at me, shocked.

"Kate. I CHOOSE YOU. *Always*. Last night, you said you chose me, too. And today…today you're all over the place. You said you wouldn't make any decisions without me and yet here we are. We have to talk about Vanessa, and Mike, and work through…"

"Mike kissed me!" I blurt out.

I will never forget the look of rage and pain that crosses his eyes in this instant. It's seared into my soul.

"HE DID WHAT?" he yells, but it sounds like a roar.

I put my head in my hands to hide my tears and I whisper softly, "Mike kissed me."

Daniel begins pacing back and forth across the room, not saying anything to me but slowly counting to ten each time he crosses the floor.

"Did you want him to?" he asks sadly.

"No." I only answer with one word because I don't want to volunteer any information. But I told him I would never lie to him and I won't.

"Did you kiss him back?" He struggles with the last word and I know he doesn't want to hear the answer he's going to get.

"Yes."

"Fuck!" More pacing and more counting. I can't help thinking he must have learned the counting trick from his mom.

"Tell me the context of the kiss, Kate. I need you to explain it to me."

"Daniel, I don't know if that's a good idea."

"Damn it, Kate! Your lips were on mine less than twenty-four hours ago. Until this morning, I *thought* we had a future together. At the very least you owe me an explanation."

He's right. I owe him this, and *so* much more.

"It wasn't planned. Hearing about Lila Hope broke him. He always wanted a family, but I never knew how much until today. He was so upset and I was trying to comfort him, we were holding each other and crying and it just happened. And I'm truly sorry if it hurts you. I pulled away once I realized what was happening."

"Do you want to go back to him?"

"No, I don't." *It's the truth, right?*

"Okay, then we need to talk and clear the air. We *need* to fix this, Kate."

"I know we do, but I'm not sure what to say. There's no way I'm going to get between you and your best friend. Period. You guys are family and need to stay that way. You're each other's support systems. Not to mention the fact you might be having a baby. That's a *big* deal. If you're the father, you're going to want to be there. I know you; you're going to want to be involved. You should have a chance at a family the right way. So should Mike, for that matter, if it's his. I need to remove myself as an obstacle between the two of you before things get any worse."

"Too late," he says as he gets up from the couch and paces some more. I've never seen this side of him. He's determined and I can tell his mind is working overtime.

"Do you remember the night we met?"

I nod and he comes forward, kneeling in front of me and lacing our fingers together.

"That night, you said you wanted someone caring and faithful in a relationship. Someone who would understand that although a relationship can be affected by outside forces, it isn't defined by them. You said you wanted someone who loves you for who you are and believes in you. That you wanted someone who would continue to believe in a relationship even if it was failing. Do you remember that?"

Holy shit, he remembers every single word I said.

"Yes, I remember," I answer in awe as he wipes away my tears.

"So do I, baby, and that's what I'm doing, and what I'm going to continue to do. I realize you're confused and this *seems* like an impossible situation, but it's not. I'm going to believe in us until we are no longer failing. Until we are not *only* surviving, *but* thriving. Our relationship is not going to be defined by this. We define ourselves; our circumstances *do not* define us. Remember, all love needs is two people to believe in it enough to resurrect it and keep it alive. That's me and you, Kate. *We* can do this, we've *got* this. Don't give up on us. Not yet, baby, not when we're just getting started."

This amazing man before me loves me with all he has to give and I'm stuck taking the moral high ground and trying to look a year into the future. "Daniel, I love you. Too much to let you throw away your friendship with Mike. He needs you, now more than ever before. Vanessa is pregnant and she needs someone there for her, too. She needs at least one if not both of you. I know Mike is going to have a lot harder time being around her than you are, which means for now, most of that responsibility is going to fall to you."

He's shaking his head at me. "We'll work around Vanessa and the baby."

"You can't work around a baby, Daniel," I snap at him

"No, you can't, but you can work around a situation and not let yourself get emotionally invested until it's necessary. You know what Vanessa put us through; I'm going into this with my eyes wide open."

I can't stand the thought that this baby may be his but it's a reality I have to face. "Fair enough, but once the baby comes, if he's yours..."

He pulls me up from the couch and holds me close. "If he's mine, I'm going to co-parent with Vanessa. We'll be friends, but I don't want to be with her romantically, not *ever* again."

"You should try, for the baby's sake at least. You could have a family—a *real* family—and that is priceless for a child."

He tilts my chin up to him, slowly backing me up against the wall. Those butterflies take flight in my stomach; it's the same wall he fucked me up against and I know he's thinking about it, too, from the gleam in his eyes.

He trails a line of kisses along my neck, pausing at my ear. "Family is what you make it, Kate, we talked about that, too. There's no reason why you can't be the best step-mom there has ever been when the time comes. *If* that time ever comes. It's still only a fifty percent chance."

I close my eyes, relishing the closeness, even if I know I shouldn't, and breathe in his scent. He cracks a grin; he knows exactly what I'm doing and uses it to his advantage by making the tiny gap between us even smaller. I want to smile back but I strengthen my resolve instead.

"The odds haven't been in our favor lately."

"Look at me, Kate. The odds are *always* in our favor. That's what you're forgetting; *we* are writing our story here. Sure, the roads may take some unexpected curves every now and then, but we are still in control of how we handle them. Don't forget I'm an expert at handling all kinds of curves." As he says those words, his hands are roaming from my hips all the way up to my breasts. I tremble in his arms while his words wash over me, filling me with warmth. It doesn't matter; I still have to convince him this is wrong.

"Look, this is going to sound selfish, but I don't know if I could be a step-mom. I'm bitter inside right now, Daniel. Bitterness isn't something I'm familiar with; it feels a lot like jealousy and I'm struggling. Vanessa has either taken away our firstborn child or she's given Mike something I couldn't. Either scenario kills me inside, but it still doesn't matter because I can't have either of you. Both of you love me, both of you are making that a well-known fact, and I can't have you! I'm doing this for all of us, and the sooner you both accept that the better."

I try and push away from him but he presses me up against the wall with force. Not a harmful force, it's an erotic force, and I wish it didn't turn me on so much.

The glimmer I see in his eyes is new, and I have no clue what it means, but he looks ready for a challenge. Whatever the look is, it's hot and it's taking all my self-control not to throw my arms around his neck and wrap my legs around his waist for a repeat of what we did last time he had me up against this wall.

"This is going to be a fight, Kate, our first, but most definitely *not* our last. I fight for what's mine. And you, baby, *you're* mine. You have been from the minute your eager lips pressed against mine and you granted me access into that fucking perfect little mouth of yours. So go ahead and be the good girl, play the martyr. Eventually, you'll figure out Mike comes in second but I'll *always* be first. You want to pretend this is about us all staying friends? Go ahead. All this really is about is *you* not being able to hurt him, even though that's *exactly* what he did to you. So if you really want to play this way, then GAME ON. I won't be easy on you and I'm going to love watching you try to resist what you crave and what you crave *is* me. Come on, baby. Tell me you aren't wet *right* fucking now, Kate. Tell me you aren't thinking about my cock being buried so deep inside you that you'll forget exactly why you're fighting us. I know just from the way your breath is hitching all you want right now is *me*. This is going to be so much fun, baby. I've always thought a challenge makes the end result even sweeter so… GAME FUCKING ON."

I've forgotten how to breathe. That was the hottest thing I've *ever* heard. He told me from the beginning he fights for what he wants. I've only seen Daniel's sweet side, his romantic side, his wooing side. I've never seen his possessive side, his alpha side, well, never outside of the bedroom. I've heard stories from Connor, though; I guess I didn't give them much thought.

Daniel grabs my wrists and holds them above my head, pinning them to the wall. His mouth descends upon mine and I open for him greedily. His body pushes against mine and his arousal is evident. My panties are soaking wet. He alternates his hold on my wrists, now holding them both with one hand as he works his way to the button on my jeans with the other. With amazing finesse, he's popped them open in a second flat and slides his fingers down into my panties where he finds my clit hard and aching for his touch. The entire time he continues to kiss me, swallowing my moans and squeals of desire. He eases two fingers into me and circles my clit gently with his thumb.

His lips leave mine only to create a searing trail across my neck and up to my ear.

"That's it, baby, fuck my hand like you would fuck me. Let me make you feel good, Kate. Let me hear you scream."

Just as I let go and come on his hand harder than I ever have before, he covers my screams with his mouth. His tongue chases mine in a passionate duel as he slowly pulls his hand back out of my panties. One by one he licks his fingers, enjoying every bit of my arousal, and not once does he break eye contact. It's a highly erotic thing to watch a man enjoy you like that.

"Hot damn," escapes my lips but I can't help it, he's really not making this easy for me.

"I've got a meeting in the morning, so I'm heading back home now. Remember who made you wet tonight, Kate. That would be me, not Mike. I bet Mike's *never* made you as wet as I just did. I bet he's never made you come that hard or that fast, either. Do you know why that is, Kate? It's because you belong with me—your body knows it, your heart knows it, now your mind just needs to catch up. I love you, Kate, and I'm *not* giving up. I'll give you some space… for now…but I'm going to win your love back. We *will* have our happily ever after and you *will* start wearing your ring again. It's upstairs in your jewelry box when you're ready to put it back on your finger. Remember, Kate, this works both ways. I'm just as much yours as you are mine. I'm not going anywhere; I would wait for you until the end of time, but please don't make me.

He backs up and takes off his jacket and then his t-shirt. It looks like he's got a bandage over his shoulder, but before I can check it out, he quickly pulls his jacket back on and zips it up. He hands me his t-shirt. "This is for when you need a reminder that I'm here and I'm not giving up on you. Goodnight, gumdrop."

He places a light kiss on my forehead and exits without looking back. *Holy hell. How am I ever going to fall out of love with him? This is so unfair.*

After a short internal debate of whether I need a wineglass or just want to drink from the bottle, I grab a bottle of wine and a glass and head to my room. After texting Jess to let her know Daniel left, I also text Vanessa, letting her know I'll call her tomorrow and fill her in about how today went and figure out move details. I feel bad I didn't talk to her today but I can't deal with that tonight on top of everything else. All I want is a long soak in the tub so I can wash this day off my skin. Then I'm going to put on Daniel's shirt and wrap myself in his love one last time. Unfortunately, before I even get the chance to turn the water on, my phone goes off in a succession of text messages. Responses from Jess and Vanessa, as well as a message from Marc, asking if we're still on for lunch tomorrow and a message from Mike; I need to program his number in.

Unknown number:

Thanks for having Jess give me your number. We're on our way back but would it be okay if I get that journal from you tonight?

I save his number and hit reply

To Mike:

Of course just come on up to my room when you get here.

I respond to Marc, letting him know I'm skipping my morning class but I'll meet him at our favorite park and bring lunch with me.

So much for my bath; there's no time, so I opt for a quick shower instead. While the water heats up, I pour myself a glass of wine and take a long drink. Wine is nectar from the gods and I drink almost half the glass before hopping in the shower. I know that doesn't sound bad but one of my glasses can hold almost a full bottle and I filled it to the rim.

Once I dry off, I put Daniel's shirt in my drawer since I can't wear it in front of Mike, and barely have a chance to get a pair of sweats and a tank top on before he knocks on my door. When I open it to let him in, I smell him before my eyes even land on him. *Shit, Jess and Connor got him drunk.* Not that I blame him; that's exactly where I'm headed right now, too, isn't it?

"Hey, Katie Grace," he slurs as he leans against my doorframe for balance. Jess and Connor are behind him and both mouth 'sorry' to me. I motion for Mike to sit on the bed and he stumbles toward it. Hearing him call me Katie Grace takes me back to a place where things were so simple for us all. I miss that place.

"Sorry, Kate, we couldn't keep him sober. You've both had a rough day," Connor says, motioning to my wine glass.

"It's fine, I understand. Guess we've got a houseguest for the night," I reply

"No, isssokay. I'll sleep in my truck. I've done it before, it's not a big deal. Well, in my Porsche not in my truck, but my truck is much more comfortable." Mike's babbling while his eyes scan my room.

"No, you can stay here; I'm not letting you sleep in your truck," I state firmly

"Let us know if you guys need anything. Goodnight." Jess blows us a kiss as she closes the door behind them. Now we're alone in my room for the first time in years.

"Are you okay?" I ask him, although I know he's anything but.

"I don't know if I'll ever be okay again," he says sadly

I nod my head because there's really nothing to say. I'm not okay, either, hence the wine I continue to drink.

"How about you, Kate? Are you okay? I'm guessing it didn't go well with Daniel from the text I got."

"He texted you?" I'm surprised, but with the way he was acting I probably shouldn't be.

"Oh yeah. He's not too happy I kissed you. He thinks I'm trying to take advantage of you," he answers sheepishly.

And this is why I can't be with them—*either* of them—in that way. *Only friends.* It's going to be a constant pissing match as it is. I know how Mike acts with Marc, and Daniel sure showed his possessive side tonight.

It was so freaking hot.

"I know you're not taking advantage of me."

"No, I'm not, but I want you, Kate. I *need* you. Am I too late or do I still have a place in your heart?" he asks, peering up at me with those beautiful blue eyes of his. I've been in love with his eyes for as long as I can remember.

Taking my time to finish off my glass of wine, I mull over in my head how best to answer his question.

Honestly.

"Mike, you shattered me when you left, but more than that, you shattered *us*. And then by some miracle you found a family, you found a job and a home and created a *life*. And I am *so* proud of you."

I take his hand in mine and squeeze, trying to pull strength from him to finish what I have to say.

"That doesn't change the fact that *you* left *me*. *You* broke *me*, my *heart*, my *trust*, my *soul*. *All broken by you*. And then I had to bury our daughter *without you,* when all I wanted was your arms around me, comforting me. I needed you so badly, I needed to hear your reassuring words, I needed to be wrapped in your love, but it was nowhere to be found and I felt so utterly alone. You left me alone for so long, *too* long. Then finally, by the grace of God, I found the strength to move forward with Daniel, and that made me less angry at you."

He grips my hand harder and I squeeze his right back. We're pulling strength from each other, just like we always have.

"I know you want to work on getting us back. Even if that were a possibility, there are more obstacles in our way to overcome than I even know where to start. You will forever have a place in my heart and that will *never* change. But how you fit there now, how you can fit there in the future… I just don't know."

He looks me in the eyes, his pooling with tears. "I'm sorry I hurt you, I know I messed up. There's so much to explain to you, and even more to make up to you, but I want to try. I need you in my life, Kate. I can't lose you again. Even when I wasn't here you were always my saving grace. Talk to Jake and ask him; he's the only one who understood." He says it with such sincerity I know he means it. Mike isn't a mean guy, he just got lost somewhere along the way. I am curious as to what it is Jake knows.

"Take your shoes off; you can stay in here tonight," I tell him as I stand to turn on the bedside lamp and turn off the overhead light. After pulling down the blankets, he crawls in and I crawl in after him. I flip the light off and we lay facing each other in the dark, just like when we were younger.

"It's going to be something we have to work at, Mike. We're going to have to talk about your past, but I know a bit about it already. We can work toward friends as our goal. I can't promise you anything other than friends. I'm in love with Daniel… but I love you, too."

Chapter Four – Kate

When I wake up in the morning, Mike is still asleep; he looks so peaceful. Mike has grown into such a strong man. The last time I was with him we were still kids and now he's this muscular, tattooed, gorgeous *man*. I try not to wake him and quietly get out of bed and head downstairs for some coffee. It's only six am but I guess my body was becoming accustomed to those early morning text messages from Daniel. Which reminds me to turn my phone back on; it's powering up as I enter the kitchen.

"I don't think I approve of you having sleepovers with random men in your room, young lady," Connor quips as he pours a cup of coffee. At least he's smirking.

"Nothing happened," I reply dryly, reaching out my hand for the cup he's offering me.

"You sure about that?" he asks, concerned.

I shoot him my 'are you fucking kidding me' look but he's still waiting for an answer. It's too early for this. He can at least wait until I get some coffee in my system for an answer.

"Look, Kate, I know you and Mike both were in a very emotional place yesterday. You know better than anyone that emotional connections bond people. How do you think Daniel would feel knowing Mike not only slept in your room last night, but in *your* bed after he left?"

"I'm sure he won't be happy about it, Connor, but that's *my* business. For the record, I told Mike the same thing I told Daniel. I'm not choosing between them. I'm going to be friends with *both* of them. They're going to have to get used to it because that's the point of all of this, for us all to be friends."

He looks like he wants to say something more but decides against it when my phone starts beeping to alert me of all my missed messages. I've got voicemails from my dad and Vanessa. My dad says he released a statement this morning personally and that the media shouldn't need to talk to me or Mike.

Thank God.

Vanessa just wants me to call her back. Then there's a text from Daniel.

Your Boyfriend:

I hope you slept well last night. Have a good day. I love you. Now. Always. Forever.

Maybe I should take a vacation, a temporary leave from school. If I did that, I could get away from all of this. I just need some space.

"I'm not trying to upset you, Kate. I get why you're doing things the way you are. I also know how much it's hurting you to have to do it. But what I haven't figured out yet is if you're doing it to take the easy way out so you don't have to actually choose, or if you're really doing it in everyone's best interests."

His words tear at my heart; I've asked myself the same thing. "It's probably a little bit of both. I do truly believe with all my heart that this is for the best. Growing up, Mike had acquaintances, but Jess and I were his only friends—his family—and he was ours. When he ran from us, I still had Jess but he had no one until he met you guys."

He looks at me with understanding in his eyes. "That's true. From what I've seen, we were his only friends. Once, in all the years I've known him, he let someone else in and that was Misty. Other than that, we've been it for him."

"Exactly, we can't take that from him, Connor. Mike's proud and protective. He would give it all up for a chance to be a couple again. While I admire his drive, and Daniel's, to get what they want, that doesn't change anything. Girls come and go but friends are forever. Bros before ho's and all that."

That earns me a smile from Connor "Kate, what about your wants, who you love and want to be with? When do you start looking out for *you*?"

"Right now, I've spent a long time mourning the loss of Mike and Lila Hope. I've accepted that and now that I have Mike back in my life I feel like… like I'm free? I don't have to hold those burdens close to my heart anymore. I've got no need to grieve, to hope, to wonder what if. As much as it hurts to lose

Daniel, and it *does* hurt, more than I'm willing to admit. We're all going to be better off, eventually. They won't stay mad at each other forever."

"So you're just going to pretend you don't love them?"

I think about that for a minute but there's no way I could ever do that.

"No, I'm just going to love them enough to let them go."

He shakes his head. "*They* don't want to let *you* go. But hey, once Vanessa pops out the baby you never know, maybe she'll get whoever back in her greedy little claws and they can all be a happy little family."

I swallow over the lump in my throat at his words, letting his meanness slide "That's what I hope for. Every child should start life off with a family, a happy one at that."

"Will you take who's left if that happens?"

My heart screams at me *in a heartbeat*, but my brain is still in control for now "I don't think so. I don't know, maybe? It's not something I can decide now."

"So what are you deciding now?" he asks with genuine curiosity

I smile up at him for the first time this morning. "I'm going to live for me. I'm going to have fun. I'm going to hang out with Marc, start working out again, go clubbing, and get drunk often. I'm going to let my inhibitions go and see where life takes me. And I'm going to be friends with Daniel *and* Mike."

"Well, what the hell, Kate? Where are you fitting *me* into this new you? I didn't hear anything about what you're going to do with me in there." I can't help laughing at his over-animated response with hand gestures and all. I think Jess is rubbing off on him.

"There's always room for you in there. When you're not having your way with Jess, we'll do our thing. Hit some bars, concerts, go to some clubs? Jess will love it. It's just time to be me—to figure out who I really am without pining away for a man again."

"So that's the plan? Just push past the pain?"

"That's the plan."

"What's the plan?" Jess asks sleepily as she walks into the kitchen.

"Kate's new life motto, out with the old and in with the new."

Jess's eyes widen. "Ooohhh, does that mean you're keeping Daniel? I wouldn't blame you, he's fuckability plus."

"I'm sitting right here," Connor states, sulking.

Jess laughs and says two words, "Jennifer Lawrence."

"Hottest alpha bitch on the planet, fuckability off the charts. *But* she's not accessible to me."

"Daniel's not accessible to me, either. He's Kate's," Jess says, chuckling at him

"Not anymore."

"Eww, Connor. *Always*. She had him first which means he's hers. We don't pass boys back and forth between us. Not ever."

Connor seems to be reflecting on her words but he doesn't say anything, just nods. For a brief moment I wonder what he's thinking until Mike walks in.

"Morning, guys. Mind if I grab some coffee?"

"Help yourself, Mike. How'd you sleep last night?" Jess asks casually, but I know she's looking for details.

His blue eyes meet mine and hold my gaze as my heart speeds up. He's gorgeous and I'd kill to get an up close and personal look at that ink peeking out from under his sleeve.

Stop it, Kate.

Only friends.

"It was the best sleep I've had in years." It's not what he says but the megawatt smile that accompanies it that elicits Connor's loud snort, I'm sure. Jess kicks him under the table but Mike doesn't let it faze him. "Aren't you guys all going to be late for school?"

"My first class isn't until ten today. Aren't you going to be late for work? You've got a hell of a drive," Connor replies

"No, I sent an email in last night letting them know I had some stuff to take care of and would be taking a vacation day today."

"Well, I'm taking today off; I need some time to decompress from the weekend. I'm having lunch with Marc after his class and then I've *got* to catch up on homework."

I don't miss the unmistakable clenching of Mike's jaw and the tight clench of his hands on his coffee mug when I mention Marc. It's comical; after all this time, he still hates him.

"Well… I decided to take the day off, too. I need girl time, so you guys need to finish your coffee and get on your way." Jess never sugarcoats anything but they get it. They both know her well.

"Fine, I can see where I'm not wanted. Want to go grab breakfast, Mike? I've got time before class."

"Sure, I could eat. Kate, can I get that journal before I go?" he asks hesitantly.

"Of course, come on up and I'll grab it for you." Mike follows me up the stairs and I pull the journal from my bookshelf. "It's not much, but I hope it helps." He takes it from my hand and pulls me into his embrace. "Thank you for forgiving me." My heart fills with love for this man. "Always," I tell him as he lets me go.

Mike walks to the door and turns around before leaving. "Kate, we're going to do this, right? We *will* be friends again?" He sounds so unsure, and even though he's the one who left, I don't like seeing him question us. "We always have been friends; we just took a break, I guess," I tell him, shrugging my shoulders.

"I want us to work hard on building it back up. I really have missed you, Mike. And now you're going to be my brother."

He chuckles, "There are so many things wrong with that I don't even know where to start, but make sure you say *stepbrother* from now on. There is nothing Jerry Springer about our love story."

He's got a point there. "You're right about that," I reply, laughing. "So are you going to see her today? Your mom?"

"Yeah, I think it's time. I've been a horrible son. I just hope she can forgive me."

I squeeze his hand, "She already has, but if you need to talk, call or text me anytime. One more thing before you go. Tomorrow, when you go to work, can you try and figure out a way to be decent to Daniel?"

"Kate…I…" He runs his hands through his hair as he tries to find his words. It's better to just cut him off.

"For me, *please*. And for the two of you. He loves you and *you* love him. This situation is just going to take some getting used to."

"I'll try, but only because you asked me to."

"Thank you"

~~***~~

A little bit after Mike leaves, Jess and I get settled on the couch so we can fill each other in on what's happened in the past day. I'm so grateful for her friendship; she's the one person I know who will always be truthful with me.

"So fill me in, what happened yesterday? First, fill me in on Mike and then Daniel and I'll do the same when you're done."

"God, Jess, it was awful. So awful. I guess I know how you felt when I fell apart at the funeral now. He was devastated. I never realized how much he wanted a baby, but most guys our age just don't want that. They would consider not having a baby a dodged bullet. It was like Mike actually was mourning the loss of not only our little girl but *our* family."

"Well, he probably was. I mean, let's face it…you and Mike didn't break up for a lack of love. I heard his story yesterday and I can't help but empathize with him, maybe even be rooting for him. I mean, hell…he bought your engagement ring our junior maybe beginning of senior year of high school."

She can't be serious. "You're joking, right? I figured he bought it a few days before proposing." She shakes her head. "No, he started looking for it after the first time you had sex, but it took him a while to find one that was perfect. And it *was* perfect."

"It took me so long to find a ring that is almost as beautiful as you."

Oh God, that's what he said that night. Every word he spoke is emblazoned on my brain. I just never put much thought into his statement, because what was the point?

"He wants me back."

She snorts. "Well, that's pretty obvious. When he heard you were at Marc's the other night, he about blew a fuse. Then he and Daniel almost came to blows when Daniel said he wasn't worried about you being with Marc."

"He kissed me yesterday," I whisper

"*Mike* kissed you? Last night in your room? Holy fuck, how was it? Did you kiss him back?"

"No, nothing happened last night; we just talked for a little while and slept. In the same bed but not together. The kiss happened at the cemetery. I did kiss him back it was instinctual and emotional and… it made my heart soar."

"Oh, shit."

"Yeah, that's kind of what I thought, too."

"Anything else happen?"

I shrug my shoulders. "No, not really. We talked and he asked if I still loved him. He told me he still loved me and always had. I told him we can only be friends and he took it well. We still have lots to talk about but it was a start."

"You must be so confused. What happened with Daniel? Did he kiss you, too?"

"Um, yeah, and then some. He seduced me with his body and his words, and fucking hell if it didn't work. That was *after* I told him about Mike kissing me, too."

"Are you *crazy*? You told him you kissed Mike?" she asks, completely shocked.

"Of course I did. We made a pact to be honest with each other and I'll never lie to him, Jess, no matter how much it might hurt. We had a very similar talk to the one I had with Mike last night. I put them both in the friend zone. But Daniel is determined to make me want him. Which isn't the hard part; the hard part is staying away from him so I don't get myself in a seducible situation."

"How do you feel, Katie Grace? I know you've got them in the zone, but if you didn't, which one would you want?"

This is the million dollar question, and I can't answer it, but I can tell her how they make me feel. "Daniel gives me butterflies that take flight in my stomach and they spread out to the depths of my being when he kisses me. But Mike… he makes my heart soar and always has. It's an amazing feeling."

"Wow, that's something."

"You don't even know the half of it. God, Jess, with Mike it was a slow burn pushing me to the heights of passion and it was amazing. But with Daniel, he takes me to the heights of passion and then pushes me above. Past limits I never thought possible. It's an indescribable freefall, a high I could have never imagined. He's *my* drug of choice. I don't know how to let him go, but I know I have to."

"So you would pick Daniel? I'm sort of surprised by that, actually."

"I didn't say that, but why would you be surprised?" I'm curious to hear her answer.

"So you'd pick Mike?" she asks eagerly. I swear it's like she just needs some popcorn and she'd be a happy camper.

"I didn't say that, either. I'm not even going to go there, Jess, there's no point. I am not going to choose between them. I want to know why you'd be surprised, though."

She flicks nonexistent lint off her pajama pants before she answers me. "Because it's Mike, and you have so much history. There's over a decade worth of love with you guys. You guys have a story fairytales are made from."

I shake my head vehemently at her. "No, Jess, we don't. Maybe once we did, but now there's almost a half decade of hurt and pain between us. There's a lot to be done to get past that. Maybe then, depending on how things turn out with Vanessa, but I just can't fall back into him. I can't let myself get lost again, not ever. I'll tell you exactly what I told Connor: I'm going to just be free for a while. I don't really know what that's like, but I'm just going to have some fun for a change. Whatever happens is going to happen, but I'm not going to worry about it."

She's stares at me with wide eyes because what I just said was very *un*-Kate.

"Before I forget, I need to ask you something important."

"Shoot."

"Do you know anything about a message from Mike? He said he sent me a message at some point, but I would remember that."

I know that look on her face. It's her 'I'm busted' face. *What the hell?* "Jess, what do you know? What am I missing?"

"Kate, promise you won't be mad at me. Please." She sounds nervous.

"You know I can't promise that but I'll do my best." She nods her head and pulls out her phone. She's pulling up her email and her hand is trembling.

"In my defense…"

Oh, this is bad if she's starting off 'In my defense'

"I thought I was doing the right thing. It came the night you were in the hospital. The night you found out about Lila Hope. You were a wreck, Kate, and I thought it would make things worse. I did what I had to do at the time. I don't think you could have handled much more. But I kept it, just in case this day ever came. I emailed it to myself—his voicemail message and my text reply. Please don't hate me." Her voice trails off in a whisper as she hands me the phone. I press play on the audio and listen.

"Katherine, it's Michael. I'm calling because I need to say a few things to you. I might be drunk, too. I'm sorry I left you like that. I'm sorry I couldn't control my temper and I treated you bad. I'm no good for you. Baby, I've done things these past few weeks I'm not proud of. Did you know I never wanted to go to school? That I was only going for you? No, you didn't because I never told you. I'm sure Jessica told you about Riley but I swear that wasn't true. I needed you both to let go. Don't wait around for me being miserable. I want you to be happy. Someday I'll come back because I need you, I'll always need you. I won't let things get lost in translation next time, I promise. I'll come back and find you when it's time. I need to truly forgive Joseph, my mom, maybe you, and definitely myself. I need to get my head in a different space. I want to be someone better than I am now, for you, for us. When the time comes, I'll have to tell you the things I've done and hope you'll find it in your heart to forgive me. I can imagine by then I'll have a lot to be forgiven for and I apologize in advance for that. Just know I love you. I've loved you since we were seven and I'll love you until I die. Then when I come back, I'll find you all over again. I miss you, Katherine. The ache that your presence has been replaced with is a pain that should be reserved for someone deep in the depths of hell. Being without you is my own personal hell. Please don't call this number; I'll change it if you do. It's better this way. I don't have the right to ask, but please trust me when I say I need to become me before we can become an 'us' again. Most importantly, I think you need to find you, too, Katherine Grace Moore. You're going to be amazing, with or without me. I just hope when I come back you'll want to be amazing with me. I'm so sorry I couldn't

be the one to catch you this time, Katie Grace. Next time I'll be a better man and I'll never let you fall again.

Tears are streaming down my face and I listen to it again, and again, before finally reading the reply she sent to him.

She didn't get your message, I did. I deleted it. She's not well but she will be eventually. We just got home from the hospital. As if you care. You really should come see her, you'll regret it if you don't. But don't come see her if you're not going to stay…if you can't be with her. I'll be her family and I'll help her with things if you can't. But you should, Michael, you have no clue, but you should. I'm deleting your number because I don't ever want to have to lie to her about knowing how to contact you. For the record, I knew you lied about Riley. You loved Katie too much to do that. I know you, Michael, better than you know yourself. Don't text me back, I can't chance it. Just come back to us.

My mind is officially blown and my heart is broken in a place I never thought it could ever be. It's broken in the place that you share with your best friend, the place where each other's secrets live in the vault and are shared with no one. The place where you know there's one person in the world who will never lie to you, the place that grows larger because you have someone you can trust filling that place with love. I'm absolutely devastated. I could have never kept something like this from her. We could have found him, I could have told him about Lila. He would have come home and he didn't, he missed it, because she didn't say anything.

"Kate please *say* something," she pleads

I'm *so* angry. She could have shown me this at any time over the last three years and she chose to keep it a secret. If I had known he was sorry, that he still cared, that he didn't hate me, things could have been so different.

"Kate *please*." She's worried, I can hear it in her tone and I see the scared look in her eyes. Good, she fucked up. Big time.

I place my hand out in front of me as I get up. "Stop. I can't… not now. I'll say something I will regret. Maybe we can talk when I get back but I've got to go get ready and meet Marc."

She's crying but I don't care. I just need to get out of here and away from her. I dress quickly, blasting Keri Hilson and singing along to *Energy*. I've always loved this song, even if it feels like it hits a little too close to home today.

Thankfully, Jess is nowhere in sight when I get back downstairs. After I get in the car, I call Vanessa on my way to the deli and arrange for her to move in on Wednesday. We agree she should wait to talk to Daniel and Mike until this weekend. There's really nothing productive that can happen right now and they still need time to calm down. It's still hard for me to believe she could have been so diabolical with them, but everyone is entitled to change and despite whatever prompted her issues, she seems much better now.

While I wait for the picnic lunch I ordered at the deli, I go back to Daniel's text from this morning and the first thing I do is change him to Daniel in my phone. Seeing 'your boyfriend' pop up each time will kill me. Then I text him back.

"Thanks I hope you have a good week. Vanessa is moving in on Wednesday she doesn't need any help. You can see her on Saturday. We'll work out the details later in the week."

He replies immediately.

"Sounds good, I'm moving into Connor's this weekend the project starts on Monday. I love you."

In the midst of all the drama the past few days I completely forgot he was moving here. Great, this is going to be torture. I don't want to be rude and not reply to him, but I have to make sure he knows I'm trying to keep my distance. So I end up sending him the lamest response ever.

"I know. Thanks for the heads up."

Oh well, I can't worry about it now. What I can do is go see Marc and let him lift my spirits.

~~~***~~~

This park is so beautiful. It's so secluded and there's never anyone here, which is probably why I love it so much. It's completely surrounded by oak trees so you never have to worry about the sun. Marc is already here and spread out on a blanket under a tree in the back. He's so sexy but he'll never let himself get tied down. It's a shame. When he notices me, he comes to meet me and takes the food from me. After setting it down, he picks me up and spins me around in a big, squeezy Marc hug. I love Marc hugs; I think he saves them all for me.

"How's my baby girl today?" he asks, shooting me his signature smile. Thankfully, I'm immune to it now or I'd be putty in his hands.

"I've been better but I'm determined to be happy." He kisses me on the cheek, and after we sit, I divvy up the food.

"That sounds like a great plan; I love my girl happy. So fill me in on your weekend. It's not like you to miss school, so I'm guessing it got worse."

As we eat, I fill him in on all the details of the weekend from when I left him at the gym. Then I tell him about Jess and I can tell from the look on his face that he's not as shocked as I am.

"Did you know?" I ask him.

"No, I wouldn't keep something like that from you even if it did have to do with Mike. I know how much you loved him. You're angry right now, rightfully so, and I'm not letting Jess off the hook but you couldn't see yourself back then. You were a scary version of yourself. We all tiptoed around you, afraid one wrong move would set you back. I think she made the choice she thought was right at the time and couldn't figure out how to come clean once she hid it."

"I don't know…maybe."

"No maybes, Kate, she kept the messages. She always *intended* to tell you, it was never a matter of *if*, just a matter of *when*." The sincerity radiating from his eyes makes me really think about his words.

"You're right. But I'm still super pissed," I reply, popping a chip in my mouth.

"As you should be. I think she was wrong but I also think she's sorry." I know he's right; she absolutely was sorry.

I decide to change the subject, "So we're still going out for your birthday, right?"

"Absolutely, and not to sound like a jerk, but I'm pretty happy you're single right now, too. No jealous men to butt into our fun. I've got a limo all set up and my friend Jack, the one who owns The Scene, is going to block off a section of the VIP for us. Invite whoever you want, but make sure to bring Jess and her man. You can even bring Daniel if you want to."

"Hey, buddy, you're treading in deep waters there." He laughs at my tone.

"I know, but I want you happy, however that comes."

He's such a good guy.

"So what if I'm happy with Mike?" I ask him seriously and he raises an eyebrow at me.

"Are you?" he asks curiously.

"I'm happy he's back in my life. But don't worry, I would never invite him to your birthday party. For whatever reason he still can't get over, you bring out his inner asshole."

"Oh, we both know the reason; he can't get over the fact that he heard me say I wanted to have my wicked way with you." I choke on my tea as I laugh, but my face is turning three shades of lobster red.

"We were what…twelve? You guys couldn't have even truly grasped the meaning of those words then."

"It doesn't make it any less true and you'd be shocked at what a twelve year old boy is thinking, let alone actually *doing*. I knew damn well what I wanted to do and so did he, which is why he still doesn't like me."

Is that really the only reason Mike hates Marc?

"Come on, Kate, admit it, sex between us *will* be hot. *Scorching*. You should stay single for a while. Maybe you'll finally give in to me before we're old enough for you to cougarize me. I promise you won't be disappointed." It doesn't get past me that he says 'will' when he talks about sex. I know he wants to, even *I* want to. Our underlying chemistry is explosive, but we aren't like that, we're better as friends.

"I don't doubt that you would rock my world, but you aren't the settling kind of guy and I'm not the one night stand kind of girl," I reply seriously.

He tilts my head toward him, keeping constant eye contact with me. "It wouldn't have to be a one night stand; we could just be friends with benefits. And just for the record, Kate, with you it would never be settling." A shiver runs through me when I let my mind wander just for a minute and think about what sex with Marc would be like.

Of course, he laughs when he sees that shiver. "Uh-huh. You just keep thinking like that and someday you'll realize you want it, too. Until then, you want to go to the gym with me and work off all this food and our sexual frustrations?"

I can't help laughing. Even though he's constantly hitting on me, I know he loves me and would never hurt me. Going to the gym sounds exactly like what I need right now. I'm going to be up most of the night doing homework, but it's worth it not to have to face Jess right now.

"Yup, let's go."

Chapter Five ~ Daniel

I've been distracted all day and my dad has already commented on it more than once. These are the kind of days that make working with family a downfall. I already agreed to go over there for dinner and I'm dreading it. Telling them about Mike and Kate isn't something I'm looking forward to. Just reading her last message was painful, even though I tried not to take it personally. She's doing what she thinks is best but I can't stand this new wall between us. Last night I pushed her harder than I wanted to, but I'm hoping it makes her understand I'm not giving up.

My desk phone is ringing and my dad's extension is flashing on the caller ID…great. As I lift the receiver to my ear, he barks out, "In my office now!" and hangs up. This day is just getting better and better. After stepping inside, I close the door behind me. The look on his face already screams to me that this is going to be a serious conversation.

"What's going on with you today, Daniel? Hell, boy, you're all over the damn place. I need you focused. This is your last week in the office for a while and you've got to get your stuff done so you can move to the next project without leaving work for others to do on top of their own."

"Sorry, Dad, I'll get it all done, don't worry."

He puts his arms behind his head and leans back in his chair, thinking. "Does this have anything to do with Mike not being here today?"

"It does," I confirm

"Should I be concerned? I have a business to run and I can't have an argument between the two of you getting in the way of my company."

"It won't, Dad, but it's a long story and I don't want to talk about it here."

"Okay then, I came in early, and you are too distracted to be productive. Let's get out of here and have a beer. We'll keep your mom company while she finishes dinner."

I know he wants to ask me more questions but decides it's best to wait. When we get to the house, he calls to my mom, "Where's my sugar?"

"I'm in here," she calls out from the kitchen.

Even drowning in my own personal misery I still imagine that one day that will be Kate and I. I can't imagine wanting to come home to anyone else but her.

"Dinner's going to be done in about a half hour so why don't we all sit down and talk?" my mom says as my dad grabs a few beers from the fridge. He offers one to my mom but she lifts a vodka tonic in response. "I had a feeling I was going to need this tonight after your call."

"Spill it, son. Tell me why one of my two best workers didn't show up today for the first time ever and why the other one was so distracted he didn't do anything today but shuffle the same papers back and forth across his desk."

They wait expectantly while I struggle with how to tell them all that happened.

"Did you know Mike had a girlfriend before he left home?" I ask them.

My dad shakes his head but my mom nods. "I did, he used to talk to me about her."

I'm shocked and yet not, my mom is one of those people you feel like you can just talk to. "Why didn't you say anything?" I ask her.

"Oh, Daniel, that wasn't my story to tell. He needed someone to listen. Mike went through so much before he came here; he was such a lost young man. I wanted to support him and secretly hoped he would come to his senses and go back to his life. He ran from sadness and made a bad situation worse. I've always hoped he would go back to that girl and tell her how much he really loves her."

Damn. I guess this is another one who will be rooting for Mike and Kate. My own mom. Shaking my head in defeat, I finish off my beer, not saying anything until I get another one and drink part of that one, too. Where do I even start?

"Mike's girlfriend, the one he left behind… is Kate," I tell them.

"Oh my," my mom says as her hand flies up to cover her mouth.

My dad doesn't say anything, just goes to the bar and brings back the whiskey and a few glasses. *Guess I'm sleeping here tonight.* "Here, drink this," he says as he passes me a double and I pound it even though it's more of a sipping whiskey. That's the least of my concerns right now; I just need to feel the burn. I *need* to feel something other than desperation.

"Are they getting back together?" he asks. Little does he know, it's about to get worse. He's going to shit his pants when I tell him about Vanessa.

"It's complicated. She broke it off with me, not because she doesn't love me, but because she thinks our friendship is worth more. She doesn't want to get in the way of Mike and me being friends."

"He was the father of her baby? The one she lost in the accident?" my mom asks.

"Yes, but he didn't know about her," I reply, watching the tears pool in her eyes.

"How long did they date?" my dad asks.

My mom answers him, "He met her when he was seven and they were best friends until they started dating in high school." It really sucks that my mom sounds so devastated for Mike and not her own son.

My dad looks at me while sipping on his whiskey. "There's something else you need to tell us, isn't there?"

"Vanessa is pregnant." There's nothing like blurting out the worst news ever.

Rage flashes in his eyes before he slams his glass down, sloshing whiskey all over the table. "God dammit! I told you that girl was trouble. Son of a bitch!"

"I know, and I wish I had listened sooner. She's sick now. She has pre-eclampsia and can't get a DNA test until the baby is born, so we have no way of knowing if the baby is Mike's or mine. She went to Kate, actually, she followed Kate home Saturday night and told her everything. It's a mess. Kate's letting her live in her other property next door for free until she can get Vanessa on her feet and settled in a job."

They both look confused so I back up and tell them everything from start to finish.

"Well, at least that pretty little thing has a head on her shoulders; she's doing the right thing."

"By leaving me? By breaking *my* heart?" I scream at him. My mom pats my hand in an attempt to calm me down.

"No, son, by being mature enough to see into the future. Your friendship with Mike, and eventually the friendship she wants with you, mean more to her than damaging lives and families so you two can run off into the sunset. She's giving up her own happiness for you two and for that baby. Someday you'll thank her, and if you play your cards right, maybe someday she'll even come back to you. But right now you need to let her do this."

"I don't need to do anything. I'm going to win her back, Mike be damned." I push myself away from the table.

"Thanks for dinner, Mom, but I'm really not hungry. I'm going to go lie down until I sober up and then I'm going home."

A little while later my mom knocks lightly on my door and brings me a bowl of chili and cornbread.

"Daniel, I know you don't want to hear this right now but I'm going to give you some advice." She sits next to me on the bed and searches my face for an indication that I'm going to stop her. When she doesn't find one, she continues on.

"Kate and Mike have a great history. And while I understand your need to be with her, you need to let her take the reins on this one. Taking a break isn't a bad idea. Use it to your advantage, get to know her. You both rushed into this and now you're dealing with the fallout. Kate is going to have to adjust to having Mike back in her life, she also has to adjust to missing you, and she has to reconcile not only how she feels for you both but what she'll do when you all find out whose baby Vanessa is carrying. That is a lot for anyone to deal with."

When she says it like that it sounds reasonable, even if I don't want it to be.

"I hope, for your sake, that it all works out in your favor because I love you and I want you to have what your father and I have. But you have to be realistic, she has a major history with Mike, and sometimes, no matter how badly you wish for something, it just isn't meant to be. Get to know her, let her get to know you. Show Kate you'll be there for her no matter what. If you're not pressuring her, it will go a long way in your favor."

She stands to leave but turns around and adds one more thing.

"I know this is easier said than done, but try to not take this out on Mike. We've all made mistakes, done things we've regretted, but if you miss Kate this much after two weeks…imagine how he feels after four years of not being around her only to find out she's in love with his best friend. You're both feeling the loss of an amazing woman."

"Thanks, Mom."

"Anytime, sweetie, I love you."

"Love you, too."

I think about what my mom said. I'm not sure about how to deal with Mike, but I get what she means about Kate. The problem is that I need to make her want me without pushing too hard. I know she's got a history with Mike but what everyone seems to be forgetting is how badly he hurt her. I can't see her ever forgiving him enough to trust he won't do it again. Especially since her top priority in a relationship is trust. I just need to make it obvious to her that she can trust me and I'm not going anywhere.

The food my mom brought has me feeling much better. A few hours have passed since my last drink and I'm sober enough to drive home now. After saying goodnight to my mom, I find my dad waiting for me out on the porch swing.

"Night, Dad," I tell him, hoping to avoid a big discussion.

"Daniel, wait. I have to talk to you about something; it's about work and it's important."

Pausing, I turn around. No matter how much he upset me earlier, work is work.

"I was going to talk to you guys about this today but since Mike didn't show up I figured we could just do it tomorrow. I've tried to come up with other options the last few hours but honestly, son, I just don't have any." He sounds defeated.

He sighs and looks up at me. "Mike is being transferred to the LA project with you. It's a bigger project and I don't have anyone with his experience who can do it. Hamilton is out on medical leave, Rogers is out because his mother is on hospice, and Martinez just doesn't have enough experience without their supervision. So I'm moving Martinez up here so he can work under me and putting Mike in LA. I'm sorry, son. I wish I didn't have to do it."

This really isn't an issue other than it makes me Mike's boss. While we're in the middle of a huge personal problem, now I'm going to have to be the bigger person and be completely professional. Which I can do since it's necessary. I love Mike; I'm just super pissed at him right now. "It's okay, Dad, I'm sure it will be fine. Thanks for the heads up."

"Daniel, for what it's worth, I hope she picks you. I love Mike as if he was my own son, but I've never seen you as happy as you were with her."

"Thanks, Dad, that means a lot."

On the way home, I decide that for now I'm going to send Kate a nightly text. If she wants to talk, she'll call or text me back, but at least she'll know I'm thinking about her. Hopefully, I'll get to spend some time with her on Saturday after talking to Vanessa.

What I don't expect to see when I get home is Mike's truck parked in my driveway. He gets out of the truck when I pull in and it's weird. He's walking the invisible line between us, because on any other day he would be waiting inside for me, drinking a beer.

"Can we talk?" he asks apprehensively.

"Sure, come on in."

His eyes are bloodshot and it looks like he's had a hell of a day. I know the feeling well.

"Do you want a beer?"

"Yeah, that sounds good. Thanks." I return with our beers and we sit in recliners opposite of each other.

"Daniel, I need to tell you the story of me and Kate. You don't have to like it, or give up on her, or even sympathize with me, but I just need you to hear it and maybe you'll understand where I'm coming from here." I've been dying to know Mike's story for years, but now I'm not sure how objective I can be to it. Doesn't matter, though; I need to hear it for my own morbid curiosity.

"You know I've heard parts of this before, from Kate, from Connor, and a little from Jess, and none of it paints you in a very favorable light. I'm having a hard time reconciling the fact that my brother Mike is the douchebag Michael whose ass I have wanted to kick since I heard what he did to Kate. So maybe it will help hearing it from your mouth, in your words."

The story flows from his mouth and he tells it with such love and emotion it's obvious that he's loved her since he first knew what love was. He holds nothing back; he talks through his tears and tells it all. I feel myself being pulled into this story and I have to hold myself back from rooting for this couple who sound like they're made for each other. Because I know if I'm cheering for them, then I'm rooting against myself. That is until he gets to the part where he left Kate. When he cries so hard about his dad and what he was led to believe. I don't understand it still, how he could have doubted Kate, but at the same time, hearing the story from his point of view doesn't seem like he had room to believe much else.

Then I hear pieces of the story I didn't know. Like how he left her a message the night he was with Lexi. I already know Kate never got it and my heart bleeds a little.

He tried.

He never told us, but he tried. We all knew he was hiding things—running from something—we should have been better friends to him. If we had pushed him instead of waiting for him to open up, maybe this would have been different. If only he hadn't kept us in the dark and ran from everyone who loved him this could have all been so different. He was just a nineteen-year-old kid. Then when he comes full circle to this weekend, after having heard how much he wanted kids from a young age, I couldn't take it anymore. I sobbed right along with him and hugged him while he grieved his biggest loss. *Lila Hope.*

While it was devastating to hear about Lila Hope from Kate, with Mike it's worse because it's fresh. For him, this loss *just* happened. He's my best friend, how do I not grieve for him and for the little girl who would have been my niece?

"And now there's Vanessa," he says sadly.

"Now there's Vanessa. What are we going to do about it all?" he shrugs his shoulders "I don't know man. I don't want to be having a baby with Vanessa, especially now, after learning about Lila Hope I just can't take it." I feel his pain.

"I don't want to be tied down to her for eighteen years. I'm not sure how she could have changed so much to have Kate snowed, but I'm not sure I buy it at all. I wouldn't be surprised if that baby didn't belong to either of us."

He looks at me sadly. "I hate to say it, but I'm pretty sure it's one of ours. I don't think she would lie about that. The more I think about it, the more it just doesn't make sense for her to lie. If the story she told Kate is true, it sounds like she'd do anything to get that Chad guy back."

I really don't want to consider her baby could be mine but I guess it's a reality I have to face.

"I love her, Daniel. With every fiber of my being. For the past four years, I've tried to figure out how to live without her and I can't. My life doesn't work without her."

The knife in my heart stabs in a little deeper.

"I know you love her and I would never undermine your feelings, but I love her, too, and I'm not willing to let her go without a fight."

"It's only been two weeks, Daniel, you can't love her like I do; it's just not possible."

I stand up from my chair and remove my shirt. I took the bandage off last night. I turn around and let him see my back.

"Holy fuck," he says, sucking in a breath and exhaling loudly.

Yeah, that's about the response I thought he would have. When I put my shirt back on and turn around, I can see the pain in his eyes; I'm sure it mirrors my own.

"You said you'd never fill that spot until you knew…' he trails off.

"It's her, Mike, and I know that it's soon but when you know, time seems irrelevant."

He sits back down; it looks like he's trying to catch his breath. I understand the feeling.

"Has she seen it yet? Does she know?"

I shake my head. "No, it was supposed to be a surprise for her after the party. We just never got that far. I don't want her to know. I don't want it to sway her feelings. She has to make this decision from her heart and I don't want her to feel responsible. I want her to want me for me, not because she feels bad or obligated because I got a tattoo."

"My entire sleeve has to do with her. All she has to do is look at it closely and she'll figure it out. But I'm not going to tell her, either; she'll have to figure it out on her own."

"What do we do now? We have to be professional at work, other than that I'm fine with just seeing where this goes," I tell him

"Yeah, I agree, and with you in LA starting next week it will be easier at work, too." He looks relieved.

"Yeah, about that, I probably shouldn't be telling you this but Pops wanted to tell you today. You're being relocated to LA, too." I explain all of what my dad told me earlier.

"Why does that not surprise me? Guess I need to find a place to stay ASAP."

"Just stay at Connor's, in Jake's old room. You know he won't care and it's pointless to stay anywhere else. We're friends, Mike. Hopefully, we'll remain so when all this is over. I'm not giving up and I get that you aren't, either, but the only person who really controls this is Kate. I know it won't be easy and we'll have our moments but we'll hardly be there, anyway. I'm sure it will be fine." I hope I sound more convincing than I feel but it's true and I'm slowly beginning to realize it. The only person who has any power here is Kate.

"I hope you're right. Kate and I talked last night. We decided to work on our friendship. I stayed there last night; I was too wasted to drive home."

"On the couch, right?" I ask him as I feel the rage building inside of me.

"No, in her bed. I don't need to explain this to you but I *want* to. Nothing happened between us, Daniel, I swear. We just talked. I'm sure it's hard for you to understand this, but Kate and I were having sleepovers together long before we ever had sex. It's what we do…well, what we *did*. After the day we had yesterday, it was just nice to have the familiarity and to be able to talk and grieve together."

I get what he's saying but I don't like it *at all*. I take a deep breath and count to ten while exhaling. "Thanks for telling me." That's all I can really say because at this point Kate is in control of this situation. But I'm definitely going to step up my game, fuck backing off.

"Daniel, there's another thing we need to talk about. I'm slowly going to come clean to Kate about my past. In order to do that, I need to tell her about Aimee and Julie and about Aimee and Julie part two…"

Damn, he's right.

"She's going to hate us. I think she would get the whole threesome thing but to tell her about us and them? She's going to freak."

"Do you think you could ever do that with Kate? Share her with someone else like we did that night?" I wonder if he's trying to trick me for a split second but I know he's genuinely curious.

"Nope, never," I tell him adamantly.

"Yeah, me either, so why was it so easy for us with them?"

"That's easy, actually. Not only did we *not* love them, but they were a couple. They were secure enough in their love to share and experiment. To share Kate you'd have to let someone else into your love and risk losing that love to them. With us, we love her too much to share; you're not a passive male and neither am I. It worked with the girls because there were two of them. There's only one of Kate and I don't want to watch anyone else pleasing her; I want to do it myself, repeatedly.

He laughs a genuine from the gut laugh and I can't help it, I laugh with him.

"I can't believe we're even having this conversation!" he chokes out.

"Yeah, well if it were any other girl we would be trying to figure out how to do it, *not if* we would."

"True that. So the reason I brought it up is I don't think she's going to be too surprised to hear anything I've done, especially after the stories she's probably heard about me. But you, I don't think she would expect it, and since we've never told anyone, she would have no reason to expect it. Do you want to be the one to tell her? Or we can tell her together. I can do it but I thought you would want to be there."

Wow, he's right. She's not going to expect it from me and I can tell he's really trying here. He could have easily thrown me under the bus with her. Mike doesn't want me to hurt any more than I want him to. We're just in an impossible situation.

"I think we should do it together. It might be hard for her to be mad at both of us."

He chuckles, "You might be onto something there."

"Alright, I should get going. Thanks for the talk."

"Anytime, you know that. All else aside, I'm here for you." I truly mean that.

"I know and I appreciate it. Do you think after it all comes crashing down we'll still be able to hang on to our friendship?" he asks tentatively

"Family is always family, Mike, and you're my brother, no matter what. When it all comes crashing down around us, we'll build it back up from there. Neither of us had a sibling growing up; it'll be a learning experience for us both."

He nods his head and gives me a guy hug as he leaves. Strange as it is, I feel a little bit better now than I did before he came over. Maybe it won't be as hard to heal this gap between us as I thought it would be.

Once I'm in bed with the lights off, I send Kate a goodnight message.

Goodnight gumdrop. Dream of me.

A few seconds later I get a text back and I'm somewhat shocked; she's been keeping her distance pretty well.

Goodnight Daniel.

Screw it I'm going to keep going.

Are you in bed?

Her reply comes just as quickly as the first text.

Yes

I'm loving this, she must be in the mood to talk.

Do you want to talk?

It takes her longer to reply this time.

Can we just text?

It's a start and I'll happily take any opening I can get.

Of course, how was your day?

It was fun, I hung out with Marc all day and then we went out for drinks.

Mike would hate hearing that. I laugh quietly at the thought.

So are you officially drunk texting me?

Maybe ;)

Oh she's being flirty, *this* is a good sign.

What are you wearing?

Honestly?

Absolutely

I hope she says nothing. I imagine her naked in bed, getting herself off, and my dick hardens at the thought.

Only your shirt and nothing else.

Holy hell that's even better than hearing she's naked.

You have no idea how hard you're making me.

So much for not pushing her too hard

Prove it.

I've never been the kind of guy to even consider sending a dick pic but the high that will come from knowing Kate is looking at me is worth the risk. If a picture of my dick gets on the internet, no one will have a face to go with it and even if they did, I've got nothing to be ashamed of. So I snap the money shot and send it to her.

That is the best thing I've seen all day. Can I make it my screensaver?

Now I'm really laughing.

I'd rather have your tight pussy wrapped around it. No screensaver but you can look at it anytime you want to get off as long as you remember who makes you feel good.

Why don't you remind me?

I would love to, sweetheart.

Can I call you? I need a speakerphone to do that.

Yes

I hit talk as fast as I can and reach over to the nightstand for the lube in my top drawer.

"Hi," she answers breathlessly

"Hey, you sound out of breath. Are you okay?"

She laughs nervously. "Of course, but I can't believe you sent me that picture!"

"I thought you needed a reminder of what you're losing out on."

"Daniel, maybe this isn't…"

Oh, hell no, I'm not letting her finish that sentence.

"How much did you drink tonight, Kate? Where did you and Marc go?" I want to know about her day, but I also want to know how far I can push this conversation since she's been drinking.

"Well, it's kind of a long story."

"I've got nothing but time for you, Kate, always." I'll tell her this until she understands it. I'm not going anywhere; she is my priority.

"Okay, well, Mike was drunk and spent the night last night." A smile spreads across my face; she's still being honest with me even though we're not together anymore.

"I heard. Mike told me. He was here for a few hours earlier."

Honesty goes both ways, right?

"He was? I'm surprised. I hope it went well?" Hearing her squeak the last part of that sentence out cracks me up.

"It was fine. We're men, Kate, and we worked some things out, or at least tried to. We're going to try and not let this come between us and since Mike's being transferred to the LA project with me next week we'll both be staying at Connor's."

"Wow, are you going to be okay with that?" I love that she cares.

"Yes, I'll be fine. I'm his boss, so if anyone isn't going to be fine it's him. Honestly, we had a good talk. I think as long as we keep our priorities straight we'll be fine. Enough about that, though; tell me about your day."

"After Connor and Mike left this morning, Jess and I had a fight. I'm still not sure how I feel about it so I'm keeping my distance from her for now so I don't say something I'll regret."

"I'm sorry, baby."

"Thanks, you know I don't like secrets and she kept a huge one from me. I just don't know what to do about it."

We've got to tell her about Aimee and Julie soon.

"What was the secret?"

She hesitates before answering. "She had a voicemail from Mike and then she replied to him via text message. He left it the day I found out I was pregnant with Lila Hope. Instead of telling me about it, Jess hid it. I know she thought she was doing the right thing, but I don't think she did. That was my chance to find him, to tell him, to see if he wanted us. And she took my chance away. The thing is, she had the messages this entire time and I got to hear and read them *today*."

Well, I guess Mike doesn't have to worry about filling her in on this part of the story now.

"I'm sorry. I know that's got to hurt." I hear her sniffling. *She's crying.* "Don't cry, Kate, it's all going to work out. You've just got to have faith."

After some more sniffling, she replies, "Yeah, that's what Marc said, too, and I know it's true, but my world is turned upside down right now and I don't know which way is up."

"I know the feeling. Can I ask you something?"

"You can ask me anything, Daniel; I'm an open book to you."

"Do you still love me?" I know she does, but if we're going to be apart I have to hear her say it when I can sneak in the chance.

"With all my heart. This was never about our love, Daniel. This is about keeping you and Mike on the right track. And I'm not going to lie; it's also about Vanessa and the baby." I don't want to talk about them so I change the subject.

"Okay, just checking. So what else did you to today?"

"I had a picnic in the park with Marc after my fight with Jess, and then we went to the gym to work out for a few hours. It was fun; we haven't worked out together in a long time. I didn't really want to come home, so he took me to dinner and then we went to his friend's club. We had a few drinks and danced our asses off. I had just finally crawled into bed after a long shower when you texted."

"I'm glad you had fun tonight; you deserve to have a good time. I just wish you were tipsy with me in my bed instead of all alone in yours." I swear I hear her inhale and picture her smelling my shirt.

"Me, too."

"Close your eyes, Kate, and imagine me there with you, naked in your bed as the scent of my cologne floods your senses. Touch yourself, Kate. Pinch your nipples; tug on your nipple ring and imagine it's my hot and greedy mouth."

"Ohhh hell, Daniel, I want you, I need you to touch me. Make me come, please."

As if I would ever deny her.

"Keep pulling that nipple ring exactly like you know I would. How you crave it. Slide your other hand down and circle your clit for me. Don't touch it yet, just soft little circles around the outside. Picture my tongue circling you, tasting you, licking your essence off my lips. You taste so good, baby."

Her moans and the slight squeals that escape her lips set my cock off on a race to the finish line without her. "Daniel, are you wet? Tell me, are there drops of cum dripping from the head of your cock? Imagine me there with my lips wrapped around you licking and sucking every last drop while you fuck my mouth nice and slow."

Fuck.

"I'm not just wet, but the thought of your pretty little lips wrapped around my dick has me ready to come. Stop circling your clit and slide your fingers into your tight little pussy. Tell me how wet you are; I need to know." The pleasurable moan that escapes her lips when she enters herself is almost enough to make me come on its own.

"I'm so wet, so ready to come. Make me come, Daniel, *please*."

Fuck me, I can't hold back much longer.

"Let go of your nipple and touch your clit, Kate. Keep fucking yourself with your other hand. I want to hear you come. Call out my name, baby. I want to *know* that *I* gave you this orgasm."

I'm stroking my cock to the sounds of her pleasure. It's so erotic and I would give anything to be there with her. I would love to watch her fuck herself, wearing nothing but my shirt, and that's exactly what I'm picturing in my mind.

"Daniel, oh god, baby. Daniel, I'm coming, I'm coming so hard." Those screams send my heart racing but her moans send me over the edge. This is the holy fucking grail of phone sex. I want to tell her I love her but I know it will push her away.

"That was incredible."

She giggles into the phone. "Yes, it was. We should do that every night."

I moan. "Oh no, I couldn't take that every night unless I was actually buried balls deep in you. I'm a tactile kind of guy; I need to touch you, feel you, and smell you. But even more than all that I need to *taste* you. We could try for friends with benefits?"

"We can't. We shouldn't have even done this but I'm a horny drunk and I miss you. But we should talk, every night before bed. It's stupid to not talk. I just needed some clarity. And who knows, with this new truce between you and Mike, once Vanessa has the baby maybe I'll get just that. Clarity."

She's backpedaling a little, but she's also giving me more than I expected so I'll take it.

"We absolutely should have done this. No regrets, Kate. Never, not between us. I don't like our new situation and I'm going to try like hell to get you to forget about all of this because I have no doubt in the end it's still going to be you and me. But for now, I would be honored to have nightly bedtime conversations with you as long as I can hear your voice. No text messages, okay?"

She sounds happy when she replies, "Yeah, okay, that sounds really good. Goodnight, Daniel. Thanks for my new picture of you. It's going into my spank bank."

I'm laughing so hard and so is she; I can't believe she just said that. "Girls do *not* have spank banks but you're welcome."

"We do so have spank banks! It's a pretty gender neutral thing. Would it make you feel better if I call it the 'rub club'?

How about 'my finger vault' or even better, how do you like the sound of 'clam dam'?"

I can't stop laughing. Oh my god, she's being so adorably funny I've got tears streaming down my face.

"Stop! Just knowing you have so many names for your spank bank makes me wonder who else lives in there besides me now."

"I'd tell you but then I'd have to kill you. Unless you're secretly bi and then maybe we could share." More laughter from her side of the call; if only she knew how close she is.

"Not bi but definitely sexually open."

"Really? Do tell."

"Nope, that's an in person kind of discussion, don't you think? And speaking of in person discussions… Vanessa is moving in on Wednesday should I come and help?"

"I think that could be a very interesting in person discussion, but I'm game if you are. And yes, on Wednesday, but she's got help…she just wants to get settled. We figured Saturday you and Mike could come over so you can all talk and figure things out."

"Sounds good. Let's try to get the Vanessa meeting done mid-morning if we can. Connor is having a barbeque and he wants everyone to come over. Sort of a welcome home party, just all of us and Mike. It can be our first chance to really try out this friendship and see how awkward it can really be." God, she's going to hate me when she learns just how sexually open I've been.

"Well, that's what alcohol is for, right?" she says with a yawn.

"Absolutely. You sound tired, but let's talk tomorrow, okay?"

"I'd like that. Goodnight, Daniel."

"Goodnight, Kate."

Chapter Six – Mike

Work was a bitch today and I'm so glad it's over and Jake is on his way up. Everything went fine with Rick and Daniel, but now with my transfer next week, I've just got way too much stuff to get done in a short amount of time. Rick was watching Daniel and me like he thought he was going to have to jump in and break up a fight. He was noticeably conflicted; I'm sure this is hard on him as well. Rick wants what is best for Daniel but I know he thinks of me as a son; he's told me so on more than a few occasions. Even so, Daniel *is* his son.

The past few days have been rough, taking me from one emotional extreme to another. Having Kate in my life again is the best thing that has happened to me in years. But learning she's Daniel's Kate… not so great. Finding out about Lila Hope absolutely ripped my heart into shreds, but being able to read Kate's journal filled a few of those wounds with love. If only I'd been there when she craved pickles and salsa, or lemons with sugar—we could have laughed about it together. I would have brought her all the Kit-Kats and chicken soft tacos her heart desired. I missed being able to kiss Kate's pregnant belly as it grew from our love. I would give anything to have been there to feel that first kick, to hear her heartbeat, to tell her I loved her, to have said goodbye. I want another chance to get Kate on a plane headed back to our island so we can create another miracle.

I loved being in her bed again even if it was innocent. I've missed being able to watch her sleep; she always looks so peaceful. Actually, being close enough that her gardenia scent could seep into my pores is better than I could have ever imagined. Slowly, we'll work on getting our lives back on track and evolve to this new normal. After the emotional visit with my mom and Joseph yesterday, I fled to Daniel's house. Relief washed over me when he let me in to talk, but I shouldn't have been surprised; Daniel is nothing if not a class act. As soon as I saw him, though, I knew we were only going to talk about Kate and telling him about my mom would have to wait for another time. In the end, it all worked out because he showed me his tattoo and now I know what I'm up against. He's never going to give her up like I hoped he would. All I can hope for now is that he's the father of Vanessa's baby and decides to step up and marry her.

Maybe Kate is right; Daniel loves her almost if not as much as I do and she loves him, too, not *just* thinks it, she really does love him. But I *know* she loves me too. I felt it in that kiss and can see it in her actions. It's not like the three of us can be in a relationship with each other and there's no way one of us won't be hurt if she chooses between us. But by not making a choice, she's not protecting her heart like she thinks she is. In reality she's only making it hurt more. I know that feeling well; it's what brought me back to her.

With a serious need to clear my head, I jumped at the chance to hang out with Jake tonight. Jake has heard bits and pieces of all the drama from Connor and was blown away to say the least. When he offered to come up with tequila and pizza there was no way I was going to turn him down. I'm glad he's coming; I need someone to talk to who isn't on anyone's side. Connor has made it clear he's not picking any sides except for Kate's but I know he's secretly hoping she'll pick Daniel.

There's a pounding on my door which practically has me jumping out of my chair. Even when you know Jake is coming over, most of the time he scares you with his knock. It sounds more like a damn SWAT team than anything. I'll never understand why he just doesn't walk in; I've told him enough times. I think he gets personal pleasure from scaring people with that knock.

"Goddamn, are you sure you aren't an LAPD dropout?"

"Funny, asshole, just get a thicker skin. If just my knock scares your pussy ass, what the hell else are you afraid of?" He's laughing as he barrels his way inside.

"Right now there are only two things that scare me: Vanessa's baby being mine and losing Kate for good," I tell him seriously.

"Yeah, I'd say you've got reason to feel that way. So let's get drunk and hash this shit out. You do finally have a bed in that spare room of yours, right?"

"Yes, there's a bed and you'll be first to break it in. Don't fucking puke in it or you'll be buying me a new one." Jake is a heavy sleeper and he's puked in a few beds because he didn't wake up in time to make it to a bucket.

"I'm not going to puke on your precious bed. I don't plan on getting that drunk; we both do still have to work tomorrow. Just drunk enough that you'll finally tell me your story. I want to hear what happened Saturday from someone other than my drama queen brother.

Those two crack me up. They love to talk shit about each other but they are actually really close. It would have been nice to have a sibling growing up. Jess was always like a sister and Daniel has become a brother, which is what makes this hard.

A few shots of tequila and a few pieces of pizza later, Jake finally starts to ask questions.

"So you're pretty fucked right now, aren't you?" he asks, smirking

"I don't know why you think it's funny, asshat. It's really not," I tell him after taking another shot, suddenly grateful I don't have to be in until ten tomorrow morning.

"Seriously, I don't think it's funny. I think it's a messed up situation. What I find funny is the timing. If you would have just come and found her three weeks ago, or showed up at Connor's party, none of this would be happening."

"Yeah, like I haven't had that discussion with myself about a thousand times already," I reply sarcastically.

"Alright, so tell me what happened. I want to hear it from you." He gets comfortable in his chair, knowing it's going to be a long story.

For someone who hasn't talked much about my life the past few years, I sure have been telling my story a lot lately. Since Jake was occupied during the party, I finally fill him in on what was going on around him, too. I guess no one really gave him any details about that. Once I finish, I notice *he* even has tears in his eyes.

"You and Kate had a baby and she…and you didn't even know. Man, I'm sorry, that is beyond fucked up. I'd seriously die if that happened to me," he says as he reaches out for the tequila, which is almost gone.

"So now what? Are you going to fight for her?"

After pounding a shot I answer him, "I'm trying to but she's not making it easy and then there's Daniel, not to mention the Vanessa situation. It's like a freaking soap opera and I feel like all I can do is wait it out and be her friend. Ultimately, it's her decision, but I know Kate and I know she can't make this kind of choice. Mark my words, she's going to ride out Vanessa's pregnancy and then slowly start dating whoever is not the father."

"You really think she'd do that? I mean no offense but that kind of makes her sound like a bitch."

Shaking my head adamantly, I let him know that is *not* how it is at all. "No, no, no, she's not diabolical like that at all. For all of Kate's strengths, she's an avoider, not because she can't deal, but because she doesn't want to hurt anyone's feelings. Kate would rather hurt than hurt you and it's one of the best things…no, that's not right. Oh, whatever…it's just one of the biggest reasons why I'm so in love with her."

"Did you hear that she's my god sister? Mine and Connor's?" He's slurring his words but not anymore than me, I guess.

"What in the hell are you talking about? I kind of vaguely remember hearing something like that the night of the party, but honestly, I was lost in my own world and haven't thought about it since."

Jake tells me what happened when Daniel and Kate got to their house on Friday. I can only imagine how worked up Kate was over the whole thing. If she could have had Linda in her life growing up, her life could have been so much better. Not that Maryanne didn't love her, or that my mom didn't, either, but having your mom's best friend probably would be beneficial I would think. No wonder she's so stuck on this whole family thing because now it's even bigger than I knew.

"Mike, for what it's worth, here's my opinion. You've gotta fight for her to the death if necessary. Well, maybe not that hard, but you know what I mean. Daniel's a good guy, he's a fair guy and I love him, but this is *your* April. I don't know how you've gone this long without her, but don't let her go.

I pour us the last two shots and think about what he said.

"For years, I pushed my feelings aside and it kills me to do it any longer. At some point, though, this has to be her choice. I let her know how I feel and I'm going to do everything I can to be her friend again. My life doesn't work without her in it, and as devastated as I'll be if she doesn't pick me to build her life with, I would be destroyed to lose her completely. But I asked her if she was still in love with me and she couldn't tell me no. That has to mean something, right?"

"Hell yeah it does! Look, Daniel screwed up getting that tattoo; it was *way* too fast. I trust his judgment and know that he *thinks* Kate is the one for him, but in reality, he really needs to back off. If it were any other situation where there wasn't this kind of history I'd be all for Daniel getting the girl because he's my boy. But in this situation she's *your* April and I just feel like…like he's ignoring your friendship. He's watched you struggle for years with your demons and now he knows what they are. Hell, he's the one who took you in and tried to fix you and make you whole again. Two weeks of insta love does not trump what you and Kate had and can have again. It just doesn't".

"Well, don't hold back tell me how you really feel," I reply, laughing

"Oh, come on, tell me you haven't been thinking the exact same thing," he challenges.

I'm at a loss for words which is unusual for me.

"Yeah, that's what I thought; you know I'm right. Look, I feel bad for the guy, but Kate's yours and he's just gonna have to deal."

"I hope you're right, but you know the messed up part of this whole thing? I know what it feels like to lose Kate and I wouldn't wish that kind of pain on anyone, let alone one of my best friends."

"Do you have any idea how glad I am that I found April in high school? I could not imagine dealing with this kind of stuff. Dating would be a nightmare for me."

"Well, I never wanted to date anyone else but Kate; it's just what happened."

Jake roars in laughter but I can't for the life of me figure out why.

"Dude, you do realize you have *never* dated right? You've fucked but that's all. In all the years I've known you, I've never once seen you approach a woman. You've always waited for them to come to you. Maybe subconsciously that was your way of keeping a part of you only for her."

"Are you going to get all philosophical on me now since you're drunk?"

"Just speaking the truth," he says with a yawn.

"Well, I think Daniel and I came to somewhat of a truce. We'll see how it goes Saturday when we're all in the same place at the same time. That dynamic ought to be interesting."

"Connor said he's popping popcorn and loading up on tequila and vodka. He thinks it's going to be the most entertaining night of the year."

Of course.

"Sounds like we need to get Connor drunk first before he can be entertained. He can entertain us instead with another rabbit hunt or something."

"As long as it's not with April, I'm down. Sorry, man, but I've got to get some sleep. I have a meeting at seven," he says, yawning again.

The clock says it's almost one; damn, we've been talking for hours.

"Thanks for coming out tonight, I appreciate it."

"Anytime, bro, now man the fuck up and go get your woman back."

If only it were that easy.

Chapter Seven – Kate

This week has flown by; I can't believe it's Saturday already. Vanessa's move went smoothly and she's been relaxing and staying stress free. I met Chad when he moved her in and I have to say they are pretty perfect together. I wish his fiancée would have come; I would love to see the dynamic between them. Chad acts like he still loves Vanessa, and from what she told me I know he does, but he seems more *in* love than just loving. Maybe some time apart will give them both some clarity on what they really feel for each other.

Shake it Off by Taylor Swift is playing, and even though the song is annoying, it's super catchy and I find myself singing along to is as I scrub the floor. Cleaning has always been therapeutic for me; it helps me clear my head and so far this morning I've done my room, two bathrooms, and now the kitchen and it's only nine.

Jess comes downstairs and starts singing along, too. Things are still tense with us but it seems to be getting slightly better. When the doorbell rings, Jess answers the door.

"Delivery for Kate Moore, needs a signature and a photo ID."

"Kate, you've got a big delivery," Jess says with a questioning tone in her voice. I'm already off the floor and grabbing my purse.

"Here you go, would you mind putting them over there in the corner?" I ask him as I hand him a twenty.

"Sure thing, ma'am, thank you."

Jess watches him bring in case after case of One Hope champagne and paces. She doesn't talk to me until he leaves. "Kate what do you need five cases of champagne for? Are you having a party you forgot to tell me about?"

"Nope."

I'm just messing with her because it's funny to see how exasperated she is while awaiting my answer. Arms crossed over her chest, feet tapping, and eyes rolling—typical Jess.

"Well? Are you going to tell me?"

"It's to celebrate the baby and also drown my sorrows. One case each for the proud parents, one case for the man who dodged the bullet, and two cases for me."

She raises an eyebrow at me, "Why do you need two?"

"One to celebrate that innocent little soul who is going to bless us with his presence and the other to drown my sorrows in because no matter how much of a blessing a baby is, this one is still going to hurt like a mother."

"I'm sorry, Kate"

"Well, it is what it is, right? Look, I'm going to go shower. Mike and Daniel will be here soon to talk to Vanessa so I need to be ready."

"Okay, I'll go check on her and see if she needs anything while you're getting ready," she says pensively and I soften a bit. I need to just forgive her but I'm having a hard time doing it.

"Thanks."

After my shower I feel so much better, that is until I start to go downstairs. Jess is talking to Connor and her voice carries up the stairs.

"Every night this week, Connor, she's come home drunk. I don't know what the hell Marc thinks he's playing at but it's really starting to piss me off. She doesn't need to get drunk every night just to avoid everything."

"Calm down, Jess. I'm sure it's not as bad as you think it is. She's seemed fine to me."

"Fine? She seems fine to you? Do you not see the five cases of champagne in the corner? That is far from fine. She's still pissed at me, so it's not like I can say anything, but I *can* give Marc a piece of my mind."

Oh fuck this, I'm livid.

"Jess if you have something you want to say, why don't you just say it to me? I think you owe me at *least* that, don't you?

Or is keeping secrets just going to be your *thing* from now on? Hmm, maybe I'm wrong and keeping secrets has *always* been your thing, is there anything else I should know? Any *other* secrets you've been keeping from me for years?" I'm freaking fuming!

"Calm down, Kate. It's not what you think; she's just worried about you," Connor says, trying to placate me.

"Do you know how many times I've seen *her* come home drunk? I don't deserve this; I've *never* talked about you behind your back like this. *Never.* If I want to go out with my friend and have a few drinks, it's my god-given right. People in glass houses, Jess—don't try to be the morality police, *not* with me. Remember I know your secrets, too!" And with that, I storm out of the house and take a walk around the block to calm myself down.

Who does she think she is? This is not the Jess I know; my Jess would talk to me. Fuck! My Jess would have told me about Mike's message as soon as it came in. I'm taking deep breaths, trying to calm down, but all I can think about is how well do I really know my best friend after all?

By the time I get home, Mike and Daniel are already with Vanessa and Jess and Connor are gone. There's a note on the counter that says 'sorry' on it but I'm getting a little tired of hearing those words from her. My phone is beeping with a message alert and I know without even looking at it that it's Connor.

Connor:

I've got a bottle of tequila with your name on it and I expect you to be here to drink it.

Kate:

I'll be there.

My thought process is interrupted by a knock at the door, it's Daniel and Mike.

"Hey, Kate, can we come in for a few minutes?" Mike asks with a killer smile. I've never been able to deny that smile anything.

"Of course," I reply, opening the door wider so they can come inside.

"Whoa, are you having a party you forgot to invite us to?" Daniel asks, gesturing to the cases of champagne over my shoulder. "No, it's just to celebrate when the baby comes," I reply sweetly and watch him and Mike exchange 'what the hell' glances.

Mike clears his throat and Daniel motions toward the couch for us all to sit. "We talked to Vanessa," Daniel says and Mike continues, "We worked out an alternating schedule so one of us will always be with her in the evenings after work. I'm taking Tuesday, Thursday, and Saturday." Daniel finishes, "And I'm taking Monday, Wednesday and Friday. Then we'll alternate on Sundays."

Well, it sounds like they've got it all worked out, so that's a start.

"That's great, you guys, I'm proud of you both. Whichever one of you is the father will really appreciate this time, and if you're not the father, at least you're helping your friend and doing a good thing for Vanessa. Tomorrow, I'm taking her shopping for the nursery so you guys can have the day off. I like Vanessa and I want to get to know her better."

Once again they exchange glances. I swear it looks like they are concerned for my mental health or something. It's time to put a stop to this nonsense. "I'm fine, you two, honestly. I've never been the girl to believe in fairytales. I've always known that life can be cruel. We're all going to adapt to this; it's just going to take some time."

"Kate," Mike speaks up, "maybe we should take Vanessa shopping, instead. It might make things easier for you." Letting out an exasperated sigh, I take a good look at them both. They're really nervous about something but I can't pinpoint what it is. "No," I state firmly.

"I want to do this, I *need* to do this. It's going to help me transition to this new reality and I know that sounds weird but it's what I need to do. Besides, it's also going to give me a chance to get to know Vanessa better. I really like her; we've been spending time together every day since she moved in. I feel bad about leaving her today, but Chad is spending the day with her so I'm not as worried as I was."

"Have you met him yet?" Daniel asks curiously.

Nodding, I answer, "Yes, and he's a sweetheart. He really cares about her. It's too bad it didn't work out between them; they seem like they would have been a perfect fit together."

"People change," Daniel says obnoxiously and it's an obvious jab at Mike. It doesn't seem to bother Mike, though, so I'm just going to ignore it.

"They do, that's for sure, but most always it's for the better," replies Mike smugly.

Oh hell, I'm not getting caught up in their pissing match.

"Well, it's time to go so I'll see you guys at Connor's in a bit," I tell them, trying to usher them to the door. They look at each other again. *What* the hell is it they're hiding?

"We thought maybe we could, um, talk to you about something else," Daniel says sheepishly.

I've got a feeling I don't want to know whatever it is that is keeping them both so pensive. "Sure we can, but I've got to make a stop to pick up some cupcakes I ordered so can we talk at Connor's?"

"Sure, yeah no problem we'll see you there," Mike says with a sigh of relief. God this must be big whatever it is. Now to go find a place with some cupcakes since I just lied through my teeth.

~~~***~~~

An hour later, after I've spent some time on my appearance and waited in line at Sprinkles, which thankfully wasn't very long, I finally arrive at Connor's. I'm already on the defensive between my blow-up with Jess and whatever it is that Daniel and Mike want to talk about. I could use a drink A.S.A.P.

"There you are! We were wondering what was keeping you." April gives me a welcoming hug and I feel myself relaxing a bit.

"Sorry I had to make a cupcake pit stop; I was craving s'mores cupcakes until I saw the coconut ones, so of course I had to get both," I tell her, laughing.

"I love cupcakes so you don't hear me complaining. Come on, let's get you a drink. From what I've heard about your week, I'm sure you could use a few." I feel bad. I should have called her to explain and I didn't.

"I could definitely use a drink. I'm sorry I haven't called things have just been…hectic, I guess."

She smiles kindly at me. "It's okay; Jake filled me in on everything after he spent the night at Mike's. Plus, I finally got some alone time with Daniel to catch up so I think I've heard most of the story. I'm sorry you're going through so much. And I'm even sorrier to hear about Vanessa. I've never liked her very much."

April hands me a margarita, which I gratefully accept, and we work our way outside. It's strange to see everyone together in one place. I'm not really sure why, the only thing different is Mike being here, but everyone seems to be getting along. Jess shoots me a pained look and I smile back at her. I'm trying really hard not to be mad at her. I know I'm overreacting, but every little thing just seems to set me off lately. At least she seems to relax a bit at my warm greeting; I'd hate for her to feel uncomfortable. Today is supposed to be about friends so we all need to make an extra effort.

"Hey, everyone, sorry I'm late but there are three dozen Sprinkles cupcakes inside to make up for it." Connor hops up and goes inside then comes back out with two on a plate.

"What?" he says with his mouthful. "Oh, come on! With the chance that this was a PMS related pick up I just wanted to make sure I got some before you three went to town." I practically ooze margarita out of my nose and a loud snort escapes me, which has everyone laughing.

When I finally compose myself, I'm able to respond, "You're such a liar, Connor Houston. You've got the biggest sweet tooth out there. Don't blame your urges on our hormones."

"Ha! I don't consider PMS hormones; it's more like the devil coming to town for a week. Now if we're talking actual hormones, I'd consider those more like carnal desires, wouldn't you?"

Thankfully, Jess reaches out and smacks him. "I'll tell you what, how about you do without your carnal desires for a bit and see if that feels like the devil coming to town, too."

He raises up his hands in defeat, "How about we just forget this conversation ever happened and to make up for it I'll go get cupcakes and bring them out for everyone?"

Jake thumps him on the back of the head. "That's probably a good idea. I swear I don't know how you ever got a girlfriend, let alone a hot one."

"I just felt sorry for him; he was like a little lost puppy wandering around campus. I just didn't think he'd be so *needy*."

Connor pounces on her and pulls her from her chair "*Needy?* You think I'm needy, huh? I'll show you exactly what I'm needy for." He throws Jess over his shoulder and carries her into the house with her squealing the entire way.

"Damn, guess I'm going to have to go get my own cupcake now," Jake pouts, but April isn't buying into it.

"Will you bring the margaritas out, too, when you come back? Thanks, babe," she tells him as she blows him a kiss.

"Only if I get drunk April tonight," he whispers in her ear but I'm sitting right next to her and I swear the tone to his voice even makes *me* blush.

"You can count on it, baby," she tells him breathlessly and suddenly I feel like the odd man out.

Needing a minute to myself to work through my thoughts, I wander over to the side yard and check on Bev's garden. This probably wasn't a good idea, though, as my body remembers how it felt to be covered by Daniel on this very grass the morning of my birthday. I can't believe that was only three weeks ago; it seems like so much longer.

"Penny for your thoughts?" Daniel asks from behind me as his hands wrap around my waist. For a moment I lean against him, close my eyes, and just breathe. The thought of Mike walking up and catching us pulls me from his embrace. Keeping my distance from both of them is key tonight.

"Just trying to clear my head, but this probably wasn't the best place to do it," I tell him after finishing off my margarita.

"Why not? Does being here bring back certain *feelings*?" he whispers over my shoulder into my ear so seductively. He knows exactly what I'm thinking about and he's trying to use it to his advantage. I'm not playing that game tonight.

Turning around, I smile sweetly at him, lean up on my tiptoes as if to kiss him, but stop just a little shy "Excuse me, but I need a refill," I say, and as I walk away, I can feel his eyes on me but I won't allow myself to turn around.

A few hours pass, and surprisingly we're all having a good time. The food was excellent and we're all three drinks past buzzed. There's no way I'm staying here tonight, though. I'll either have Marc come get me or call a cab. It's so weird to think Daniel and Mike are going to live here with Connor now. I can only imagine how awkward it's going to be for them, but at least they'll be close to Vanessa, which is great.

"Aaaapprrriiilll," Connor says as he slurs, "want to come find Bugs Bunny with me?" And even though Connor is laughing, I don't think I've ever seen Jake look so alpha male before.

"Hell no, we're not doing that again," Jake growls at him. Everyone else is laughing but Jess and I have no clue what's going on. Mike takes mercy on us and explains. I don't think I've laughed that hard in a very long time. My stomach hurts so bad and Jess and I both have matching tear trails down our faces.

"Fine," Connor huffs. "If we can't play Bugs Bunny then can we at least play truth?"

"You mean truth or dare?" Jess asks.

"No, just truth. Truth or dare is for pussies. Everyone takes the dare to get out of telling the truth. We're all friends we should know each other's truths even if it means admitting our dares." Connor has the biggest shit eating grin on his face and I can only imagine his questions. It actually sounds intriguing. I'd like to get to know their secrets, and since I don't really have anything to hide, I'm in.

"Sounds good to me, do you play with different rules?" I ask him with genuine curiosity.

"Kate! My favorite sister! I knew I loved you for a reason, that's a really good question. We play in a circle and go clockwise from the leader, who would be me. I'll ask a question and then everyone in the circle answers it. *Honestly.* If you know someone is lying, you have to call them out on it. There are no secrets in truth. Then after my question, the next person asks one, and so forth."

"I'm in," says Jess as she plops on Connor's lap.

April and Jake shrug their shoulders like they couldn't care less and they probably don't since they've been locked in a kiss for the last five minutes or so. Daniel and Mike don't look as excited, which reminds me… they wanted to talk earlier. Maybe I'll make that my truth to ask them what they wanted to talk about. I'll have to word it carefully since everyone gets the same question.

"Alright! It's truth time," Connor says excitedly. He looks like a little kid on Christmas morning.

The first round of questions are kind of silly, but when the second round starts they get a little more intense, and by round three it's an all-out truth war.

"Have you ever had a threesome?" Connor asks. "We all know I have." *That* is a fact I didn't know and I choke a little on my margarita, even though it doesn't surprise me.

"Nope, thankfully you're a bigger whore than me," Jess says with a giggle.

"Nope." I reply. "I'm even less of a whore than she is," I say laughing and Jess is busting up. Jake and April both answer no. I was actually curious if we'd get some interesting information from their answer.

"Yeah, but…um…most of you already knew that," Mike answers sheepishly, and even though it doesn't surprise me, it still hurts to hear it. That would have never happened if we'd stayed together and a little piece of me breaks for him and for us. Never in a million years did I expect the next answer. I would have lost my ass in a bet on this one for sure.

Daniel avoids my gaze as he answers and all hell breaks loose. "Yes." It's all he says but Jake and Connor both exclaim, "What the fuck?" at the same time which mimics my thoughts exactly. Mike is the only one who doesn't look surprised and I can tell Jess notices that, too. She gets a determined look on her face and I have a feeling I'm not going to like her next question.

"Was it Aimee and Julie? Come on, Daniel, you can't say threesome and not dish… we're playing truth."

Connor is on the border of mad and excited and I'm not sure which emotion is going to win this battle with him. But Daniel looks pissed, so I'm guessing mad is going to win.

"We're playing truth, which means I have to answer the question, but I don't have to give you any details of my private life."

"Fair enough," Connor pouts.

It's Jess's turn and she doesn't hold back. "How many of you have had foursomes?" Right then when I see the look Daniel and Mike exchange, I know it's game over. *I'm going to be sick.*

It's a continuous round of 'No's' as we go around the circle, and instead of this being fun, a somber mood has settled over us all. Surprise, surprise, Mike and Daniel both answer yes. I pull out my phone and text Marc the address and ask him if he can please come and get me. He immediately replies he'll be here in twenty minutes. I pull the bottle of tequila off the patio table and pour myself a double shot. Connor and Jake look dumbfounded; they aren't even asking questions at this point. Probably because they know that both men just stepped into a steaming pile of shit.

"My turn," I say, and by now even I'm slurring my words. "I want to know by a show of hands how many people here have not had sexual relations with Julie and Aimee."

Like I thought, Connor, Mike and Daniel have all been with the same two girls. I turn to April and ask her sweetly, "April can I have your turn too? I have one more question?" She nods and no one says anything about me breaking the rules. So I begin my rant that eventually turns into a question.

"Today, Mike and Daniel wanted to talk to me about something and I could tell it was something I didn't want to hear so I was avoiding it. In the back of my mind, I remembered something Daniel said the other night when we were having phone sex. Oops, I probably wasn't supposed to mention that, was I? Well it's not like we *actually* fucked, so I guess it's okay. Don't worry, Mike, if it upsets you too much maybe you can take a turn next week."

They look scared because out of everything I've ever done, this is *very un*-Kate. "Come on, guys, lighten the hell up would you? This is my truth isn't it? Well, my turn to ask one so I might as well tell it. Anyway, Daniel said he was and I quote 'definitely sexually open' and I wondered what that meant. I'm not a prude, and I've never had a threesome, but I still consider myself sexually open as well. Whatever floats your boat, right? This truth is for the men in this group. I want to know by a show of hands, please. How many of you have been in a threesome or foursome with each other?"

Ever so slowly, Daniel and Mike's hands both slowly creep up and I'm not the only one in shock. Jake's voice thunders through the night, and for whatever reason it makes me laugh uncontrollably. "Are you fucking kidding me right now? You two and who? God, please tell me you guys weren't fucking each other. That is just TMI."

Jess replies, "I don't know, the thought of that could be *really* fucking hot."

All I can do is laugh. She's completely right and the absurdity of this situation is comical. Mike jumps up, running his hands through his hair as usual, but Daniel actually speaks, "Kate we wanted to talk to you about this. This isn't how…"

"This is not how we wanted you to find out, Katie Grace, I'm so sorry," Mike says sadly, and for some reason that *really* pisses me off.

"Look, you know what? I don't care if you're sorry! I'm so sick and tired of hearing both of you saying you're sorry. Your past is just that, *your* past. You have every right in the world to have one and if you both fucked Aimee and Julie, together *and* separately, more power to you. If you've fucked each other, that's even better, because maybe you can understand why it's so goddamned hard to choose between you two. Both of you have fucking fantastic cocks. But this…" I say, waiving my arm around in a circle at all my friends "This isn't working for me right now."

A horn honks and I start to gather my stuff before the dam of tears building behind my eyes bursts. They're not even sad tears, they're pissed off tears "Do not, let me be absolutely clear, do *not* call me. Do not come by, do not send me packages or letters or flowers or coffee, or any other thing you can think of to make contact. Let me breathe for *at least* a week. If you try, you'll push me further away and *trust me* when I say you do *not* want that right now."

"Kate, are you okay?" Marc's concerned voice asks from behind me.

"Sorry to just walk in, but I heard her yelling, and after the text she sent me I was worried," Marc tells Connor and Mike throws his chair. I've never seen Mike get violent. Is this how he deals with his shit now?

"Are you kidding me with this right now? This isn't how you were supposed to find out and you know that! You're all pissed at me for running away and never looking back, but what are you doing right now, Kate? You're fucking running! And with HIM! Don't you understand how much worse that makes this entire situation?"

Marc is standing like a bodyguard between Mike and me. I've never seen Mike so angry, but he's never seen me this angry, either. "It's none of your business if I call Marc to pick me up, *Matthews*. I'm not your girlfriend, I'm not your fiancée, I'm *nothing* to you but a friend. You don't get to tell me who I can and can't be friends with. Hell, you don't even get to tell me who I can and can't fuck anymore. That was *your* decision, not mine, so get down off your high horse and leave me the hell alone!"

"Kate, can we please just go somewhere quiet and talk to you? We'd like to explain…" I shove my hand out in front of me to stop Daniel from going any further. "So now you'd like to talk to me? Now you want to explain how 'sexually open' you are? No. I'm not interested. You should have told me this the other night. We never should have waited for that in person discussion."

Daniel glances to Mike for intervention. "Kate, we wanted to tell you together. That's the truth and why we came over earlier, but like you said, you cut us off. You're wrong about you being nothing to me because… dammit, Kate, you're my *everything*." And even though his tone is laced with nothing but pure emotion, I'm too worked up to care.

"Well, you have a great way of showing it, don't you? It's been three and a half years, Mike. Somewhere in that time, if I was really 'your everything', you would have let me know it! You sowed your oats and now it's time for me to do the same. I've been doing my best to look out for all of you, to make sure that you're all okay, so we can *all* be okay." I'm so mad and upset, I'm sobbing through my words at this point but I don't even care. "I'm done, you guys, it's time to look out for myself. All this…" I say, waving my arms wildly around me, "I didn't sign up for all of this. I don't know much right now, but I know this is *not* what I want for my life. I'm done walking the tightrope between you two. Let's just get this out in the open now. Mike, I can *never* be with you, because for all the times you lifted me up and made me whole, you ultimately let me crash and fall. I broke into pieces that are yet to be fixed. There's no way in hell I'm letting the person who destroyed me try to fix me. I'd be a flipping fool. Daniel, as for you, I'm sorry but you're just a casualty of war. You're his friend, his family, and I've never been the kind of girl to be passed around an inner circle of friends."

Marc places his hand on my low back and guides me to the gate. Everyone is still gaping at my outburst, but as we walk away, I hear Jess and April's statements almost overlap each other. "See, guys, I told you. She's different; now we're going to lose her again," says Jess, while April is saying, "She's just drunk, she doesn't mean it. Tomorrow things will be better, you'll see."

Jess's comment pisses me off, so I pivot on my heel and storm back over, getting in her face. "Let me make something perfectly clear to you, *Jessica*. I'm not that fragile girl I was four years ago. That broken, pathetic excuse for a human that I was no longer exists. I've buried a child, *my* child, and I'm still standing. If that didn't break me and send me into a padded room or into a full-blown alcoholic binge trust me, this won't, either. Just because I'm showing some backbone for the first time in my life does *not* mean something is wrong with me. On the contrary, it means *everything* is right with me."

Now I've said all I need to say, I need to get out of here before her tears make me feel bad for what I just said. As I walk to the car with Marc, it's obvious I'm a lot drunker than I thought because he has to keep me from falling quite a few times. Marc doesn't say anything until we get to our favorite taco place. "Come on, baby girl, let's get some food into your overly drunk but very fine ass." Leave it to Marc to make even the drunk nights sexual.

After he orders us both carne asada street tacos and some bottles of water, he comes and sits with me. "You look like hell; maybe you should go in the bathroom and splash some water on your face." That's actually not a bad idea because I've had to pee for what seems like forever.

"Since I need to use the facilities anyway, I'll see what I can do." Once I take care of business, I look in the mirror and saying I look like hell was a compliment. I look like death warmed over. My makeup is smeared and tear-streaked, my eyes bloodshot, and even my nose is red from crying.

Once I wash my face, I feel a little better and look it, too. Marc and the waitress are flirting when I get back and I'm in no mood to watch. "Don't let me interrupt." *Damn the snarky bitch that lives inside me is on point tonight.* Marc has the decency to look embarrassed as I slide into the booth but this girl...Ugh, this girl flashes me the universal look for 'I'm gonna fuck your man' as she passes Marc's phone back to him. Psht. Little does this bitch know that even if they hook up she'll only be a booty call. I doubt he'll ever settle down, but he seems okay with that so more power to him. She lets her fingers caress his, and in what I assume is *supposed* to be her sexy voice says, "don't forget to call me," but seriously she sounds like a cat in heat, all high pitched and squeaky.

"What are you thinking, Kate? I know something is going on in that head of yours." Marc's eyes are sparkling; he's enjoying this.

"I'm thinking that tequila makes me a mean drunk and maybe I should drink something different next time. And I'm also thinking if you screw that waitress you've got lower standards than I ever could've imagined."

He lets out a good laugh, "Why? Because she's a waitress?"

Really? Why would he go there? "What? No one should be looked down upon because of their job. A hard worker is a hard worker. It's because..." I lean across the table and whisper loudly at him. "She's a ho."

Marc looks at me for a long moment and doesn't say a word. Finally, I'm blinded by his megawatt smile. "I've never seen you this drunk before, baby girl. It's a good look on you. You're finally taking down your walls and speaking what's on your mind." He takes my hand in his across the table and kisses the top of it. "Now, if only we can get you to do that when you're sober."

"I'm already getting there, buddy old pal," I tell him right before devouring one of the best tacos I've ever had. *Why does food taste so much better when you've been drinking?*

We eat in peace for a few minutes, both of us just enjoying our food. I know I'm sobering up because I'm tired and starting to feel guilty about all the things I said tonight to my friends.

"So you want to fill me in on what happened tonight? What did Mike do to set you off? I've never seen you go off like that before on him *or* on Jess." He's really serious all of a sudden. I do my best to fill him in and he nods and comments in all the right places, but it seems forced somehow.

"You think I'm wrong, don't you? That I had no right to go off on them the way I did?" I really want to know what he thinks.

"No, Kate, I think that you have the right to feel however you need to in order to process and deal with this situation you're in. But I also agree that their past is their past and they are entitled to it. You can't tell me that just because someone has had a ménage that you would stop dating them? Especially since it's before you were ever even in the picture."

Begrudgingly, I admit he's right. "No, I wouldn't but what bothers me is that they had one *together*. It makes me mad and I can guarantee you if I asked them both into my bed they would turn me down. So what made those two so special?"

"Oh, Kate, you really don't get it, do you? Nothing makes them special. But everything makes *you* special. They didn't care about those girls. Sure enough to have sex with them and still look back fondly on it, but the fact that they wouldn't want to share speaks volumes about how they feel about *you*. When you've got something amazing, you don't ever want to let anyone get close enough that it can disrupt your environment. It's like asking for trouble."

"I guess," I reply with a frustrated sigh.

"Think of it this way: if you and I had sex, it would be great and maybe a little awkward afterward for a quick minute, but everything would still be okay later. If you and Daniel and I had sex, it would be fun but your love lies with him. I could still walk away and we could still be friends with fun memories to look back on. I'm sure that's how it was with those girls.

However, for the sake of the argument, which by the way is weird because I don't want to picture you all freaky deaky like this, but if you and Daniel and Mike were to do it, trying to separate after and make sense of it all would be very difficult. Trying to do it in the first place would probably be difficult because of your feelings for them and theirs for you. Make sense?"

The look on his face is so genuine. I know he's trying to help, and I agree with most of what he's said, but I do have a question. "Do you really think you and I could have casual sex and then just go back to being friends?" I ask him incredulously.

"Out of everything I said that's what you're going to focus on?" He's amused. "Okay, I'll play along. Yes, I *absolutely* think we could have sex and still be friends. You know me, Kate, I'm not the settling kind of guy and the only person I would *ever* try for would be you. At least at this point in my life, anyway. But your heart lies elsewhere, so I'd never let myself get attached. I'd just be in it for the smoking hot sex. You know you want to and that's the true reason you focused on that part of what I just said."

He's making light of the situation because he knows me well enough to know I asked that question because it was the only part of the conversation that was safe. Talking any more about Mike and Daniel is just too much right now.

"One of these days we're going to have sex and it's going to be so amazing that we'll both wonder why we didn't do it sooner. I know that for sure. We'll wish we'd been friends with benefits all along, but that's all it would be. You're right, my heart is with someone else, I just need to figure out what to do about it," I tell him honestly.

"Keep doin' what your doin', baby girl. Life has a funny way of working itself out. Things happen when you least expect them to. I'll always be your shoulder to cry on and you'll always be mine. Take comfort in that, a lot of people don't have anyone they can truly trust. You've got more than you realize; you just need to get past the hurt and come out on the other side stronger. Come on, let's get you home."

Chapter Eight – Kate

The last two weeks have been very peaceful. Marc ended up taking me home long enough to pack a suitcase. Thankfully, no one was home and I was able to get in and out without an issue. I ended up renting a room at the Lowe's Hollywood hotel and that's where I've been for the last fourteen days. The thing I felt the worst about was canceling on Vanessa, but what was interesting was that Daniel had shown up in my place. He told her I had a bad night and that I would make it up to her later. Even though I was thankful, *very* thankful since I didn't even wake up until three hours after I was supposed to meet her, the whole thing irritated me because he knows me so well already and I wish he didn't.

I've had two mani-pedi's since I've been here, two massages a week, room service at least once if not twice a day and caught up, actually even gotten ahead on my assignments. When I emailed my advisor that I was having some personal issues, she assumed it was because of all the stuff going on surrounding Tom's arrest. She was very supportive and emailed all my professors and worked things out for me.

Marc has come by a few times to take me to dinner and talk. He's also been my go-between since my cell phone has been on silent. I see their messages and missed calls but I don't answer them. Marc is the only one who knows where I am so he's been getting daily calls from Jess asking me to please call. I still haven't. I'm still a little angry, but mostly I'm ashamed I let everything get so out of control. Not ashamed of what I said, necessarily, just how it all happened.

Marc also ended up bringing me my car so I could go visit Vanessa during the day while they're all at work or school and that's been really nice. I'm glad I'm getting to know her; she is *such* a sweet girl. I told her all about my freak out on everyone and why I'm spending time away and she told me she confessed to Daniel and Mike that she did drug Mike. Not with a roofie— she thought she could slip him a couple of Xanax and he would loosen up enough to give her a chance. Mike's a lightweight on drugs, which she had no way of knowing and she gave him two double-strength Xanax.

At least she came clean; she could have kept that secret forever and no one would've ever known. She said even though the guys were mad they forgave her and that Mike even felt better knowing it was only a bad reaction to Xanax. I'm really proud of Mike for forgiving her; it really shows he's trying. I should probably follow his lead and forgive Jess but I don't know if I'm ready yet. Ready or not, I'll be home in about five minutes after two weeks of peace. I've never been an anxious person, but going home and facing the firing squad has me on edge.

When I open the garage, Jess's car isn't even here, which is a relief, but Mike's truck is next door. Today must be his Sunday with Vanessa. Vanessa knows I'm supposed to be back this afternoon so I'm sure she probably told them and Mike will stop by later on. It's okay, though, because I'm finally ready to have this conversation with him now.

After spending some time unpacking, straightening up my room, and throwing my clothes in the washer, I settle down with a glass of wine and my kindle. I'm trying to decide if I'm in the mood for romance or mystery when there's a knock at the door.

It's go time.

"Come in," I call out.

The door opens slowly and Mike walks in, taking in the surroundings before speaking. God, he looks good and my heart races a little. I really wish it would stop doing that. "You know, I could have been an ax murderer," he says cockily, leaning back against the door with his arms crossed in front of him.

"I knew it was you," I tell him dismissively while sipping on my wine.

He walks closer and stops right in front of me. "Oh yeah? How?" He's so close to me and I can feel the sexual tension radiating off of him. If I said I wasn't affected I would be lying.

"Because I saw your truck out there when I got home a couple of hours ago, and I knew Vanessa would tell you I was supposed to be home today."

"May I?" he asks, gesturing toward the seat next to me.

"Suit yourself." *Dear lord, he smells good and he's so close.*

"Look at me, Kate; it's time we talk this out. Connor took Jess to SeaWorld so they won't be back tonight. Do you want to order dinner and talk?"

I nod my head but I'm afraid to speak. The feisty mood I'm in coupled with being alone with Mike for the first time in years might be a bad mix. As I watch him walk from the couch to the menus on the fridge, I'm reminded of what a nice ass he's always had. *Shit!* Time for a refill.

"Chinese okay?"

"Sure," I reply as I refill my glass. "There's beer in the fridge and more wine, or if you want something harder it's in the cabinet next to the sink on the right."

Once he calls in the order, he stalks back and sits down, gently removing my glass from my hand. "I'd like to be sober for this talk and I wish you would be, too." His voice radiates sincerity but the underlying tone is *need*.

"I'm not drunk, Mike, I'm just taking the edge off."

The narrowing of his eyes shows me he's not happy. "Like you took the edge off on Saturday? Talk to me, Kate. Tell me what you're feeling. I can imagine but I want to hear it from *you*."

Guess it's time to put up or shut up. I can't judge them for keeping secrets if I don't talk to them. "You want to know what I'm feeling? You need to be sure, Mike, because I'm not going to sugar coat it."

"I don't want you to. We can't move forward with anything until you lay your cards on the table, Kate. Don't you realize yet that all the power in this situation is with you? Daniel and I can want to be with you until the cows come home, but you're the only one who can make a decision. You hold all the cards here… not us."

"Look, I said some things Saturday that…"

"That were said from a place of anger. If anyone gets that, it's me, trust me when I say that. But tonight I want to hear from your heart, Kate. Good or bad."

"Alright then, I'm confused and I don't know what to feel. One minute I want Daniel and the next I want you. I know with all my heart that we should all just be friends. But then my heart, body, mind, and libido tell me I want something different."

"Go on," he urges and I pause, reaching for my wine, shooting him a 'don't mess with me' look.

"So when I heard about what you guys did with those girls and each other…"

"I'm going to stop you right there. We did not do *anything* with each other; I just want you to be clear about that. Neither one of us are into that," he states adamantly.

It's a relief to hear that even though in the deep recesses of my mind I still agree with Jess that seeing Daniel and Mike together would be totally hot.

"Well, it sounds like you're into a lot more than you used to be," I snap at him, but before he replies there's a knock on the door. Mike answers the door, pays for the food, and brings it back to the coffee table.

"Where are the forks?"

"First drawer left of the sink." Silence has descended upon us as he gets the forks, a few bottles of water, and sorts the food. He hands me the chicken chow mein and he takes the broccoli beef, just like old times. We eat quietly, both of us deep in thought.

"Will you come somewhere with me? Please." What am I going to say…no? He went somewhere with me not too long ago with no questions asked.

"Sure, let me grab my sweater and some shoes."

It's weird riding in his truck. He's changed, not just because of his car but he always had that preppy boy feel to him before. That was Claire's doing… and the Porsche… that was his dream car but it looks like his dreams have changed. Just as Sara

Bareilles belts out the last notes of *Gravity,* we arrive at the beach. I had a feeling he was bringing me here, to the place where I'm the weakest because every single memory of this place that I have includes him.

As we exit the truck, he grabs a blanket and takes my hand, leading me to our spot. This place looks the same but I haven't been here since that night. The sun just finished setting and there's no one around except us and the stars.

"Why are we here, Mike?" I ask hesitantly.

"I've always been able to talk to you, Kate, but what we need to talk about tonight is hard and emotional. This has *always* been our safe place. So whatever happens tonight, whatever we say, it needs to happen in a safe haven. I need you in my life, Kate, and I know that's selfish after everything I've done, but it's the truth. If we're going to talk about my many transgressions, I feel it's important to do it here."

"Okay." My voice comes out strong, which is good because I feel anything but.

Once he lays out the blanket and we both get comfortable—and by comfortable, I mean me between his legs with his arms wrapped around my waist just like old times—he finally starts to open up.

"You're right, Katie Grace, I am into a lot more than I used to be and I feel like I need to explain it."

I cut him off quickly, "You don't have to explain anything to me."

"Yeah, I do. I owe it to both of us to get this off my chest, even if it's hard for you to hear. Just know that I'm not telling you this to hurt you, but for you to understand. When I left, I was a mess; my mind wasn't in the right place. I was grieving, and after all the proof my mom and Tom showed me that you and your dad were behind everything I was *beyond* devastated. I couldn't reconcile how the girl who I knew and loved could do anything like what I was being shown. Even so, I *knew* my mom and dad wouldn't manufacture proof. Tom, I wasn't so sure about; I always thought he was a shady fucker."

His arms wrap tighter around me and I feel him tense up a bit. "Once I left, I just drifted for a few weeks. I finally came back this way and stopped off for coffee about fifteen minutes from your house. By then, I knew in my gut you had nothing to do with it, but I still wasn't sure about Joseph. I was embarrassed and angry at myself for treating you that way. I didn't want to give you a chance to forgive me for something I couldn't even forgive myself for. I should have *never* doubted you or your love. I realized then that I needed time to figure out who I wanted to be. I never fit into that preppy boy mold, but I filled it well because it's what was expected of me. All I ever wanted was what I told you that day on the beach."

"Me, you, and a few kids for Jess to watch in our own island paradise," I whisper.

"Exactly. God, Kate, the only thing I ever knew was real in my life was that you were meant to be my wife, *my* happily ever after. Everything else I was never sure of. I never wanted to work with my dad, never wanted to even go to college. The best thing that could have ever happened would have been us having a baby and me being Mr. Mom. At least for me, and when that didn't happen and my world started to fall apart… I let it."

A shiver runs through me as I try not to let my emotions get to me after finally hearing his side of the story. Gently, he tucks the blanket around my legs to keep out the cold; it's a sweet gesture. He continues, "When I went into the coffee shop, that's where I met Aimee and Julie."

Ugh, I so do not want to hear this but I let him continue.

"Aimee gave me her number and invited me to her birthday party. Initially, I told her probably not, but as the day went on I needed a distraction. I was running out of money and had no clue what to do with my life. I had to become the man you deserved before coming back. When I got to the party, I found out the girls were lesbians. Well, technically I guess they are bi and they have a real BDSM fetish. They are also now happily married; I think it's important you know that."

He pauses then kisses me on the cheek and whispers in my ear, "I missed you so much, Kate. Every breath I took without you by my side felt like it was stealing the air from my lungs instead of keeping me alive."

Damn him.

A single tear escapes from my eye and I quickly wipe it away, hoping he doesn't notice.

"That night we got drunk, very drunk, and Aimee and Julie showed me a new way to have sex. Yes, it was a threesome but it was more than that. I don't think it was their intention at all, but I learned you can have sex without emotion by doing a few simple things."

My body tenses up, bracing itself for all that's about to come and he hugs me tighter. He knows this is going to hurt.

"There's no way to sugar coat this. I've had a lot of random sex the past few years. The vast majority of the girls, if they told me their names I don't even remember them. There were always rules in place; not being allowed to touch me was rule number one. Most of them let me tie them up. They thought it was part of the kink, but for me it was insurance they couldn't touch me. I don't like intimacy with my sex, Kate; that's reserved only for you."

Deep breath in and exhale.

"Nothing crazy, I promise, all light stuff. Usually with my belt or a tie, it's not like I have a closet filled with BDSM tools, so you can relax. Although, I have noticed over time I enjoy it, especially if she lets me spank her. There's just something about a woman submitting themselves completely to me that's a major turn on."

Holy fuck, why is this turning me on?

"Even so, I still missed you. I've thought about what it would be like to tie you up, to spank you, to make you come over and over again. We never got to do any of that but I know if we did it would be *so* fucking hot."

Oh good god, I'm going to have to go jump in the ocean to cool off if he doesn't stop.

"You need to understand this is all one hundred percent consensual. They all know ahead of time that I like it rough and it's a one-time deal. The only other rule I had was that no one could even come close to looking like you. Anyway, I've gotten completely off topic here. The night I met Daniel and Connor was the night I was with Aimee and Julie. If I had never met them who knows what would have happened. I was sad and desperate and quickly running out of money. Daniel gave me a home and a job... he rescued me from myself. If I wouldn't have met those girls, I wouldn't have my family."

"I've heard some of this from them, it's just when they told me the story I didn't know we were talking about you," I say sadly.

"Yeah, I know the feeling, Connor talked a lot about his friend Kate but I never knew it was you, either. Let me fast forward a bit here. Obviously there were girls, lots of them, and after Daniel was with those two I inadvertently found out about it. He can tell you his story, but when they asked for a foursome, well, we're guys and we like sex... I don't know what else to say. It's something that happened and I, well, we all enjoyed it. That was actually the night Daniel met Vanessa."

"Wait, what? So that was only a year ago?" I ask incredulously.

"Yes, but a lot can change in a year, Kate. People can live a lifetime in a year, especially if it's a bad one."

He's got me there; I know that all too well.

"Anyway, I was getting really burned out by then and thinking about you more and more. Finally, on your birthday weekend I decided enough was enough and I had to do whatever it took to get you back in my life. Unfortunately..."

"That was the weekend I met Daniel," I finish for him.

"Exactly, and to be honest with you, I've always thought part of the reason I kept intimacy out of my sex was because to let someone in would be like cheating on the best part of us. Sex is physical but love and emotions are connected to the soul. The only person connected to my soul is you, Kate. I'm not saying that sex isn't cheating, but we weren't together and I *still* felt like an emotional cheater. Then the other day, Jake pointed something out to me."

He pauses and all I hear are the waves crashing against the shore and our hearts beating as one while he holds me tight.

"What did he say?" I finally ask him, not able to take the wait any longer.

"Jake said that in all the years he's known me I've never dated and I've never *once* approached a girl. He reminded me I always let them come to me. I realized how extremely true that was and took a while to think about it and figure out *why* that was. And then he said something else: he kept calling you *my* April and I finally figured it out. In my mind, sex is just a physical act when there's no emotion going into it. No feelings for the other person, no love being poured into it. But to approach someone, to let them in, to let them touch, in my mind that would have still been cheating, and even though we were apart I never wanted to cheat on your heart, Katie Grace, not ever." He whispers those last words and tingles caress me from head to toe.

He didn't want to cheat on my heart but he sure as hell just stole it with those words. Not that I agree with his line of thinking but I can *completely* understand it.

"Daniel and I have done some talking the past few days and we think we might have an idea about how to deal with things. Before we go there, I want to know if you came to any conclusions while you were gone the past few weeks. I cut you off back at the house when you were getting ready to talk."

Do I tell him? Mike was just brutally honest with me about things I never wanted to know about him and yet somehow the fact that he was comforts me immensely.

"When I was at the hotel, I tried *not* to think. I got massages, manicures, room service, did tons of homework, basically anything to keep my mind off of you guys. But at night, when I would close my eyes, you two were all I could think of."

His hand is tracing circles on my thigh, slowly inching up higher. My breath catches but I try to ignore what he's doing and continue.

"What I said Saturday night is true, Mike. I might have been drunk but I wasn't lying," I say breathlessly and the circles stop. When they do, I tense up a bit…out of reflex maybe? Out of want most likely, because I'm still turned on by his words. He picks up on it and starts up with the circles again. My body instantly relaxes. *Damn him.*

"I know you meant what you said, but I also know that we're working on this, and over time you'll trust me again." His hand is now stroking my upper inner thigh. He's so close to me and my body floods with need.

I need him.

"You're right; eventually, I will trust you again. I've never been able to stay mad at you for long." My heart is racing and I'm so distracted by what he's doing it's hard to stay on topic. I should push him away, I know I should, but my body *wants* him, or maybe it just needs what he's doing and I'm beyond caring anymore.

"Go on and tell me what you figured out," he says, but his hand is now cupping my pussy and my body betrays me by leaning back into him as a moan escapes my lips.

"I'm…I'm trying…to tell you…distracting…you're…" It feels so good, I can't even form the words.

"I'm distracting you, Kate? Let me make you feel good and then maybe you'll be able to concentrate. Can I make you come, baby?" he asks, whispering in my ear, with a slight nibble on my earlobe.

Fuck it; I deserve to have some fun don't I?

"Yes, Mike, make me feel good." As soon as I finish saying yes, he already has my shorts unbuttoned. He slides his middle finger up and down my slit, spreading my wetness around and circling my clit while he still continues to cup me in his hand…hard. It feels absolutely amazing. Maybe it's the wine I had beforehand, or maybe it's him and this setting. Hell, maybe it's just because I'm horny as hell but I don't remember it ever being this good with him before.

His tongue traces down my neck, and as he connects with my shoulder, he bites down gently but with just enough force that I moan in a combination of pleasure and pain. At that exact moment, he slides a finger inside me while still circling my clit. My arm finds its way behind his head and I run my fingers through his hair. He slides another finger in, and then another and I'm fucking his hand with wild abandon. The presence of his erection behind me makes itself known, and for a fleeting second I feel bad. Then I begin to grind harder against him and he turns my head to his with his free hand and captures my lips with his. There are no words; I'm absolutely captivated by his kiss. There's so much passion and fire between us and I'm building higher and higher with every stroke of his tongue. Each thrust inside me and every flick of my clit bringing me higher and higher until I finally explode, and when I do he kisses me even deeper and releases himself. It's so fucking erotic and all I want to do is take him home and fuck him but I know I can't.

One by one he pulls his fingers out of me and slowly licks them off. I gaze up at him curiously because he's *never* done that before "I have always regretted never tasting you, but damn, Kate, that taste was worth the wait. So. Fucking. Exquisite." I feel myself blushing at his words, thankfully he can't see me. That was so un-Mike but so damn hot.

Then he laughs, a huge rolling laugh, and as I feel a little wet underneath my backside I realize why and I laugh, too.

"I haven't come in my pants since that night on the boat when you agreed to be my girlfriend." I love that he's still laughing; I've missed that sound.

"Here you go," I tell him as I pull some tissue from my purse. Thankfully, there are two packs. I'm still loaded up from our trip to the cemetery so there's enough for both of us to clean up. Once we're all clean, I sit between his legs again and take a deep breath of ocean air.

"So I have to ask, was that you one-upping Daniel because of the phone sex?"

"What? No absolutely not! That was only about me and you and what was happening in the moment. Anything that is between us is between us, Kate. Daniel has *nothing* to do with it.

Now that you have a clear head, can you tell me what you decided at the hotel?"

Clear head, my ass.

"The only thing I decided at the hotel is that I need to learn to be more forgiving. I need to get to know Daniel better, and I need to get to know you again. Oh, and also that tequila makes me a mean drunk and if I'm going to get wasted I need to do it with something else."

He chuckles at that last part. "So no big decisions on who you love and who you want to be with?"

"The point of this whole thing is that I'm not dating *either* of you, remember?"

"Yeah, I can see how well that's working out for you," he replies sarcastically.

"That obvious, huh?"

"Well, maybe just to me," he teases.

"I love you both in different ways and in the same ways. I thought I loved you enough to let you both go but now I'm not so sure I can, or how that would even work. I just need some time."

Mike places a kiss on the top of my head. "Well, we think we figured out a way to give you that if you're open to it. Don't get all freaked out; just hear me out for a minute. Daniel and I talked about the three of us having a threesome."

"WHAT?" He *did not* just say that to me.

"Calm down, Kate. We talked about it and there's no way we could do it even if it was what you wanted. There are too many emotions that are all over the place and you're admittedly in love with both of us, and us with you. It couldn't work."

I breathe a sigh of relief because I seriously don't think I'm ready for anything like that, especially not with them; it would make *everything* worse.

"So what did you figure out then?"

"We think you should take some time and get to know both of us better by dating us both."

"You guys think *that's* a solution?" My mind is officially blown.

"Yes, we do."

"You actually got Daniel to agree to this?" I don't buy it; there's no way Daniel would capitulate to this idea.

"Actually, no, the other way around; Daniel got *me* to agree to it. After a lot of convincing, too, I might add." What kind of alternate reality have I stepped into? Then I hear Daniel's voice resonating in my head '*I'm very sexually open'*. I really don't know anything about him.

"I'm not a whore!" I yell, jumping up and walking down to the water. The waves wash up over my feet and the waters freaking cold but I don't care because I'm flaming hot.

Mike's arms wrap around me from behind. "I'm sorry, Kate, truly. We don't think you're a whore and we would *never* want you to feel like that. And what I'm suggesting doesn't have to be like that *at all*."

That makes me relax a bit but I feel like I'm going to cry. My emotions are all over the place lately. I hate feeling this way.

"So what are you suggesting?"

"Just what I said; you date us, separately not together, and *never* around each other. I don't want to see him with you any more than he wants to see you with me. You don't have to sleep with us, or make out, or anything. But we've both kind of accepted that those things could happen and it's just going to have to be part of this process."

"Sounds like a whore to me," I snap back at him

"Stop it, Kate. You're not a whore, you've never been a whore and no one will think you're a whore. WE all know you're in an impossible situation. This is a way to allow you to get to know Daniel because obviously you don't know him as well as you thought."

What... is he reading my freaking mind?

"But it's also a way for you to get to know me. The man I am now is a lot different than the boy I was back then. The only thing that's ever been consistent is my love for you. That's why I agreed to this because it's what's best for *you*."

This can't actually work, can it?

"So how would this work?" Not that I'm even entertaining this ridiculous idea. *Am I?*

"That's up to you, but we were thinking since we're all close by each other now it's pretty easy to date. We can alternate dates based on who isn't spending time with Vanessa. Dinner, movies, miniature golf, whatever you want to do to help bridge this gap between us and for you to get to know me again."

This is a lot to take in; I don't know if I can do this.

"Think of it this way: there are people doing online dating who go out with a few different people to try and get to know them and find the one they want to actually be with. This isn't much different; just consider it being down to your final two choices. We won't be able to do it forever, but long enough for you to figure out who really owns your heart."

"Mike, don't you see the downside of this? I'm already conflicted! I already love you both, so how is this going to make me pick one of you? It's just going to make me fall *even* more in love with you guys. It's not a good idea." My words are filled with desperation.

"You don't have to make a decision now, Kate, or even tomorrow. Just think about it, it's an option and it's a better option than you pushing both of us away. Of course, my reasons are selfish; I want to get to know you, too, and this will give me the chance."

For a moment I just close my eyes and relax in his arms, wishing for simpler times when it was the two of us and I would have never considered letting anyone else disturb our bubble.

"Okay, I'll *think* about it, but I'm not making any promises."

"I'm not asking you to. Once you decide, you can let me or Daniel know. Come on, it's late; I should get you home."

Mike insists on walking me inside once we get back to my place.

"Thanks for dinner and for…the interesting evening?" It comes out like a question but what was I going to say? Thanks for the orgasm and the BDSM discussion? Or how about thanks for wanting to whore me out? I'm not sure what the proper etiquette is in this situation.

"You're welcome for dinner, but thank you for the rest, it was very…stimulating." Oh my god he's too funny; that is a *perfect* word for it! Mike pulls me to him and covers my mouth with his. I immediately wrap my arms around his neck, closing any gap remaining between the two of us. This is different; it's always been good between us, but it's so much hotter now. He bites my lip and my body floods with desire, but I can't let this go further—not until I figure out what it is I want to do. As I pull back, he tapers off the kiss, and for the first time in a long time I'm happy he knows me so well.

"Goodnight, Kate," he says longingly.

"Goodnight, Mike," I tell him breathlessly as I close the door behind him.

After showering, I crawl into bed and fall into a deep sleep.

When I wake up in the morning, Jess is spooning me from behind. I must have been sleeping deep because I never even heard her come in, let alone felt her climb into my bed. That's actually kind of scary.

"Are you still mad at me, Kate?" She sounds so sad.

"I'm trying really hard not to be," I tell her honestly.

"I've missed you so much; we've never gone that long without talking or seeing each other. Please don't do that again." She's crying and I snuggle into her tighter.

"I won't, Jess, I promise. It wasn't just you, it was everything all together. I had to take a break from it all and try to get my head on straight."

"Well, why is Marc so special? You talked to him…"

"Marc is my inner circle but he's separate from all of you. You two talk but you're not really good friends. Trust me, I think Marc would rather I not drag him into all my stuff, either." I'm trying to stifle a yawn but I'm still tired.

"So did you figure anything out while you were gone? I feel so completely left out of your life right now." She's pouting but it's shrouded in sadness.

"After last night, I'm even more confused than I was before." And that's the God's honest truth.

"What happened last night?" Now she's curious. I've always loved how fast she could switch her moods. I wish I could do that. I spend the next half hour or so filling her in on *everything* that happened last night.

"Shut up! You and Mike? Hot damn! I was hoping, but whoo-freaking-hoo!"

"We didn't…"

She interrupts me, "You did enough. That's awesome; you need to enjoy this. Mike's right, you should totally date them both." She's so excited, I can't help but roll my eyes.

"I don't think it's right."

Jess jumps up and pulls me with her, looking me dead in the eyes "It's perfect, Kate, *really*. This is going to give you the chance to figure out which one of them it is. It's not like I'm completely all 'TeamMike' and not 'TeamDaniel', but I do think it's fucking awesome that you got the chance to do something HOT with Mike instead of just making love. My god that is *so* overrated. Kinky, hot, erotic, sex is better than making love any day. And don't even get me started on make-up sex." She is way too enthusiastic for it being so early in the morning and I love her for it.

For a moment she pauses and just looks at me, "Don't overthink it, Kate, just do it. You've played the safe card all of your life—done all that's been expected of you and then some. This is your time to experience life, because as soon as you pick one of them it's as good as being married. This isn't just dating, Kate, it's picking who you want to spend your life with. No one is going to think you're a whore. In all honesty, it's the perfect way to make sure you're making the right decision."

I know she's right, and god knows people have done far worse than date two men at once.

Just do it, Kate.

Just.

Do.

It.

Chapter Nine – Daniel

Tonight, I finally get to see Kate. It's been almost three weeks since the fiasco at the house when she left with Marc and all hell broke loose. Connor and Jake were mad as hell that they didn't know about the Aimee and Julie stuff. I get it because I would have been, too, if it had been reversed. Even April was mad, but I think she was more disappointed than anything that I didn't trust her with my secret when she's always trusted me with hers. Before talking things out with them, we first had to calm Mike down. I knew he didn't like Marc from the night of the engagement party, but *damn* I've never seen him like that before and I hate to admit it, but I think I felt almost as angry as him. Seeing the way Marc jumped between Mike and Kate was unreal; it was like he thought Mike would actually hurt her. If there's one thing I know, it's Mike would never hurt Kate, well, at least not physically. We all know he's absolutely crushed her emotionally.

Once all our skeletons had been let out of the closet and everyone was filled in with what few details we gave them, they all went to bed… except Mike and I. By that point, any buzz we had was long gone and we were both just really concerned for Kate. I was terrified she was going to cut us out of her life completely. We were both grasping at straws when I finally brought up both of us dating her. It's honestly the last thing I want, but I feel like it's my only chance in this game. The look in her eyes when she's around him is a combination of pure adoration and fear and it terrifies me. I don't want to think she's going to choose to go back to him, but they've got *so* much history.

These last two weeks, she was completely silent, and for the first week neither of us dared to reach out, per her request. Marc was keeping Jess updated so we knew she was okay, but knowing Marc was the only one she was letting in was putting us all on edge. Connor's pissed and I can't say I blame him. He's the only one she had no reason to cut out but she did because he's part of our circle. When the second week passed with no contact, we were all about to go have a little sit down with Marc, until Vanessa told us she was coming home.

Even with everything going on she still kept up with her visits to Vanessa. That speaks volumes about her character and is just one of the many reasons why I love her so much. When Mike came back to the house Sunday night, I don't think I've ever seen him so happy. Immediately, I knew something had happened between them but I just kept reminding myself this is going to happen until she figures it out. I'm not okay being in the middle of a love triangle for long, but until Vanessa has the baby I can try to deal with it. Mike said he thought his talk with Kate went well and she actually texted me back shortly before I went to bed.

It was…awkward…which really sucks because I don't want to have awkwardness with her. She had a study group on Tuesday and she was with Mike last night, so here we are—it's Thursday and I finally get to see her. I've been trying to figure out what we can do because we haven't really actually dated outside of the bedroom. It took me a bit to figure it out, but I think I came up with the perfect plan. I'm as nervous as a twelve-year-old boy when I knock on her door.

"Hey," she says, flashing me a gorgeous smile as she opens the door. At least she seems happy to see me; that's a good sign.

"Hey, yourself. Are you ready to go?"

"Absolutely, just let me grab my coat. You're being awfully mysterious about where we're going."

She looks amazing; those jeans hug her ass in a way that should be illegal. Thankfully, we'll be alone all night with no chance of any other guys around. Two is already one too many for my tastes; I don't need anyone else trying to date her, too.

"I thought women liked men who have a mysterious nature to them," I tell her with a wink and she starts cracking up.

"Oh my god, what is with that wink?" she asks through the laughter.

As I usher her outside and into my truck I explain, "It's Connor's new thing. Jess showed him this video of some super stud winking, which was not at all sexy, and Connor laughed for like an hour straight. Now every time something happens he feels is 'wink worthy', his words not mine, he winks."

Kate is laughing hysterically, and I realize how much I've missed that sound—how much I miss *her*. I'm not ready to live without that laugh in my life, without her smile to brighten my day, without her body to drive me insane. Not now and not ever. Suddenly she's very serious, somber even.

"Daniel, I'm really sorry about the way I've been acting. Our circumstances changed so dramatically and unexpectedly and I didn't handle it well. I'm sorry I was such a bitch to you and I really have a lot to make up to Connor, too. I've acted unfairly to you all."

Reaching across the cab, I take her hand in mine, pressing it against my lips. "Don't apologize, Kate. We're all going through this and we all understand the emotional toll it's taking on you." I'm trying to gently remind her that we're all in this together.

She's looking out the window, watching the world pass by in a blur. "You know I wasn't the biggest advocate of your idea to date you both and honestly, I'm surprised it's really what you want." Finally, she turns and looks at me. "Is it, Daniel? Is this truly what you want?" Her tone is laced with desperation and I have no clue what she wants to hear: that it is what I want or that it isn't *at all*. It doesn't really matter, though; I have to tell her the truth.

I fidget with the steering wheel for a minute, turning off Gavin Rossdale's *Love Remains the Same* and putting all of my focus into the best way to answer her.

"Honestly, Kate, all I want is to make this as easy as possible for you. Let's be real for a minute… your way wasn't working—at all. Maybe this won't work, either, but it's a *chance* and right now I need all the chances I can get for you to get to know me, and realize that *you* still want there to be an *us*. Hell, it's not going to be easy, thinking about you being out with Mike when you're not with me is a slow form of torture if you want the truth." She's nodding.

"But the thought of losing you, the thought of you closing off your heart and not choosing either of us because you want to do what is right…well, that's an even worse form of torture, baby. That's hell."

"I'm worried," she whispers.

So am I.

"About what?" She's back to looking out the window but eventually looks back at me.

"This is going to change me, Daniel. I'm not built to do this. While I agree at this point it's the best option, and I'm so happy to see you and spend time with you…I'm terrified the whole thing is going to backfire and I'm going to fall even more in love with you both."

And that is my second biggest fear, right behind her choosing Mike.

Exhaling, I nod, acknowledging her fears. "You have the power here, Kate. This doesn't have to change you if you don't let it," I tell her honestly.

"That's what Mike says, too."

"Then believe it, Kate, because as much as I hate to admit it, this is *our* only shot. Your history with Mike speaks for itself. This time with you is all I have to prove to you that your instincts weren't wrong and that we will be together no matter what. Is it confusing? Hell yes, I'm sure it has to be. Will it be worth it in the end? I think so, because no matter what, we're both getting to spend time with you and I don't think that's something either of us will ever regret." There, I've said all I can on the subject; the ball is completely in her court.

"We're here?" she questions as I pull into the harbor.

"We're here," I reply, trying to gauge her reaction.

"Do you have any idea how much I love it here?" she squeals as she hops out of the truck before I can even open the door for her.

I'm relieved she's happy again. "Good, I'm glad. Come on, I have a surprise for you." I'm nervous as I lead her to the boat. Hell, it's a yacht and I've never brought a girl here before. The perplexed look on her face as we board says it all; she had no clue my personal fortune isn't all that much less than hers.

"Whose boat is this?" she asks as she looks around the deck.

"It's mine," I reply casually.

She sputters; it's actually very cute. "Yours? You own a *yacht*? Please tell me you're not a member of your local country club, too," she says with disdain.

Busted.

"Well, I am, but only because some of the clients we deal with are very…" *God, I don't even know what the word would be for most of those guys.*

"Say no more, I get it. Joseph Moore's daughter over here… I know all about the stuffed shirt club. You know I don't care if you have money or not, right? I'm just surprised because you're so normal." Her cheeks flush and I can tell she's embarrassed.

Placing my hand at her low back, I lead her inside. It's perfect; just as I requested—no lights, a completely candlelit atmosphere, champagne on ice, dinner covered on the table, and no staff in sight. A small gasp escapes her perfect lips and a beautiful smile emerges.

"Okay," she says, but to what she's referring, I have no idea, and from the perplexed look on my face, she knows it.

"I'm going to assert my power and not let this change me. I love you, Daniel, and I want to see where this goes."

That's my girl.

The urge to kiss her is stronger than ever before but I don't want to push. "I love you, too, Kate. Thank you for trying."

After filling our glasses, I pass one to her and motion for her to have a seat and then lift my glass to hers "To new beginnings and the chance to see where life takes us."

"Are we moving?" she asks excitedly.

"I thought it would be nice to go out for a few hours, maybe dance under the stars?"

"That sounds nice. I've really missed you." The words cross her lips as a whisper.

"Me, too, Kate, so much, and we have so much to talk about. Why don't we start while we eat?" She agrees by nodding her head. I pre-made my grandma's lasagna and the captain's wife heated it and plated it for me. They set everything up, actually, and did a fantastic job.

"Back to your first question: this is my boat. I know it's technically a yacht but it's a small one and the word yacht is just *too* pretentious; I like boat."

She giggles. "Mike and I were the same way when we were younger. We spent a lot of time on our parents' yachts but they were always just boats to us." Her smile lingers and I can tell she has a lot of fond memories of her childhood.

"My dad actually bought it for me; it was one of our big fights. You know he lives modestly but his net worth probably exceeds the Houstons'. When I bought my house, he was so mad. He wanted to build me one from the ground up and pay for it all. I didn't deny him that, but I *did* insist he had to wait until I got married so he could have the privilege of building the house his grandkids would grow up in. That way my wife and I could make it *our* dream instead of just *my* dream."

"That's understandable."

"Rick McCormick doesn't like to be told no, especially when he's trying to do something for his son. When he gifts me something, it's usually from the heart no matter the expense or lack of it. One time, he gave me this quarter like it was a prized possession. The prize was the story that came with it. My grandmother had dropped the quarter and my grandfather picked it up for her and that's how they met. They held on to it through the years. It's still the only thing I own that I would probably run through fire to try and save."

"That's beautiful," she replies with tears glistening in her eyes.

"I think so, too. Anyway, after my grandfather died, he knew how much I missed going out with him on his boat. When I say boat I mean *old* houseboat, but it was always fun and we had some great times. This was my dad's way of giving me a chance to go out again, but in a way he didn't think would kill me."

"Your parents love you and they want what's best for you. Have you told them about Vanessa yet?" She reaches across the table and grasps my hand gently.

"I have and I'm sure you can imagine my dad's reaction. As a matter of fact, he built a paternity lab about five years or so ago. The owner has already given him his top technician on call, so as soon as Vanessa goes into labor, my dad is to page him and he'll meet us at the hospital. They said the results take between twelve and seventy-two hours typically, but he'll be sure we get them in twelve."

"Wow."

"It's good; I'm so glad he had that connection. I can't touch that baby until I know if he is or isn't mine and I know Mike feels the same. I couldn't imagine waiting two days or even two weeks to find out. I just want it over with. Don't get me wrong, if he's mine I know I'll be happy." My tone is filled with sadness and she grips my hand tighter. I'd much rather Kate be the one pregnant instead.

"I get it," she says with a forced smile. "Babies are blessings, Daniel. They may not come when we're ready for them, but if you were the kind of guy who could deny his flesh and blood I wouldn't want to be with you, anyway. Things will work out how they're supposed to; we just have to have faith."

There's a comfortable pause in the conversation as we both eat and I refill her champagne.

"Is this your grandma's recipe you were telling me about? Mmmm, it's to die for, seriously. You're still going to teach me how to make it, right?" The noises she makes while eating remind me of the noises she makes while having sex and I have to adjust myself under the table.

"Absolutely, anytime you want just tell me and I'll show you how. I'm a pretty hands-on teacher, though, so you'll need to be ready for me. We could easily have a repeat of the cupcake frosting incident."

The hooded look in her eyes as she licks her lips, remembering back to that night, is more than I can take.

"Too bad we don't have any cupcakes now," she replies seductively.

"Are you done with your dinner?" I ask impatiently and she nods affirmatively and excitedly.

"Good, let's go dance under the moonlight." I can't wait to get her in my arms.

It's a gorgeous night—the sky is clear, the moon is almost full, and it's cold enough for Kate to want to snuggle against me, but not cold enough for a jacket. *Mine Would be You* by Blake Shelton is playing softly, which couldn't be more perfect. Then again, this entire playlist is my 'Kate' list and every song on here reminds me of her in one way or another.

I've got her wrapped tightly in my arms and she snuggles against me, breathing me in. When I chuckle lightly, she knows I'm on to her.

"What?" she says innocently. "I've missed this smell...I've missed *you*."

"What happened to the shirt I left you?" I'm genuinely curious if she's used it more than just that once. "Well, after we had phone sex, I kind of had to wash it; it got a little messy."

Oh, I know all about her kind of messy. The girl comes like a fountain; it's so fucking hot.

"Well, if you want, I'll give you this shirt tonight. I have more in my room."

"Oh, I definitely want."

The song changes to *Thinking Out Loud* by Ed Sheeran and Kate sighs "I absolutely love this song; it encompasses everything love should be. Love isn't just about the good times, it's about taking care of the one you love during the bad times as well."

"This song reminds me of us," I tell her, placing a kiss on her forehead, and she sighs again. I wish I knew what she was thinking.

"I think we need to talk about the elephant in the room," she says after the song ends and I follow her lead to the on-deck couch. She kicks off her boots and curls her legs up underneath her, reaching for her champagne on the table.

"Admittedly, I freaked out a bit on Saturday night, but I'll try not to now. I really think we need to discuss how sexually open you are and exactly what that means." It's not like I didn't know this was coming, but it's hard to talk to the girl you love about your ex-girlfriends and hookups.

"Look, Kate, when I said that, it was because I knew eventually we'd have to have the talk about Aimee and Julie." She cringes when I say their names and I can't say that I blame her; both of the men in her life have been with them. Thank God they moved and hopefully she'll never have to meet them. That would likely be a disaster.

"The truth is probably not as bad as you think it is. I feel like such a jerk even having to talk to you about this." I'm so frustrated and consider not telling her. It wouldn't be lying, it would just be withholding information she doesn't need.

"It's okay, Daniel. I need to hear it." Her eyes are pleading with me to tell her the truth.

"Connor was the first to be with them. They tried to get me to hook up with them for a few years but it just wasn't my thing. I'm sure Mike told you he did the night we met, right?'

She nods.

"Okay, so they were Mike's first experience after you and I really wish that wouldn't have happened because I think it led him down a destructive path. But that's his story, not mine. Anyway, one night I was staying at Connor's and everyone was out of town. They came over and we started drinking…a lot…one thing led to another and it happened."

Hesitantly, I ask her, "How much of this do you really want to know?"

"All of it," she replies firmly.

Shit.

"It started slowly with them kissing each other, which I'd seen a million times before, but then they surrounded me—one on each side—and drew me into their kisses. First separately and then together, a lot of it was me watching them. I was enraptured, not exactly by *what* they were doing, but by how *much* passion they were doing it with."

A look flitters across her face...maybe realization? "Kate? Are you okay?"

Snapping back to reality, she responds, "Yeah, I'm fine. Sorry, keep going." I glance at her, unsure if I should, when she laces her fingers in mine. "Really, Daniel, I'm fine. Just keep going."

"The whole thing was pretty surreal; they're both very sexual and extremely sexually open. This was common for them; they had at least weekly threesomes. And well, up until you and I had sex, I've never seen a woman come so many times so easily. Honestly, that was more them because they know each other so well."

Again, I pause because I want to make sure she's okay. She seems fine so I continue. "I watched them play out a scene. They like to tie each other up and eventually they worked me into the scene. It was one of the most erotic things I've ever done. That night, I watched them make each other come repeatedly. I watched them seduce each other, make love to each other, and all the while I was accepted into their world. I fucked them both, made them come with my mouth, and they fucked me with their mouths. Until our foursome, it was the most erotic thing I had ever done."

Now she looks like she's going to be sick as her hand flies to cover the sob that escapes her.

"Enough, Kate, this isn't good for you."

"No, I have to hear this, Daniel. Don't you understand? Until I know, I can't move forward because the scenes that play out in my head are so much worse?" She's crying now, but they're silent tears and I battle an internal war because I know she thinks she wants to hear this, but I'm really not comfortable telling her. *Why do girls always want to know the details?*

Reluctantly, *very* reluctantly, I continue, "Before we were together, they had mentioned it was their one off-limit desire to be with both Mike and me at the same time. It was a big fantasy of theirs to watch each other having sex at the same time but yet be close enough to touch and kiss each other. At first, I was a little turned off by the idea because I had never done anything like that before. Once they clarified they had no desire to see me and Mike together that made it a little easier to swallow.

She's still crying; this is unbelievable.

"No more, Kate, I can't. I'm sorry; I can't be the one to make you cry." Now I'm getting choked up because I'm hurting her and I *never* want to hurt her. I want to heal her, I want to be the one to make her whole! *Fuck!*

"You have to! I can't hear it from Mike; I have to hear it from you, Daniel. I don't…I don't…dammit, I don't trust him to tell me the truth and I *need* the truth!" Her body trembles as she screams. "You're the only one I know who will be honest with me," she whispers.

And if I'm not already feeling asshole enough, now I have a glimmer of excitement that she still doesn't trust him.

"Fine, but I'm going to bullet point it. They like to be tied up and they like to be spanked. In the foursome, they tied us each up, but not at the same time. One of us got to watch as they tied the other up. One of them would ride us and the other would ride our face. We're guys, Kate, and it was fucking hot. That was basically it; we took a lot of turns, they sucked us off, we came, and they came. There were three emotions that came with it: erotic, excited, and turned on. Do I regret it? Absolutely not, and I'm sorry if that hurts you, but I try to live my life with no regrets."

Her knees are now pulled into her chest and she's rocking back and forth, absorbing all of what I just told her. I pull her into my lap and lean my head against hers.

"You wanted the truth, so let me finish telling you the truth. That was their thing; it's what made their relationship special to *them*. They liked to experiment and it didn't diminish their love for each other, but instead made it grow. Other than Mike and me, they had never once had a repeat with a man. They don't like emotions with their outside sex. Their focus was always on each other—turning each other on, watching each other being turned on, and working that passion into their sex. They're bi, so they like dick, but they love each other and this kind of thing fuels their love for one another. Can you understand that?"

"Sort of?" she replies, hiccupping and questioning. Since she's only been with two men and is pretty sheltered sexually, I can see why.

"Alright, well just so you know, they're married now and Julie's friend donated sperm and Aimee is pregnant. They're really happy, Kate, and I'm happy for them. Aimee told me not too long after that night that threesomes were fun and the foursome was flaming hot but it made them realize they want more out of life than random hookups. Shortly after, they decided to expand their vibrator collection, move closer to family, and get married."

I see the beginning of a smile on her face and I don't know if it's because they're gone or because she's happy for them, but I wouldn't be surprised if it was a combination of both.

"Now, here's the most honest thing I could ever tell you; are you ready to hear it?" She nods and I tilt her chin up to face me. "No, I need to hear you say it because I need to know you hear the words that are going to come out of my mouth next."

"Yes, I'm ready," she says with a shaky voice.

"Kate, I'm sexually open to new experiences and new ideas; that's obviously a given with my history. Never in my life has a woman turned me on more than you do. *Not ever*. Never has someone made my heart skip a beat. Never before has a girl wrapped me around her finger so tightly without me trying to get away. Instead, I'm hanging on for dear life. Not in my entire life has a girl made me feel passion from the top of my head to the tips of my toes, not ever. I've never been with a girl that made me *feel* the electricity between us with a simple touch. I've never made love, fucked, or had sexual relations with anyone where my body felt connected with theirs from the inside out…until you."

A surprised gasp escapes her lips and I lean closer, placing feather light kisses on her earlobe as she shivers in pleasure.

"I've never met a girl who trembles for me the way you do, who comes for me the way you do, or who calls my name out when they come the way you do. More importantly, Kate, I've never wanted to lay claim to anyone the way I *need* to lay claim to you. I need you to be mine, baby, as much as I need the air to breathe, water to drink, and food to nourish my soul. None of those things will help me if you're not in my life making me *thrive.*"

Tentatively, I begin kissing my way across her jaw and hover just a whisper away from her lips and then pause. "All of that stuff was erotic and hot, but it was also *before* you. Anything before I was with you pales in comparison; they were just shadows but *you* are my light. I know we've got a long way to go, but trust me, baby, I'm in this for the long haul. We have the once in a lifetime love people look for their entire lives right at our fingertips. It's within our grasp, and when we finally reach out and take it, our lives are going to be better than they've ever been. I can't wait for the day I get my ring back on your finger, but I hope that when you finally *do* put it back on you're ready to marry me, Kate, because I don't ever want to go through *this* again."

Her lips are parted, her breathing escalates, and I'm done talking. Before my lips are fully on hers, she opens her mouth to me and I take what's mine, relentlessly. At first it's a dueling of tongues, biting of lips, and grasping on to each other with all we have. Then I slow it down, making love to her senses by caressing her gently as my tongue slowly and tentatively meets hers. As much as I want her to *feel* the passion we share, I want her to know the love even more.

Taking control, she straddles my lap, places a hand on each of my cheeks, and pulls me in for a passionate kiss. My hands immediately move to her hips as she moves up and down against my painfully hard cock. A pained sounding moan escapes her but I'm not offended. I know that sound; it's the sound of wanting something you can't have and it's exactly how I feel right now.

After another long, slow, and torturous kiss, she pulls back and rests her head against mine. "Don't ever doubt that I love you, Daniel. No matter what may happen, just know that I. LOVE. YOU." She emphasizes each word with a kiss. There's nothing more I want to do than to take her to my room and make love to her, but I know that would be the wrong choice for both of us.

"I love you, too ,Kate, never forget that. Come on, let's go inside. I have something for you." The dinner plates have been removed and in their place are a dozen cupcakes—chocolate, coconut and s'mores—all from Sprinkles.

"Cupcakes! You remembered!" she exclaims excitedly, flashing me a dazzling smile.

"Of course I did," I tell her, wrapping my arms around her waist. "I remember everything, Kate, or at least I try when it comes to you."

"I've noticed, and that's one of my favorite things about you."

"Well, this is probably going to be one of your not-so-favorite things. I told myself I would never ask but I have to know. Did you have sex with Mike?"

I really don't want to know this answer.

As she licks the frosting off of her cupcake, she contemplates her answer. Before she replies, I lean over and lick the frosting off her lips, just like I did on her birthday. Putting her cupcake back on the plate, she pulls me in for another kiss but pulls away too quickly for my liking.

"Mike said you guys discussed the possibility of things happening," she says without making eye contact and my heart plummets.

"We did, and I know there's a real chance, but I want to earn your heart, Kate, not fuck it into submission. I don't think we should have sex while getting to know each other, but you tell me *your* thoughts on the subject. *After* you tell me if you slept with Mike," I say firmly.

"Mike and I kissed and we did get swept up in the moment…things happened…but we didn't have sex. When I made my decision to date you both, I made a choice to not have sex with either of you and Mike knows that. I don't feel bad about what happened between us because let's be real here, we've done way more in the past. But I'm not going to be that girl—I feel bad enough dating best friends, *loving* best friends, I'm not going to sleep with you both, too. Making out with you guys is hard enough." She's pouting and I laugh at the way it came out. She catches on quickly and corrects herself.

"Okay it's not a hardship by any means; it's actually quite easy to lose myself in either one of you. It's hard because I still feel like a whore and I've never been the girl to bounce between friends. That part of this is what I hate the most."

"Hey now, stop that. You're not a whore and the only opinions that matter are the three of ours. You've got to let that go, sweetheart; don't let that negativity consume your soul. Are you ready to go yet? We can stay here tonight if you want to…the choice is yours."

We docked a few minutes ago and it's getting late. I know she doesn't have class tomorrow but I have to go to work.

"If it's all the same to you, I'd like to go home. I've spent way too many nights away and I'm really trying to work things out with Jess."

"Sure, I understand. Just wait here for a minute, I'll be right back."

After a quick trip to the bathroom, I take off my shirt and put on a new one. On the way back, I stop in the dining room and grab a bag of leftover lasagna and cupcakes I had the captain's wife pack up for Kate. As I approach her from behind, she's lost in thought, looking out at the view.

"Why did you bring me here tonight, Daniel? We could have gone any number of places, but why here?" she asks with genuine curiosity. I set down the food and the shirt and hug her from behind.

"Because I wanted to bring you someplace special to me, a place where no other women have ever been before. I thought it would be nice to have a place to create new memories after all the bad ones we've had lately."

"Thank you," she replies softly as I place a kiss on the top of her head.

"Anything for you, Kate, don't ever doubt that. Even if things don't work out with us, I'll always be your friend."

Kate fell asleep on the way home and doesn't wake up until I'm lifting her out of the truck; she must be exhausted.

"You know you don't have to carry me. I can walk," she tells me with a yawn. "I know you can, but I'd like to tuck you in." *I'd love to do more than just tuck her in.*

"Okay," she replies, laying her head on my shoulder. Connor must have heard the truck door close because he opens the front door for me.

"Hey." He's smirking at me and I know he's thinking that I one-upped Mike. If only he knew…

"Hey, Daniel."

"What…no 'hi Kate'?" she asks him.

"Well, I'm still pretty pissed at you. In fact, I'm so pissed that I'm kidnapping you tomorrow and we're spending the day together, just the two of us. Get some sleep, princess; you're going to need it." He says it with a smile; even Connor can't be pissed at her for long.

"I love you Connor," she tells him sleepily.

"I love you, too, Kate. Goodnight."

I proceed to carry her up the stairs, close the door behind me, and set her down. Leaning up against the door, I see her expression change from sleepy to aware. "Strip," I instruct in a firm tone. Kate cocks an eyebrow at me and then slowly turns around, bends over, and takes off her shoes. She did that on purpose so I could watch her ass as she did it and my dick responds just like I'm sure she intended. After the shoes come off, she removes her shirt, then shimmies out of her should-be-illegal, ass-hugging jeans.

She stands before me in only her bra and panties—a sexy, black lace set. It's an image that will be at the forefront of *my* spank bank for a while.

"Is this how you want me?" she asks innocently, even though we both know she's anything but.

"Do you sleep with your bra and panties on?"

"No, Mr. McCormick, I don't. Would you like to see what I wear under my pajamas?" Her tongue licks across her bottom lip as she bites down. She's so fucking hot and I don't think she has any clue.

Inching closer to her, I reply, "Yes, Ms. Moore, I'd very much like to see."

As she removes her bra and I watch it fall to the floor, it takes all my willpower not to take her perfect nipples in my mouth. They're so nice and big, and that nipple ring just calls out my name.

Willpower, Daniel. Willpower.

"Panties?"

"Unless I'm going to get myself off, the panties stay on."

Fuck willpower; it's overrated.

Reaching behind me, I lock her door. "Panties off, now," I demand.

I begin to strip out of my clothes, but at the last second decide to leave my shirt on. She cannot see this tattoo. I use my hesitation to my advantage as she starts to stutter over her words, "Daniel, I thought we weren't going to have sex."

"We're not," I reply, pulling her to me and taking her mouth with mine. Releasing her from the kiss, I lead her to the bed and lie down next to her. Guiding her hand in-between her legs, I tell her what we're going to do, "I want to watch you make yourself come, Kate, and you're going to watch me. We don't have to have sex to give each other pleasure, but this is so much better than phone sex."

Her free hand reaches up and caresses her breast while the hand I placed between her legs circles her clit, teasing it until it's a hard nub. Climbing between her legs, I reposition myself so I'm up on my knees. This is the best goddamned view I've *ever* fucking seen.

Slowly, I start stroking my dick while I watch her. "You're so beautiful, Kate, let me see how bad you want me."

She looks at me with hooded eyes, lips parting slightly with the most erotic sounds escaping her as she watches me stroke myself right between her legs. "God, Daniel, I want you, I want you *so much,*" she says and then slides two fingers inside her pink pussy. Propping herself up on her elbow so she can get a better view, she forgoes the breast play to watch me instead. Damn, I could come now I'm so turned on. I'm so close to her, I'm fighting every urge to just slide inside her. It would be so easy—she's so wet, her tight pussy would grip my dick so tight I'd forget everything else except how perfect she is for me. I groan just thinking about it and squeeze my balls when I see her slide a third finger inside.

"Oh god, Daniel, this is torture. You're so close and I want you so…so bad." Her breath hitches and she starts fucking her hand with an even harder intensity.

"I'm right here, baby, and I'm so close. Just let go, Kate, let me watch you. Let me hear you, baby."

The second she screams my name and I see her tight pussy convulse around her hand, I call out her name and come all over her already wet pussy and hand. "Oh yeah, Daniel, make me yours!" Her body is still trembling, and as she slowly pulls her fingers out, I lean down and suck them into my mouth, one by one. *My personal fucking gumdrop.* I'll never get enough of her.

Covering her body with mine and placing my hand behind her head, I lower my lips to hers and kiss her tenderly.

"I love you, Kate," I tell her as I pull away.

"I love you, too. Stay with me?" I'm already off the bed heading to the bathroom. I hold a finger up so she doesn't think I'm ignoring her as I warm up a washcloth for her to clean up and grab a dry towel, too. She accepts them with a grateful smile.

"It's not a good idea for me to stay; I don't think I could keep my hands off you all night. But I'll see you Saturday?"

"Absolutely."

After I'm dressed, I hand her my shirt from the boat. It's the reason I had her strip in the first place. "Here you go, let me know next time you have to wash it and I'll bring you a new one." I'm chuckling as I hand it to her.

"Hey, McCormick, it's your fault…you're the one who sent the picture."

"That I did," I say, placing a kiss on her forehead. "Goodnight, Kate."

"Goodnight, Daniel. Thank you for tonight, honestly, for everything. I really did have a good time."

"Me, too, Kate."

Me, too.

Chapter Ten – Kate

Last night I had the best sleep I've had in weeks. I almost forgot how good Daniel makes me feel when we're together. Things are just so easy with him, almost effortless. I'm smiling like a fool when Jess knocks on the door, except it's not Jess—it's Connor.

"So I heard a little bit of fun escape these walls last night, which means you should be in a great mood today. Get up and shower, I'm taking you to breakfast. Nice shirt, by the way," he says with a smirk and then closes the door behind him.

Shit.

Not that it matters what he heard; I'm pretty sure Connor wants me with Daniel and not Mike, anyway. Those two, my god they're going to drive me into an early grave. I need to do a better job at keeping my distance because they both turn me on beyond measure.

Before leaving, we quickly go check in on Vanessa. Jess is already over there making her breakfast and shooting the breeze.

"Kate, you look beautiful this morning!" Vanessa exclaims when she sees me and I blush.

"Oh, I get it," she says with a laugh. "Well, for what it's worth, your secret is safe with me."

Connor laughs, "It's not you she has to worry about; it's those two and their not-so-subtle pissing match they have going on."

"So how are things going over here?" I ask, sitting next to her at the table.

"Things are good, really good," she says with a beaming smile. "Chad and his fiancée broke up and he says he misses me."

I'm stunned.

"Wow, Vanessa, that's really great!" I'm excited for her. I know how much she loves him and the fact that he's taking the first step so she knows he cares is wonderful.

"What about Daniel and Mike?" Not that I've been encouraging them to be with her. I've finally realized a family won't be an option until they know whose baby it is, but at least they're getting to know her now so it might be an option later.

She shakes her head at me. "You know my heart is with Chad. He might not be the father but I think we'll be able to co-parent pretty easily with either of them. I was open to a family, Kate, but now everything is different. Chad *is* my family and always has been."

"So are you going to move back in with him?" Connor asks incredulously. I can see he's ticked that I'm supporting her and now she's going back to Chad.

"No, we're going to try dating. There's still a lot to work out and the two of us living together didn't work out so well the first time. I'm trying to do the responsible thing for once. I want to learn how to be a mom and a co-parent before *anything* else. We're just going to take baby steps. And I'm really excited to get into the internship program Kate is setting me up with. I finally feel like my life can be good—that I actually *can* have a purpose." She flashes me a beautiful smile and I take her hand in mine. I'm so proud of her and so happy for her that things are working out.

"Oh, sweetie," Jess says, "you've always had a purpose, you're just finally finding out what it is."

"Okay, enough sappy shit. Can we go, Kate? I'm wasting away, let's go eat, woman!" Connor loves to demonstrate his impeccable whining skills.

"Sure, Connor, let's go get you some food before you waste away in front of us. We're still on for Sunday, right, Vanessa?"

"Absolutely, I can't wait to go shopping for the nursery," she replies happily.

"I can't wait to go shopping for the nursery," Connor mimics when we get to the car.

"Connor Houston! Be nice! She's having a baby with one of your best friends."

"Yeah, she's such a peach. Not only does she *not* know who the father is, *and* letting you support her, but she's getting back with her ex. I don't know, Kate, I still don't buy it. I wouldn't be surprised if that baby was Chad's. Admit it…doesn't it seem a little coincidental that she's getting back with her *engaged* ex?"

He's such a negative Nancy. I know she's played them in the past but people change and that's exactly what I tell him.

"People change, Connor, sometimes for the better. I'm happy for her that Chad realizes how much he misses her. Getting back together with a pregnant ex can't be easy. I'm still holding out hope that she makes a family with the baby's father, though."

"Ha! The only reason you want that is because it will make your choice for you. You've got it easy right now dating them both. When that baby comes, if they don't make a choice, you'll have to, and you're not even prepared for that." What he says is the truth, even if I don't like it.

"Whatever," I reply, frustrated, and he pulls into the diner we went to on my birthday. "Besides I wouldn't say that dating them both is easy. It's nice to get to know them both, but the problem is that I love them both for different reasons."

Of course, Mike's old pal Misty is our waitress again and she's just as chatty as last time. "Hey there! Is it just the two of you today?"

"Yup, just us two. We've got a lot of catching up to do today, right, Katie Grace?"

When he says that she literally stops in the middle of the restaurant and spins around, "*You're* Katherine?" she chokes out, obviously shocked.

Connor shrugs his shoulders. "I am," I tell her, and she seems to get her wits back again and walks us to our table.

"I'm sorry; I've heard Mike talk about you before. You guys were together for a long time; you're the reason he could never give anyone a chance. He never got over you…" her voice quietly trails off.

"Yeah, they're trying to work through all that now," Connor tells her nicely. Mike has obviously told this girl more than he ever told the guys, which is interesting. Suddenly, I'm looking at her in a different light, a jealous light, and I don't like the feeling...not one single bit.

"Well...um...good luck and I'll be back in a few minutes to get your orders. Oh, sorry, can I start you with some drinks?" She's completely flustered and I wonder how much more there actually is to her and Mike's story.

"Water and an orange juice for me," I say distractedly.

"Same," Connor tells her and we both watch her walk away. "What was that all about? She sure does seem to know a lot about you and Mike. I know they were friends but *I've* never heard him talk about you before. How did she know?"

"He must have been closer to her than he let on; she seems to still have feelings for him. I can empathize." Then he does it, he flipping winks at me and I burst into uncontrollable laughter. "Hey, what can I say? You're wink worthy." And I laugh even harder. He did that just for me and I love him for it. A new waitress brings us our drinks.

"Where did Misty go?" Connor asks her with his dazzling smile. This is the one women get flustered by and it works like a truth serum.

"Oh...um...she...she...uh wasn't feeling well and had to go home. Are you ready to order or do you need a few more minutes?" she asks, regaining her composure. We place our orders and sit in silence for a few minutes.

"Okay, that wasn't just me, right? That was really, really weird?"

"No that wasn't just you." I let out a sigh. "I think we need to have Mike come and talk to her sooner rather than later."

After our food arrives, and we're pleasantly stuffed, Connor informs me we're driving out to see his mom. That gives him over two hours to drill me on recent events so I might as well give him the opening I know he's going to take anyway.

"I'm sorry about how I acted at your house a few weeks ago and I'm really sorry I've been such a crap-ass friend to you," I tell him sweetly and with a smile.

"I know you are and it's okay. We just haven't had any time together and with things strained between you and Jess I thought a day trip could do us good. Besides, I have to know…Are you fucking them both?"

Well, that didn't take long.

"Hey, if you are, more power to you. Seriously, you've needed to make up for lost time for a while now. I just like the insider's point of view is all."

He's lying; he wants to know if he should be worried about me. It's sweet.

"I'm not exactly having sex with them but we've done sexual things. It has to stop, though. It's not good for any of us to let these feelings get deeper and stronger than they already are."

"Well, it sounded like you were enjoying it. Too bad you want to put a stop to something that sounds so fun."

My eyes are growing wider, I can feel them. "Connor Houston, how much did you listen to last night?"

"Anything that was audible, not gonna lie. I'm a perve and I'm going to ignore the fact that we're like siblings right now and tell you the truth. You sound really *hot* when you come." He's being completely serious.

"Oh my god! Connor!"

"What? You do. Ask Jess, even she thinks so. She also thinks it ups Daniel's fuckability rating, too. Watch out…if you don't pick him, she's going to leave me and snap him up, I can see it now."

All I can do is laugh. I learned a long time ago that Connor could mortify me in so many ways and I had to learn how to brush it off. "I think you're just trying any angle you can to get me to pick Daniel."

He's shaking his head. "Do you want to know the truth? It might sting a little, and I don't mean for it to, but I feel like I should warn you." He's so solemn; this is going to be bad.

"Yes I want the truth, always. Don't ever sugar coat it for me."

"Alright, here it goes. I honestly don't think you should pick either of them," he says, blowing out a breath.

What?

"Why?" I'm stunned by his answer.

"Look, they're my brothers and I would give my life for theirs, but I lost a lot of respect for them when they decided it would be a good idea to ask you to date them both."

Silence.

Deafening silence.

"So now you think badly of me because of it?" I ask, my voice flooded with sadness.

"No, Kate, not at all. If it were you dating two guys just in general I'd be telling you to fuck them both and see who was better suited for you. Now, after your outburst the other night, we both know they have…oh, how did you so eloquently put it? That's right… 'fantastic fucking cocks'. Kudos to you for that, too; I think you shocked everyone with that one."

Oh shit, I forgot about that one. Oops.

"I'm confused."

"Your determination was, and still is, admirable. You were trying to keep them away to preserve friendships and also to give Vanesbitch a fighting chance with her baby daddy."

Oh shit. Vanesbitch. That's hilarious, but I'm not going to encourage him

"They were more concerned about who was going to get in your pants to see that *you* were looking at the bigger picture. I'm disappointed in them; they're being really selfish."

"They're not, Connor, really. When Mike first talked to me about it, I was beyond shocked, but the more he explained it, the more I got it. Mike isn't the boy I knew four years ago; he's a different man now."

He's nodding along, which means he's listening. Good.

"As for Daniel, as much as I love him, and what I know of him, I don't *actually* know him yet and that was a hard realization to swallow. This is giving me the chance to see which one, if either of them, is the right man for me. Now with Vanessa being back together with Chad, I feel a little less crappy about the whole thing. But I'm still not having full on sex with either of them. We're just testing the waters."

"You just said if either of them are the man for you. Does that mean you're having doubts?"

"That means I'm still reserving the right not to choose between them. I'm trying to find the balance. There are things about both Mike and Daniel that I love, and things I'm realizing I didn't know about them."

"Like what?" He's awfully curious today, but we haven't talked in a few weeks, so I guess it makes sense.

"Well, Mike seems to have some anger issues he didn't use to have and his sexual preferences have changed a lot since we were together."

"All true."

"Daniel...well, he's a little different than I thought." *How do I explain this without sounding bitchy?*

He looks perplexed. "Different how?"

"Daniel is very dominant in everything he does—the way he moves, the way he says things—it's like every single move is calculated. It's not a bad thing. In fact, it can be really hot, but I didn't see it at first. I noticed it in sexual situations but the rest of the time he was sweet and doting."

A smile spreads across his face like he knows an inside joke. "Daniel likes control and I think that's why he agreed to the night with Mike and the girls. It's a level of foreplay that he enjoys, and for most women it turns them on. Don't get me wrong, he's a nice guy anyway, but when he met you, he was thrown for a loop."

He glances at me to see if I'm still following along and I'm really intrigued so he keeps going.

"That night you met, he was so nervous around you. I'd *never* seen him like that. When he decided he wanted to send you gifts and decorate, I was floored because he seemed completely out of his element but yet still in it. Everything he did was planned and done his way. Decorations, flowers, coffee, pizza…see a pattern? Most girls would have gotten some flowers or dinner but he was *completely* taken with you. The sweetheart, baby, gumdrop, and whatever other pet names he might have had are normally something he *doesn't* do."

But he does it so well.

"Now that you're taking the time to get to know each other, he's trying to let you get to know *him*. Daniel the man, not Daniel the smitten, pussy-whipped manchild he was for those first two weeks. I kind of think he was somewhat relieved when he was able to go back to being himself. None of this has changed his feelings for you. If anything, they're stronger now than before. It's just now he gets to man up and actually compete on an even playing field with Mike.

I've got nothing to say to that. I'm totally speechless.

"Look, Kate," he says, reaching for my hand, "in all fairness, if you *do* choose one of them, either one of them, I think you'll be happy. They both do love you with all they have to give. Aside from all the dominant, possessive, angry, sexually strange alter egos they have, they're good guys. And both of them are head over heels in love with you."

When we pull into the Houstons' driveway, I finally ask Connor what I'd been meaning to since we left the diner, "Why are we here, anyway?"

"My mom wants some mom and daughter time with you. She knows what you're going through and she and Bev want to talk to you."

"Bev's here, too?" *Great, all I need is Daniel's mom pushing me toward him.*

"Ye of little faith. Bev isn't going to push you toward Daniel; she's going to encourage your heart, and she's good at it, so watch out. I bet you didn't know this because I just found out, but Mike and Bev have been secret buddies all these years. Bev has known all about you since the day he moved in and has been praying to the heavens for you to come back into Mike's life. Of course she didn't know that Katherine was Kate; she just knew that her boy was hurting, and now *both* her boys are hurting and she wants to help fix it."

"Let's just go home," I say quickly.

"Not a chance. It's time for you to go get some advice on love from some women who know what it's really about. Between the two of them, they've got over sixty years of happily wedded bliss under their belts. I love you, Katie Grace, now get out of my car and go face the music."

Leaning over, I give him a kiss on the cheek and grab my purse. "I love you, too, Connor but you're going to pay for this one."

~~~***~~~

Twelve hours later, I'm lying in my bed, exhausted after a trip to the gym. I had to go let off some steam and think about my day. It wasn't a bad day at all; we actually had a lot of fun. They weren't bringing me up there to talk—they wanted to get my mind off of things. Now, when Bev drove me home, *she* wanted to talk.

"You know Kate, from the day I met Mike I've treated him as if he were my own son. He was so lost, and when he decided to confide in me, I was honored. All these years I knew there was a girl out there who would make him whole again and I kept wishing she would come along."

She chuckles to herself for a minute the way older women sometimes do before picking up where she left off.

"I don't think any of us could have imagined that when she came back into his life it was going to be in quite this way."

"No, I don't guess you could have, I know I sure didn't," I tell her honestly.

"Sweetie, there are no right or wrong feelings here. You just have to search deep down inside and ask yourself if one of these two men is the right man for you. And if the answer is yes, you need to decide which one."

I nod thoughtfully at her.

"Kate, I think deep down you already know which one of them you love and which one you're in love with. You just have to admit it to yourself. And if you're waiting for that baby to come so you don't have to make a choice, that's just the easy way out, because, sweetheart, it's only got a fifty percent shot of being the man you're truly in love with. Baby or no baby, the heart wants what it wants and everything else is just details to be worked out. Don't limit yourself or settle based on who does or does not have a baby. I know you want the father to be a family with Vanessa, but based on history, I don't see that happening. If you're going to wait until after the baby comes to announce your decision, do yourself a favor and write down his name now and date it. Put it somewhere so that once the baby comes, you can show him that you made your choice long before."

Wow she's really long-winded but her advice is excellent. When we reach my house, she reaches over and pulls me into a loving hug.

"I know you love them both and no matter who you choose, someone will be hurt. You have a good heart, Kate, and they know it. Eventually, you'll all be able to move past this, and while some of the memories may be painful at first, it will get better."

She looks at me thoughtfully and speaks one last time.

"When I was a teenager, I was dating someone when I met Rick. Little did I know that my beau had also recently met someone else who tugged on his heart strings a little more than I did. I was devastated at the time and so was he; we were childhood sweethearts. Over time, as he fell in love with his new girl and I fell in love with Rick, we realized it truly was for the best. If he had never had the courage to call things off we would *have married and I would have never been loved so fiercely by Rick and wouldn't have had the utmost pleasure of being Daniel's mom. Trust me, Kate, the best things in life come from the worst kinds of pain. You have a beautiful past with Mike that has to be considered carefully before even contemplating a life with Daniel. I'd love to have you with either of my sons, but for the right reasons. If you ever want to talk you pick up that phone and call me."*

"I will, I promise. Thank you for everything," I tell her, trying to keep the floodgates from opening once again.

"Anytime, sweet girl. Anytime."

So now, here I am hours later with the same sentence resonating in my head, over and over.

Trust me, Kate, the best things in life come from the worst kinds of pain.

It's so true, and as I sit on my bed with a journal in my hands dated for today, I write a brief note about my talk with Bev and then write down a name and lock the journal in my desk drawer. I don't know if I'll ever tell them or if I'll break both of their hearts, but I know whatever I do, it won't be until after the baby comes. I'll just enjoy whatever time I have with them both now before it ends.

I'm glad Jess is spending the night with Connor tonight because I spend the rest of the night curled up in a ball, crying hysterically. I cry for the man I didn't choose and for the one I did, but mostly I cry from the excruciating pain of knowing I have to let one of them go and there's not a single part of me that thinks I'm strong enough to actually do it.

~~~***~~~

I'm having the best time with Vanessa today. I rented her one of those portable scooters since she's supposed to be on bed rest, and even though she didn't like the idea, she knew it was the only way we could shop properly.

We've picked out everything so far except for the crib and matching furniture. Since she doesn't have a lot of friends, she didn't want a baby shower, which was fine by me because it gave us even more shopping to do. Retail therapy is highly underrated. I feel so much better today after shopping than I did last night.

"What do you think of this one?" she asks and I love that she actually wants my opinion. I'm not sure why she does, but I give it to her.

"It's my favorite," I tell her, and it really is. It's a gorgeous, white-washed pine crib that's been lacquered to a gleaming shine. There's a matching rocker, dresser, and changing table—it's perfect.

"It's a lot of money, maybe we should look somewhere else." It doesn't matter how many times I tell her not to worry about the money, she still worries.

"You guys are family now, and family helps family. I want to do this for you and your baby boy."

She flashes me a beaming smile and reaches for my hand. "Thank you, Kate. I really don't know how I would have gotten through this without you."

I'm feeling a little emotional, of course, because I'm a sentimental sap. "You would have been fine but I'm happy to help. Come on, let's go pay for all of this and get home so we can decorate everything."

We had everything delivered and Daniel and Mike are both coming over to put it all together. So is Chad—it will be interesting to see how they all react to each other.

"Kate, can you bring that box up, too, when you come upstairs? I'm sorry I can't carry much; I feel so unhelpful," Vanessa says this while she is using one hand to hold her back and the other to hold on to the stair rail.

"Unhelpful? Vanessa, if you tried to carry anything up these stairs you would topple over! Not to mention you're starting to get winded. I think it's time you start considering sleeping on the pull-out couch until the baby comes. You really shouldn't be climbing these stairs much longer." She laughs but I'm legitimately concerned for her health and for the baby.

"My doctor said to limit my trips up and down—try to keep them to fewer than two a day. So far, I haven't been able to keep it under three. He also told me at my last appointment that now that I'm in my seventh month my pressure is likely to get worse and the baby can pretty much come anytime." She pauses at the halfway point to catch her breath.

"Okay, well we don't need to have that happen any sooner than it should, so tonight we're moving you down here."

"Really, Kate, I'm fine."

"You might be fine now but we're going to keep it that way. I'm sure the men will all agree with me, too." Grabbing the chair out of the hall, I pull it into the nursery for her to sit.

"So what's in the box?"

"Letters to put up on the wall above the crib that spell out his name." She suddenly seems shy, I wonder why? "Really? You didn't mention you picked out a name yet. Have you talked about it with the guys?"

"No, I haven't, but I've had his first name picked out for months, before they were even involved. His middle name I just decided on recently. I'm naming him Lucas, Lucas Hunter."

Lucas Hunter.

Lila Hope?

Vanessa notices my reaction and confirms it, "I wanted him to share something with his sister. I figured their initials would work." I'm crying. She's doing something so sweet to honor Lila Hope. "Don't cry, Kate. You're going to make me cry, too."

"I can't help it, I'm sorry, but that is just…it's just so sweet. But, Vanessa, you don't know that the baby is Mike's." She smiles at me like she knows a secret I don't and pats my hand.

"Kate, I know you all are going through something big, but from the moment I saw you and Daniel together, I knew you two were meant to be. I'm pretty confident you're going to work through this and in the end you'll still be with him. I know Daniel and I *know* he would have treated Lila as his. So no matter what, however this turns out, Lucas is named after his sister."

She's so kind-hearted, I'm so proud to call her a friend. "You know I still want you and the baby's dad to be a family, right?" And then she laughs at me and I watch her belly shake; it's super cute.

"Oh, Kate, sweetie that was never going to happen. I know you wanted it to but there's too much between us to make it work. Besides, I am head over heels in love with Chad—always have been and always will be. Mike and Daniel, they're great guys but they're not Chad. This baby is going to have an unconventional upbringing, but that's okay because he's going to be surrounded in love and that's all any mom could want for their child."

I couldn't have said it better myself.

"We're here and we brought food!" Mike's yelling up the stairs and I quickly try to wipe away my tears.

"Kate, why are you crying?" Daniel asks, concerned and looking between Vanessa and me.

"They're happy tears… what's going on?" Mike knows me well…*too* well.

"Just two girls having a moment. I told Kate the baby's name and she got a little emotional."

"Wait, you named him?" they ask in unison.

Uh-oh.

I haven't seen Vanessa's strong side yet, but from the stony look on her face it's about to come out. "He's my son and I have the right to name him whatever I want to. Neither one of you even want to *talk* baby because you're both hoping you're not the father. As much as I appreciate your help and your company and getting to know you again, this is *not* up for discussion."

"It's a good name, you guys, and maybe if you ask nicely she'll tell you what it is." Hopefully, my gentle tone will snap them back to reality. It would be nice if they had all agreed, but

Vanessa has a point. If they won't talk to her about him, she can't just put her life on hold.

"We're sorry, Vanessa. We shouldn't have jumped your shit. What are you naming him?" At least Mike can think coherently, Daniel is still pouting like a little kid.

"His name is Lucas Hunter…last name to be determined, obviously."

And there it is. Mike gets it before Daniel does; I see the light bulb go off in his head. "Is that a coincidence?" he asks and she gently shakes her head no.

"I like it, a lot, actually," Daniel says.

"Me, too," Mike agrees and finally all is right with the world again.

"Anyone home?" Chad calls out from downstairs.

"We're all up here!" I call back to him and exchange knowing smiles with Vanessa. Now we get to see how they all act around each other.

"Hey, everyone, I'm Chad." He reaches for Daniel's hand and then Mike's as they do introductions.

"Hey, baby, how are you feeling today?" Those seven words tell me my first instincts about him were right—he absolutely adores her. We all watch as he drops to his knees and rubs her belly, kisses it, and says hello to Lucas. Mike actually leaves the room, so I go after him.

"Are you okay?" His back is to me, but when I place my hand on his shoulder he grabs on tight.

"I'll be fine," but his voice doesn't sound fine, he sounds really choked up.

"I'm sorry Mike, for what it's worth, you're not the only one who wishes you could have been there."

Mike turns around and pulls me into a fierce hug. "I love you, Katie Grace." His words almost bring me to my knees. Not because they're romantic, but because they're not. He's just loving me as a lifelong friend right now and that's exactly what I need from him in this moment…to be his friend.

"I love you, too Mike. You missed out with Lila; don't look back and regret missing out with Lucas. Even if he's not your son, he'll still be your nephew and there's nothing wrong with rubbing and kissing a belly that holds a loved one. You'll feel worse if you don't."

"You're right, as usual," he says, laughing. "But if I'm being completely honest, I just don't think he's mine. Call it naïve or stupid because the odds are that he is, but something deep inside me says no."

After pulling away, he goes back into the room and I can hear them discussing what to put together first. With the three of them it actually goes pretty quickly, especially since two of them are builders by trade. They brought grilled chicken and vegetables, which is good for Vanessa since she's supposed to avoid salt as much as possible. I quickly run home to get a tablecloth and a picnic basket so we can all eat in the nursery.

When I get back to Vanessa's, Daniel is in the kitchen getting some water. It's really uncomfortable at times being around them both while I'm still so confused about my feelings for them. For example, right now just seeing him standing there in his tight black shirt and loose blue jeans makes my heart race. I'm completely undressing him with my eyes and really wish I was home, wearing his shirt, and looking at that picture of his dick that he'd sent me.

Holy Hell.

The smile that flashes across his face tells me he knows *exactly* what I'm thinking. "Not really the time or place for those kinds of thoughts now, Kate."

Bastard.

"I don't know what you're talking about, Mr. McCormick," I tell him in a sultry voice. "It sounds to me like *your* inappropriate thoughts are seeking company."

"Damn straight they are," he growls.

"Well, like you said, this isn't the time or place but I can see if I can squeeze you in one day this week," I say, batting my eyelashes at him.

"Just one day this week?" he says, winking at me.

"Well, maybe I could spare *two* days since I'm obviously 'wink worthy' in your opinion."

His arms find their way around my waist, his lips press against my neck, and he whispers, "You're more than just 'wink worthy' but the question is, am I worthy enough for you?"

Always.

"Well, I guess we'll need that third date to figure that out, won't we? Now come on, we've got a hungry pregnant woman upstairs to feed." *Good god, the two of these men are going to bring me to my knees.*

When we walk in with the food, Chad is rubbing Vanessa's feet and I *know* how good that feels; Jess used to do it for me all the time when I was pregnant. The crib is done and the changing table is almost done and the dresser came as one piece. Even I'm getting excited about Lucas's arrival and he's not even mine.

You'd be a great step-mom, Kate.

Daniel's words come back to me and I try to shake them off. I've never thought about being a step-parent. I guess I'm not opposed; I've just always thought I'd never be in a situation where that would be a possibility.

Once we're all sitting cross-legged on the floor, plates piled high with food, Daniel starts firing off twenty questions to Chad and he sounds like a jealous boyfriend. I have to say it *does not* sit well with me.

"So, Chad, what do you do for a living?"

Fair enough question.

"I'm still in school. I'm pre-med and I do volunteer hours at the free clinic."

"How do you afford everything?"

Uh-uh, he's getting snippy.

"My parents saved for years for my college but I got a full ride. They ended up giving me all the money so I wouldn't have to work *and* go to school." Chad's starting to get defensive; you can hear it in his tone.

"That's cool, man. Glad it worked out for you."

Ahh, Mike's way of trying to diffuse the situation, too bad it's not working.

"Do you have enough money to raise a family? Will you *even* be able to give them attention? Pre-med is a time sucking major."

Oh my God, I can't believe he just said that.

"Daniel, that's enough!"

This is so not good. He's not supposed to rile up the pregnant one.

"Calm down, baby. It's okay, I've got this under control…" Chad's trying to stay calm but there's unmistakable anger in his eyes. Daniel, on the other hand, keeps digging himself into a steaming hot pile of shit.

"I mean, do you even love her? You were engaged all of five minutes ago and now suddenly you're back? How does that even work?"

And now they're up and in each other's faces.

Mike tries to pull them apart and I scoot behind Vanessa and start rubbing her shoulders. "Breathe," I tell her. "Just breathe. This is nothing; don't let it stress you out *at all*. They're just being men." She nods but I can feel the tension in her shoulders.

"Look, Daniel, until we know if you're the baby's father, this really isn't any of your business. However, since I don't want to stress Vanessa out any more because it's really not good for her *or* the baby, I'll answer your questions. My family isn't poor, so even if I run out of money I can get more. They love Vanessa and are fully supportive of us getting back together. Jesus, we were high school sweethearts, of course I love her. When we moved here, I needed space. I questioned everything I knew was right because I didn't want to make a mistake and marry her right out of high school."

Chad takes a deep breath and clenches and unclenches his fists.

"Leaving her was the stupidest thing I could have ever done besides getting engaged to someone else. Do you have *any* idea how bad it feels to know that I'm not this baby's father? You have no clue because both of you are just wishing it isn't you!"

I know exactly how he feels.

"I'll give them all the time I possibly can. I'm going to be there *every single step* of the way, happily too, I might add. Vanessa wasn't herself when we moved here. She changed… we both did…and now we've grown from our mistakes. I've realized I can't live without her, that my life is better when she's in it. Kate has given her the confidence she's lacked for so long in just a few short weeks. She's going to make her life better for her and the baby and she doesn't need any of us to do it. I'm just glad she gave me a second chance so I can *show* her how much I love them both."

An uncomfortable silence falls over the room until Chad asks a question of his own.

"My question to you is, why do you even *care*, Daniel? You broke up with her and wanted *nothing* to do with her. This line of questioning makes me think you've got more feelings for her than you're letting on. If you do, now would probably be a good time to let all of us know about them."

Damn straight it would be.

Mike seems curious to know that answer, too…

"Because I'm human? Yes, I thought Vanessa was out of my life but she's not, and you're right, she *has* changed. No offense, Vanessa, but you're a much better person now than you were before. I'm enjoying getting to know you and I'm concerned for you and your child. Father or not, I still consider you my *friend*. One thing you should know about me, *Chad*, is that I look out for my friends."

He's pissed and that just doesn't sit well with me, and that tells me two things. One, I need to cut back on how much I see him so I don't continue to get attached. Secondly, I'm already attached to them both so I'm royally screwed, anyway. I've had enough.

"Enough already! This isn't good for the baby. I've had to watch the two of you," I say, waiving my fingers between Daniel and Mike, "in a continuous pissing match for weeks and I'll be damned if we're going to have a pissing match threesome up in here. NO more ménages allowed in any form. Now since everyone is done with dinner, I think it's time to say goodnight. This works much better when you're all on separate shifts."

Vanessa pulls my hands and wraps them around her belly so I can feel Lucas kick. "Thanks, Kate. You can tell he's a boy; he gets active when there's rough housing," she says, giggling. This could be my little girl's brother in there and I'm suddenly overcome with nothing but absolute love and adoration for this baby.

"Chad, can you help move Vanessa's necessities downstairs, please? She should not be making this trip up and down the stairs more than once a day until the baby comes."

He looks grateful for the reprieve from the tension. "Sure, Kate, I'm on it." Mike seems happy but Daniels looks confused. He probably is after what he did.

"You guys should just go home and get some sleep. I think you're done here for the night. Thanks for coming by to help."

Mike leans over and gives me a kiss on the cheek, Vanessa, too, and leaves. Daniel stays behind.

"Kate do you think we can talk?" He still doesn't seem himself but I don't care; I'm over it for tonight. "Not tonight, Daniel, I'm tired and still have homework to do. I'll just see you Tuesday, okay?"

I can tell he's not happy but he reluctantly agrees. "Okay, see you tomorrow, Vanessa." I think this might be the first time I've ever seen him leave a room with his head hanging down. I almost feel sorry for him. *Almost.*

"You do realize that was his possessive side coming out in all its glory and has nothing to do with his feelings for me, don't you?"

"I don't know," I tell her as I continue to rub her belly, feeling more connected to this baby every second that I do. "Maybe, but I think I need to step back a bit from both of them and keep things a little more casual for the time being."

"Can I ask you something without offending you?" she asks hesitantly.

"Ask away."

"Does you not making a decision fully ride on who the father of this baby is or is it because you're not ready to admit to yourself who you want to be with? Because if it's still about you wanting the father and me to have a chance, that's not going to happen. But if it's about you not wanting to accept someone else's kid in your life…well, I totally get that."

"Aw, sweetie, it has nothing to do with that. At first, I wasn't sure if I could be a step-mom but Lucas is Lila's brother or cousin and that makes him family. I love him already, even more just sitting here feeling him kick. Sometimes I think the easiest choice is just to not choose between them. I'm still trying to figure out what my heart wants over what my mind says is right. Then if I finally *do* listen to my heart, I'll have to break one of theirs. There will never be a time when I'm ready to do that. I'm just postponing the inevitable, I get that completely, but sometimes living in denial is the only option."

"I'm sorry you're going through this, Kate. For months I hoped to have a chance with them both. I don't know why it was so important to me. I guess I was seeking an outlet since I couldn't have the man I really wanted. It's one thing to want them and them not want you. I think that's a lot easier to deal with than trying to choose between them. I never loved either of them, not like I love Chad, so my heart was never at risk.

Whichever one of them you don't choose isn't the only one that's going to be brokenhearted. You love them both; your heart is going to shatter right along with them, unfortunately." Those might be the wisest words anyone has said to me yet and it's true—I'm avoiding my own heartbreak as well.

"Hey, baby, are you ready for me to help you get ready for bed?" Chad asks her sweetly from the doorway. "Well, actually, maybe I should help you off the floor, first. I don't know why pregnant girls always think it's more comfortable to sit on the floor when you can't even get up," he says, laughing.

"It just is more comfortable down here for whatever reason." After I scooch out from behind her, Chad helps her up. He's so adorable with her.

"You're really okay with all of this, aren't you?" I ask him, genuinely curious.

"Babies are a gift from God, Kate. They come to us in the way they were meant to, *when* they're meant to. Sure, I wish he was mine but he will be in lots of ways, just like he may be yours, too, in lots of ways. Blood doesn't make a parent, only unconditional love does that."

"If you ever get tired of this one, you send him my way and I'll give you the other two back," I tell her over my shoulder as I leave.

"Thanks, but no thanks. That's your mess to deal with. I'll keep this one right here all to myself."

Chapter Eleven – Kate

As it turned out, keeping Daniel at arm's length wasn't much of an issue. It's been almost two weeks since that night at Vanessa's house, and between Mike and Daniel's project and my upcoming mid-terms, we haven't seen each other at all. Mike and I have managed to grab a few quick lunches but not much more. I feel like the two of us are falling back into a routine and I've never been happier.

Daniel sent me flowers today with an apology note asking me out on a date tonight. We need to talk, but tonight is Marc's party.

"Why do you look like someone just pissed in your Captain Crunch?" Connor always has such a nice way of putting things.

"I don't."

"Um, yeah you do, and if those flowers are yours I'm thinking you should be going for the opposite kind of look. You know, one that says 'I'm happy'?" *Smartass.* "They're from Daniel, I haven't seen him in a few weeks and he wants to go out tonight but I've got Marc's party."

"Okay...well, didn't Marc say you could invite him?"

"He did." The perplexed look that crosses his face is almost comical. "Well then, I don't see what the problem is. Just invite him to come out with us."

"It's not that simple. Aside from a few basic text messages, we haven't seen or talked to each other since that weird night at Vanessa's. I think we both needed space but now we need to talk, and clubbing isn't talking."

"Talking is overrated sometimes," he says with a beautiful smile. "Come on, Kate, I thought you were going to loosen up and see where the road takes you? It seems to me the signs are telling you to take Daniel with us to the club tonight."

"I don't know..."

Connor sits next to me and pulls me close. "Stop over thinking it. One night out isn't going to make or break you guys. Get your frustrations out while you dance and build up your sexual frustrations instead."

Laughing, I push away from him. "That is *not* going to help! The last thing I need is to be sexually frustrated around him."

"No, the last thing you need is to make this *any* more complicated than it is. You can't be friends *or* lovers if you can't even hang out. You're supposed to be getting to know him again, remember? So what if he got a little jealous over Chad? His heart is with you even though some of his feelings are a little mixed up right now. You should understand that more than anyone right now since you're dating two men at once."

I hate it when he's right.

"You're right; I'll go over there and ask him if he wants to come meet us at the club after I get ready. He's got the early shift with Vanessa today; it seems to be working out well for them splitting Saturday with her now that Chad has taken over the Friday and Sunday shifts."

"Well, I'd be happy, too, if I had to spend less time with Vanessbitch."

"Connor…" I scold him gently. "I know, I know, she's a changed woman. Blah, blah, blah. I'll believe that when the DNA test comes back and actually shows she's not lying. Even so, the fact she's even in this situation says it all."

"I don't know, I can kind of relate. The way she went about it wasn't right, but come on, look at *me* right now. If I started having sex with them I could easily be her. No birth control is one hundred percent. This is just as much their fault as it is hers. Well…not Mike, he was sort of innocent in it all. But you know what I mean."

"Kate, I'm ready for you," Jess calls down from upstairs. Good timing, too. From the look on Connor's face he was probably going to tell me all about how this is not even the same.

"I love you, Connor," I tell him sweetly as I pop a quick kiss on his cheek.

"I love you, too, Kate, now go get all sexied up for your man."

After slapping him on the shoulder I feel better. "He's not my man"

"Oh yeah, I forgot; he's just one of your men."

Sarcastic asshole.

"You're an ass, Connor," I call out behind me as I go up the stairs.

"Maybe, but you love this ass!" he yells up after me. God, he cracks me up.

"Shower fast, Kate, we don't have a ton of time to get you ready and I need to take my time with you."

"Got it, but you're going to have to speed it up a bit. I'm going to go next door and see if Daniel wants to come with us."

"Connor got his way after all?"

"Doesn't he always?" I ask her, stepping into the shower.

"Yep, he sure does. There's this thing he likes to do with his tongue, oh my god. At first I was creeped out, but…"

Oh no. TMI.

"Stop, Jess, I don't want to have that image in my head. I get it, he rocks your world. Let's just leave it at that, okay?"

She's cracking up. "You guys are too much. You'd think you're actually related. He can't stand to hear anything to do with you and sex, especially if it's *gumdrop* related, and you can't listen about him, either."

"Yeah, well, some things are just better left unheard," I tell her, stepping out of the shower. "Even if he seems to think my orgasms sound hot," I say with a pointed tone and she at least has the decency to blush, but it's fleeting.

"Whatever, just hurry up and put this on. We've got work to do, woman!" She rolls her eyes and thrusts a skimpy black dress at me.

"This? You want me to wear this? It barely covers my ass on a *good* day."

"I know," she replies, smirking at me. "That's why you're wearing it. Daniel isn't going to be able to keep his hands off of you."

"Tonight isn't about that," I tell her as she zips me up.

"Maybe not, but it can't hurt to show him what he's missing. He screwed up not talking to you the past few weeks. Let him regret it a bit, and while you're at it you'll be humoring me. Dress and black six-inch Louboutins—we'll be picking guys off of you all night."

Great.

There's no point in arguing; the easiest thing to do is just give in.

"Too bad Mike won't see you in that dress. He'd go super-hot alpha over it."

Thinking about Mike's reaction, I have to squeeze my thighs together a bit. Either one of them would have plenty of ways in their heads to get me out of this dress.

"Earth to Kate! Jesus, woman, you're in la la land tonight. Sit so we can turn you into a vixen and get out of here. Marc will be here in about thirty minutes, which doesn't give me much time at all."

This is nice; things are almost normal between us right now and it feels good. Jess is chatty as usual while she does her thing. When she finishes, I almost don't recognize myself. She is a master with a brush. Instead of going into nursing she should be a make-up artist to the stars; she's got a real gift.

Connor whistles from behind us, "Hot damn, you two look gorgeous! I hate to break up the party but Marc and the limo are waiting outside."

Shit.

"I've still got to go talk to Daniel." I grab my shoes and hand Jess my clutch.

"Take this to the limo and I'll meet you guys there in a few minutes."

After running down the stairs, I stop long enough to put my shoes on. Marc is standing outside the limo and *damn* he looks good. Dark jeans, black button up shirt, sexy-ass look on his face. Some girl is going to get very lucky tonight.

"Damn, baby girl, you look hot! Hurry up and go get your man before I keep you all to myself." I think he's joking, but when I look back over my shoulder he's watching my ass walk away with a very intense look on his face.

Pausing outside for a minute after knocking on the door, I smooth my dress down. When no one answers, I let myself in. I hear Vanessa laughing upstairs so I quickly pull off my shoes and head up. What I hear next stops me in my tracks right outside the nursery door.

"Have you told her yet?" Vanessa asks him breathlessly.

Too breathlessly.

"Not yet, I asked her if we could meet tonight but I haven't heard back yet."

"Daniel, you have to tell her before this goes any further. It's not fair. It's better if everything is out in the open. It's the only way we can move on from everything."

What the hell?

"Ohhh," Vanessa squeals out, giggling.

"Careful there, we wouldn't want to hurt Lucas now, would we?" he asks her seductively.

Turn around Kate.

Turn Around Kate.

TURN.

AROUND.

KATE.

I've never been good at listening to my inner voice though as much as I wish just this once I would have. As I peek around the corner, I can't believe my eyes.

Daniel is sitting on the loveseat in the corner of the room and Vanessa is straddling him. Her bulging pregnant belly doesn't seem to be getting in the way at all, they're so close. *Too close.* Her head is pressed against his, her long blonde hair is covering both of their faces and the only sound is their heavy breathing. They have no clue that I'm here. She's wearing a beautiful sundress that's pulled up a bit since her legs are spread out over his.

"Ohhh," is the sound she makes as she rises up just to move down again and I can't believe what I'm seeing.

"Careful, just go nice and slow," he tells her.

He's fucking her.

He's FUCKING her.

FUCKING HER.

I'm already running down the stairs and I can't get the 'ohhh' sound out of my head. With every step I take, my heart races faster and faster until I feel like I'm going to pass out. Clumsily, I manage to get my shoes on at the door and open it to Mike's surprised face.

"Wow I didn't even knock, talk about timing…Kate, what's wrong? Are you okay?" I can't look at him; I don't want him to know I'm upset.

"I'm fine… I'm just in a hurry. I've got to go."

"Stop, Kate, look at me please." The smile falls from his face when I do and he pulls me into a fierce hug just as Connor yells out for me to hurry up.

"What's wrong, Kate?"

"Go ask your friend, but you might want to give him a few minutes to finish what he's doing. I've gotta go, I'm sorry. Call me tomorrow, okay?"

"Kate," he calls out after me and I turn around. "I'm sorry you're hurting, but you look beautiful tonight," he tells me with a sad smile.

"Thank you."

When I climb into the limo, it's so quiet you could hear a pin drop.

"He's not coming?" Connor asks incredulously.

"He was otherwise entertained."

Jess and Connor exchange concerned glances. "What does that mean?" Connor wants to know as Marc passes me a glass of champagne.

"Can I have tequila instead, please?" Nodding appropriately, he passes the champagne to Jess and pours me a tumbler full of tequila from the bar. In this moment I'm thankful for how well he knows me.

"Kate, don't you remember you're a mean tequila drinker?" Connor asks seriously.

"You don't want to see me without this tonight, trust me on that."

Thank God this is Patron because I down it like it's water. The burn feels good as it goes down and I'm thankful that in a few minutes I'll start to feel numb.

After a few minutes pass, I'm indeed becoming less aware of my senses and it's a wonderful feeling. Tonight I'm going to forget the world and just have a good time. I'm not even going to give Daniel or Vanessa a second thought.

"So," Connor begins hesitantly, "can you tell us what the fuck just happened back there?" *Can I?*

Can I actually say the words out loud?

If I want to believe it's real I guess I have to.

"No one answered when I knocked on the door so I went upstairs. When I got up there, I heard them talking about me so I paused, trying to decide if I should leave or go in. They were in the nursery, but I heard some noises. So I...I waited because I couldn't just walk away; I had to see the train wreck in front of me with my own eyes."

Jess's eyes grow wide and I hold out my glass to Marc who promptly fills it with more tequila. Not a lot, but enough.

"When I peeked around the corner, *Vanessbitch,*" I say, fully emphasizing Connor's lovely nickname for her, "was on top, straddling Daniel... fucking him."

"No, that is not one bit possible," Connor states firmly while pulling out his phone.

"Put your phone down, Houston. It is one hundred percent possible. They were talking about 'Had he told me yet? Things were going to come out and the sooner I knew the better for everyone'. Of course they're getting back together; I mean, he did *love* her. The Chad thing was probably just a scam to win him back."

"But the baby could still be Mike's. Hell, the baby *most likely is* Mike's," Jess squeals. I really wish I could figure out whose side she's on in all of this.

"I don't buy it, not one single bit. Did she drug him? Daniel wouldn't do this. Not now, not when he's so close to everything he's ever wanted. Are you sure you saw what you think you saw? Sometimes things can look far worse than they actually are." I know he's trying to rationalize with me but all I feel is that he's treating me like a child.

"Hmmm let me think... 'you have to tell her before this goes further... ohhh' in a crazy, breathless sex voice. Don't forget about her being on top of him. I'm pretty sure I saw what I think I saw."

God, I'm pissed!

The limo slows and Jess and Conner get out when it comes to a stop. Marc grabs my hand and pulls me close. "Baby girl, we *do not* have to do this. Let me take you home."

I feel like such a jerk. It's his birthday and I haven't even wished him a happy one yet.

"Are you kidding me? Hell no, we're *not* going home. This is your night, *our* night, we're going to have so much fun. I'm sorry I didn't say it sooner, but Happy Birthday. You're my soul keeper, remember? All will be right with the world once you and I get on the dance floor. Come on; let's go have some birthday fun." Yanking his arm with enthusiasm I don't really feel yet, I pull him from the car. Connor is texting furiously away on his phone and I do my best to ignore it.

Immediately, Jack greets us at the door and ushers us to the VIP section. The club is packed already and the music has a pulsating beat that I just want to lose myself in. Marc whispers something to Jack and then Jack punches a few buttons on his iPad. Within two minutes our table has appetizers, tequila, and shot glasses, as well as champagne on ice, and a few bottles of water. I'll give it to him, Jack has built this club up from nothing and it's one of the most prestigious clubs in Los Angeles now. Bands will even rent this place out for small concerts and events. Marc has hinted in the past that there are things that go on here behind closed doors which aren't for the faint of heart. I've always wondered what that means exactly but Marc is seriously guarding that secret with his life.

"Why is your phone going straight to voicemail?" Connor is super irritated right now.

"Because it's off."

"You need to turn it on, Kate. Read your text messages, *listen* to your voicemails. Please."

"Not going to happen. I'm going to have fun tonight and let loose. I'll deal with everything else tomorrow," I tell him stubbornly.

"Kate, I wouldn't tell you to do it if I thought it would hurt you. Please. You didn't see what you thought you did and now you need to hear that from them."

Taking in a deep breath, I count to ten as I exhale very slowly. "Connor, sometimes ignorance is bliss. Tonight, that's the case. I'm going to celebrate Marc's night. You only turn twenty-four once and we're going to do it in style. Drop it for now. I'll deal with it tomorrow."

After pounding two shots, I pull Marc onto the dance floor leaving Connor staring after me. Iggy Azalea and Rita Ora's *Black Widow* is playing and I completely lose myself in the beat. If there's one thing Marc is my soul mate for, it's dancing. Our bodies meld together in the most sensually erotic way. His hands rest on my hips, my arms wrap around his neck, and since he's behind me, my ass grinds right into him. His erection is obvious but over the years I've learned that it's just his reaction to our dancing. His hands leave my hips and roam all over my body. When I turn around, he pulls me close to his body, his hand strategically placed on the top of my ass, resting against that erogenous zone on my low back. We're grinding face to face and it's fucking hot.

The song shifts to *New Flame* by Chris Brown and Usher and our dance becomes even more sensual. I'm losing myself in the sensations and the feelings, and I don't know how to describe it, but there's a point where something shifts. My heart beats faster and his clutch on me gets harder...*tighter.* Marc pulls me deeper into his body, if that's even possible because we're already as close as two people can get. When his hands each grab an ass cheek, I know that this night is going to end with us together and I'm surprisingly okay with that.

Connor shoots me an evil look from across the dance floor but I just ignore it. He's the one who told me to let loose tonight and that's exactly what I'm doing. Marc bends down and his breath caresses my ear, immediately making my nipples hard and my body tremble.

"Why don't we get a drink and sit for a few minutes?" The words float into my head and I don't hear them as much as *feel* them as he kisses my neck lightly. Nodding, I let him lead me off of the dance floor and back to our table.

We both drink some water, and even though we're sitting in silence, his hand explores my thigh under the table. At first, he rubs closer to my knee, but then, as if seeking a hidden treasure, his hand stealthily moves up my thigh. Normally I would move away, because this isn't what our relationship is, but not tonight. Our relationship has been leading up to this for a long time and I'm tired of denying our attraction. Even if I know it will only be a one night stand, I know it will be hot. So instead of moving away, I move closer to him, giving him easier access to claim what he's seeking.

Reaching for the tequila shots already poured and waiting on the table, he passes one to me with his free hand.

"Happy Birthday," I toast to him as we take the shot and he passes me another, "To taking things to the next level," he says, raising his glass to mine.

"Friends with excellent benefits," I reply, clinking mine to his as his fingers find my clit and graze across it. The burn of the tequila isn't the only fire I'm feeling right now. Marc licks the taste of tequila from his lips as his eyes gaze into mine. He places the palm of his hand on the back of my head and pulls me close to him, so close he's whispering in my mouth.

"Now or never, Kate. Once I put my mouth on yours I'm not going to want to stop. Do you really want this? Tell me now if you don't, and I'll back off."

In response to his question, my lips meet his and my body trembles in excitement. *Why have I waited so long to do this?* His lips are full and soft and meld to mine perfectly. It's like he's making love to my lips with his and it's beyond erotic. When my tongue finally meets his, my world spins, the fire spreads, and no joke—I'm contemplating fucking him right here, right now. It's. That. Good.

When he pulls away from the most exhilarating kiss I think I've ever had, my body craves more of his touch.

"Damn girl that was…"

"Beyond words." I'm breathless and reach for another shot when his hand reaches out to stop me.

"Last one, baby girl. I want you buzzed enough to want this but not too drunk to enjoy it, remember it, or tell me no."

"Got it, but for what it's worth, I've waited just as long for this as you have and I'm not turning back now. Tonight is our night."

"Let's dance then."

Connor and Jess come back to the table as we're getting up. Neither of them looks happy and I'm positive they saw us kissing. "Kate, can I talk to you?" If I go talk to Jess she's going to try and kill my night and I'm not going to let that happen.

"In just a little bit, okay? We're going to dance for a little while and when I come back we'll talk." I say the words with a smile but don't mean them at all. I'm going to get Marc out of here before she gets a chance to wreck my night.

"Alright," she replies hesitantly.

I let Marc lead me to the dance floor and Jason Derulo's *The Other Side* comes on. There could not be a more perfect song to be playing right now.

Dancing with Marc makes me feel alive! All of my senses awaken and I'm in tune to everything around me—the pulsating music, his body against mine, how turned on I am knowing what we're about to do. I don't have a care in the world right now and I like it that way. We're in our own bubble, and even if it may burst eventually, I'm enjoying it for all that it is right now. His hands caress every part of my body as he grinds against me.

Why didn't I do this before?

It feels so fucking good.

I let myself get lost in the music, in the dancing, in his touch; it's the only thing I want to feel right now. I've been watching Jess and Connor out of the corner of my eye. They're up to something but I don't know what. When they head to the door, I've got a feeling someone is going to try and break up my party. Marc pulls me close and kisses me breathless. We need to go *now*.

"Can we get out of here?" I yell out to Marc over the music and his eyes follow mine. Now Connor is arguing with the bouncer. They're trying to get someone in. "Follow me." Marc grabs my wrist tightly and weaves through the crowd. He pushes through a door at the end of the hall marked 'private' and pushes the up button on an elevator.

Maybe he's taking me to Jack's office?

When the door opens and we step inside he pushes the five button; I didn't even realize this place had five floors. "Kate, you have to promise me you won't freak out, okay?" My confused state of mind must reflect on my face because Marc laughs and pulls me close. "I love the look you get on your face when you're confused or thinking hard. It's cute."

As we exit the elevator, he walks me past twelve or so doors until we reach the one at the end of the hall. It looks like a hotel and since this door is by itself maybe it's a suite? I'm super buzzed and don't really care but it's just so odd that a club would have rooms.

Marc pulls out a key card and my eyes widen in surprise. This is his room?

Don't.

Freak.

Out.

His words repeat in my mind as we step inside the room.

"Wow." It's all I can say; this room is amazing. It's like a loft—everything is here and it's an open floor plan. There's a kitchen, bedroom, living area, and one giant glass wall overlooking the city. It's not a great view because we're not high up, but in Los Angeles, when the city is lit up at night, any height advantage will give you a beautiful view of the city lights. It's probably not as pretty in the daytime. Thankfully, at least the bathroom has walls.

Marc is standing back, letting me take all of it in and process it. The bed is a huge king size bed, and I don't know how I missed it before now, but there's a sex swing hanging in the middle of the room.

What the fuck? "Marc, I think you need to start talking."

He holds a finger up to me, indicating he needs a minute, and then goes into the kitchen. When he comes back, he's got two bottles of water and two shots of tequila on a serving tray then motions for me to have a seat on the couch.

"The Scene is successful because it's a sex club. Well no, that's not really accurate… it's not a place to watch or pick up other people publically. It specializes in one night stands, people looking to spice up their marriage for a night, or for people who are unhappy in their current circumstances to take a…" I'm dumbfounded as he struggles over the words.

"A place for people to go and cheat?" I ask him incredulously.

"Well yeah, basically." *I'm stunned.*

"Look, Kate, Jack doesn't make them cheat and he actually lets it be known he frowns upon it. His hotel fills a niche. People want to go to places that are fun, the club is fun but the rooms are each stocked with fun things—swings, toys, edibles, bondage kits—pretty much anything you could desire. There are also rooms that are set up more romantically—bath oils and salts, fresh-cut flowers, in-room fireplaces—things that will restart a romantic spark."

"So this is the secret you've been keeping this whole time? This is what you haven't been able to tell me?" Now seems like a good time to take that shot of tequila because my buzz is rapidly fading. Marc can sense it, too, because he hands me the other shot and goes back to the kitchen and brings the tequila bottle to the table.

Smart man.

"Kate, I couldn't tell you; I signed a contract and I'm bound by the terms. Until I actually bring someone to a room, I can't tell them anything about this place."

Holy shit…he's a member.

"You…you're a…oh my God, Marc, you *belong* to this club?" I'm officially freaking out and reaching for my third shot of tequila.

"Not exactly, I'm Jack's silent partner. Because I own half the club I'm automatically a member."

God, do I know any of my friends anymore?

Needing some space from him, I walk back over to the window. He's not having it, though; I can see him in the reflection of the glass as he approaches behind me and wraps his arms around my waist.

"Baby girl," he whispers in my ear, "you should know I've never used one of these rooms before tonight. Jack issued me a key tonight because I asked him to. I've watched you struggle with secrets for a while now and I didn't want to keep this one from you any longer. Look at me, Kate."

He turns me around in his arms and pulls me close. I'm really feeling the effects of the tequila right now.

"If you and I are going to do this, and I hope we are, I wanted it to be in a place that doesn't have any associated memories. You're my best friend and I don't ever want to lose you. My place is your second home; your place is my second home. I don't want you avoiding my house because it reminds you of this night."

I didn't even think about that.

"I told you I'm open to all kinds of sexual ideas, that's why I have no problem being a partner in this club. But I also wasn't kidding when I said that you would be the girl I would settle down for. I'm confident I can separate my feelings for you because I know your heart is somewhere else, but being here makes doing that easier."

The sparkle in his beautiful eyes is blinding and what he says makes so much sense.

"You're the only girl I've ever wanted to bring here. The only one I've ever wanted to tell all my secrets to. And now that you know them, Katie Grace, do you still love me?" There is so much trepidation in his voice, it's heartbreaking.

"Of course I do! There will never be a day that I don't love you, Marc, even if I'm not in love with you." Best to be honest and make sure those lines aren't blurred.

His mouth descends onto mine and I open immediately to him. When his tongue strokes mine, it's as if he's turned on all the senses in my body. I feel it everywhere. Kissing Marc is a transcendent experience, maybe because it was so forbidden for so long or maybe because we've had built up sexual tension for years. Whatever the reason, I don't want the feeling to stop.

Marc leads me to the bed, kissing me the entire way, his hands glued to my ass. God, I love how he squeezes it, like he just can't get enough. His hands work their way to my zipper and he peels the dress off of me. It's tight so it takes a minute to get it all the way off. Once it is, I'm left standing in my black demi bra, black thong, and my six-inch fuck me heels. His eyes take me in and he subconsciously licks his lips as he does; he likes what he sees.

When he finishes taking me in with his eyes, he starts with his hands. He's not really seeing anything he hasn't before since he's seen me in a bikini. Well, a little more ass cheek this time around, I guess, but that's about it. He turns me around and bends me over the bed so my ass is in the air.

"That is one beautiful sight; I could look at your ass all day." And that's when I feel the bite, he bit right into my ass cheek and I'm not going to lie, it feels good.

"Marc!" I cry out his name and his hand lands a firm slap on my ass.

"Yes, Kate?" His tone is teasing. He's enjoying this, and so help me god, so am I.

"Fuck me," I cry out as the next slap comes down on my ass.

"Oh, baby girl, I plan to, *all night long.*"

The moan that escapes my lips at his words turns him on even further. Suddenly, he's flipping me over and pulling me to him. Bending forward, and with precise control, he opens my bra with his teeth. *Fuck that's hot.*

For a split second he backs away, enjoying the view of my breasts being bared to him. Taking one in each hand, he squeezes them together and pulls them to his mouth. "Damn, Kate, I had no idea you were pierced here, too," he says and his mouth descends onto me, giving each one of the girls attention. Laving my nipples with expertise, sucking my nipple and playing with my piercing with his tongue, my senses are hyperaware of everything.

"Marc, oh god, yes," I call out during his relentless assault, which only makes him work harder. Marc kisses his way up to my mouth, tasting me. I throw my arms around his neck and wrap my leg up over his hip and he holds on tight. I take that as my cue to wrap my other leg around his waist. Marc is strong, so strong, and he holds me up effortlessly. He continues kissing me as he lays me back on the bed.

His hands reach for my panties and he slowly slides them down my legs and groans. "Damn, girl, that pretty pink pussy is glistening just for me. You're so wet and it's a beautiful fucking sight." He props my feet on the bed, heels digging into the duvet, legs spread open, completely bared to him except for my shoes.

Licking his lips, he backs up and slowly unbuttons his shirt in such slow motion. I'm left anticipating every single move. I swear I can feel myself get wetter as each button comes undone. I've seen him without a shirt before but never in a situation like this. I bite down on my lip when it finally comes off. *Good God, his body is amazing.*

"Fuck, girl, I can't wait any longer; the clothes will have to come off later. My mouth needs to taste you *now*."

He slides his hands up my legs, kissing the inside of my thighs as he inches closer to what he wants to taste. Then he uses one hand to spread my lips open to him, and with one long stroke, licks me up to my clit and then back down. When his tongue enters me, I cry out in ecstasy. My arms are flailing, trying to grip on to the blankets for traction because I can't stop squirming. Firmly, he places his hand on my abdomen, essentially holding me down as he feasts on me. I'm building at a rapid pace, my cries escalating higher and higher, until I come hard, screaming his name.

He doesn't let up, instead he's moaning as he swallows every last drop, using his finger to press lightly on my clit. The vibrating sensation from his moans coupled with the pressure on my clit sends me into a second orgasm, this one longer but not as strong. The feel of his tongue licking up my come sets me on fire, and the longer he does it, the wetter I'm going to get. Finally, he pulls his tongue out and slowly licks around my clit, working his way up my belly, stopping to tug on my belly button ring with his mouth. This man is an expert in making my body succumb to his touch.

As he continues his way up to my mouth, he licks his lips with a smile. "Baby girl, you taste excellent on my tongue. Kiss me and find out for yourself just how good." Eagerly, I open my mouth to his and kiss him until my taste covers us both. Everything I need tonight he's giving me, and more. *So much more.* His erection presses hard against me through his jeans and I wrap my legs around him, pulling him to me, grinding on him through his clothes.

"Marc I need you," I whisper the words in his ears but rub against him desperately so he realizes just how much. When he backs away, I lean up on my elbows so I can watch him disrobe. Once he's down to his boxer briefs, I'm breathless with anticipation. As I watch them come down and see his perfect cock for the first time, all I want is for it to be in my mouth. Flipping around quickly, I reach out for him and pull him into my mouth.

"Damn, Kate, that feels so good." Marc puts his hand on my head and pushes me down further onto his cock. I try and open my mouth wider to take more of him in. He's a big boy, so it's a little stretch, but *fuck me* he tastes fantastic.

I'm working him with my hands and my mouth and I swear he's still growing. The growls that are coming out of his mouth are sexy as fuck! Finally, right when he's about to come in my mouth, he pulls back and away from me. Looking up at him with hooded eyes, I swipe my tongue across my lips, licking his essence from them. He pulls me up to my knees and kisses me hard and forceful, enjoying the taste of himself on my lips.

His hands glide down my body and finally his fingers touch my clit. "Yes!" I call out as he slides a finger inside of my tight pussy.

"Oh, baby girl, you're so fucking tight and so fucking wet."

I feel my wetness spreading and he uses it to his advantage, slipping another finger inside of me. Marc has big hands, so even his fingers give me a new sensation of fullness. My lips find his as he continues to finger fuck me. I'm building again and then he does the unexpected. Suddenly, he takes a coated finger and works his way to my ass. Sucking in a breath, I tense up.

His breath caresses my ear, "Relax, baby girl, I promise you'll enjoy this." His movements are slow and calculated; he knows exactly what he's doing and I do trust him with my whole heart. My body relaxes into his and he kisses me again as his finger penetrates me. At first it hurts like a bitch, but after he lets me get used to the feeling, it feels fucking fantastic. He's got three fingers in me—two in my pussy and one in my ass—and I can't get enough. I'm riding him with reckless abandon and I don't care. This feeling is amazing and I don't want it to end. I'm fighting off my orgasm but I know when it hits I'm going to scream my head off.

When he pulls my nipple ring in between his teeth, I lose it. "Marc! Fuck, Marc! Oh God, yes, Yes, YES!" When I finally collapse, he slowly pulls out each finger and goes to the bathroom to clean himself up while I come down from this all-time high. Every nerve ending in my body is fully alive right now.

Marc comes back with some water, which I take gratefully, and then I curl up into his embrace. I've always felt so safe with him and this is no different. He's still hard and I know he's got to be dying to come. Turning onto my side, I begin to kiss my way across his chest and to his mouth and we share an all-consuming kiss. Reaching over to the bedside table, he rips open a condom packet.

"Marc…" I start to say but he cuts me off.

"I know, Kate. It's not latex, it's polyurethane, much safer than lambskin and completely latex free."

Wow, he really did think of everything.

I watch, enraptured, as he tugs the condom on, pulls me on top, and lets me take control. "Start at your own pace, baby girl, and when you get comfortable we'll really get things going."

Slowly, I lower myself onto him. He feels so damn good. His hands go to my hips and hold on tight, just following my lead. Tentatively, I rise up and down until my body gets acclimated to him. He hisses and pulls me down to kiss him.

"You're so tight, so perfect, this is so much better than I *ever* could have imagined."

He's got that right.

His hands caress every inch of my body he can reach and I let myself go completely, losing myself in him. Marc changes position, sitting up with me still on top, but he starts controlling how I move. It's so deep like this; the noises that escape me let him know that with every thrust he *owns* me. My body finally can't take anymore and shatters around him in a mind-blowing orgasm. That's when he kisses me in a way I've never been kissed before and there are no words to describe what he does but it makes me need him again already.

Marc moves to the bottom of the bed, and one by one, removes my shoes. Gently, he massages each foot and my body is putty in his extremely capable hands. As he climbs my body, he does this combination of licking, sucking, biting, and kissing the entire way and it's heaven. Finally, he enters me slowly but in absolute total and complete control.

His hands press into my stomach, spanning me from hip to hip, as he moves in and out of me at an achingly slow pace. I manage to wrap my legs around him, pulling him in deeper, getting whatever leverage I can to make him speed up the pace. His tempo does speed up but in small increments. He's taking this time with me, relishing this, *us,* and so am I. But when his love making becomes a hard, relentless fucking, and I'm screaming his name over and over again—that's when I lose all control. My orgasm hits almost without warning and as it does I scream, and that's when he comes. Watching Marc come is enthralling; you can actually see his entire body shake and tremble from his head to his toes. You absolutely know that he *feels* every little bit of his orgasm and *relishes* it. Out of all the things I've seen in my life, the men that I've been with or will ever be with, I know without fail this will always be the hottest sexual moment I will ever witness. This is a memory I will keep with me forever and it will be a secret and a great memory that only the two of us will share. For whatever reason, that is a very comforting thought. Marc disposes of the condom and curls up in bed with me, covering us both up. We cuddle together, naked, just like we have a million times before with our clothes on. He presses a kiss onto my forehead as if nothing has changed, even though *everything* has just shifted.

"Are you okay, Kate?" Concern oozes from his voice; he's looking for reassurance that this wasn't a big mistake.

Determined, I look him in the eyes and hold his gaze. "We're okay, Marc. I'm okay, too. That was everything you always said it would be and more. I don't regret a single thing we just did." That is the absolute truth, too. Whatever issues Mike and Daniel have with it are just going to have to be theirs. My buzz is wearing off and I'm super sleepy.

"Okay, baby girl, but if at any point you start having doubts or you regret this in any way, you need to come and talk to me. No running, Kate, not from me, not ever. Sex is just sex, but our friendship means everything to me and I'll never be okay losing it."

Snuggling into him tighter, a yawn escapes me "That's not going to be okay with me, either, Marc. We'll be fine."

~~~***~~~

A few hours later, I wake up startled and with a massive headache. It's almost five in the morning and I'm in bed with Marc. A wave of nausea washes over me as the night floods back to me. I'm sleeping in a sex club.

Holy shit.

There's no way I can wake up here and walk out with the rest of the cheaters and people trying to get their sparks back. Not to sound like a judgy bitch, to each his own, but that's just not the kind of walk of shame I want to do today.

"Kate, are you okay?" Marc asks sleepily.

"I'm fine…I just need to get home. It's late, well, early and I know Jess is probably freaking out. I haven't had my phone on all night."

"Okay, get dressed and I'll have the limo pulled up." After Marc gets dressed, he helps me zip my dress and suddenly, I'm so sad I start crying. "Hey," he says, pulling me close. "Kate, it's okay, nothing is going to change. I won't let it, I promise."

"I know you mean what you're saying, I do. But last night was amazing and beautiful and now it's over. How can things just go back to the way they were?"

After kissing me gently on the lips, he replies, "Because we love each other enough to not let this get in the way. I know your heart belongs to someone else, baby girl. We're good, I promise. Someday maybe that will change and this can be something we can explore because you have to admit it was off the charts hot!"

Now I'm laughing, my emotions are a mess. "It was…I love you, Marc, so much."

"I love you, too, and that's how I know this is going to be okay. Let's get you home to face the music."

When the limo pulls up to my house, we share one last lingering goodbye kiss. The culmination of all our years of wanting and needing finally came to pass. This kiss is sweet but it's not full of sparks. It's bittersweet because a part of me deep down inside knows Marc would love me the way I deserve to be loved. If only I loved him that way, we could be happy.

As I close the door behind me and fall to the floor, I burst into tears. Everything I've lost in the last few weeks crashes down on me. All the mistakes I've made and the decisions to come hang heavy over my broken heart. I messed up so bad last night, and even though I don't regret what came from it…I know I'm not cut out for covering pain with pleasure.

When Connor makes his presence known, I cry even harder. Even though he's pissed at me, he's still here and waiting, hoping he can help make things right in my world.

God I love him.

Chapter Twelve – Daniel

Saturday

This morning I sent Kate flowers and asked her on a date. The past few weeks have been really awkward for us ever since I acted like a jealous fool at Vanessa's house. I don't know what was with me that night. All I kept thinking is that we don't know Chad and we need to keep Vanessa and Lucas safe. In no way did I mean that to cross over in a way which seemed like I still had feelings for Vanessa.

How could I? Every time I see Kate there are only two thoughts that cross my mind: making her my wife and making love to her. I've never loved someone the way I love Kate. And for that reason only, I've backed off a little the past few weeks. I know she's still trying to figure things out and my feelings for her are only growing so much that if I see her, she'll be able to tell.

Mike has taken her out to lunch a few times, but since we've been swamped at work, he hasn't seen her much, either. I've never seen him so happy, so in love. Maybe he's part of the reason I've backed off a little, too. Watching them rekindle their friendship almost has me rooting for their reunion. *Almost.*

Tonight, I'm going to tell her what's been going on, why I've been so distant and hope that she can understand that I *was not* jealous of Chad. Mike and I are alternating Saturday shifts now so I'll have all night free to be with her. Today, I'm going to hang up Lucas's name for Vanessa now that the nursery has been painted and her labor is likely to start soon. The doctor says she can go anytime now that pre-eclampsia patients rarely go full term.

We try to keep her sitting as much as possible, so when I get to her house, I just let myself in so she doesn't have to get up. I'm happy to be here, but I'd rather be next door with my friends.

"Hey, Vanessa."

"Hey, Daniel! I'm so excited to finish the nursery today, thanks for offering to help." She flashes me a beautiful smile; she's positively glowing today. *Will Kate glow like that pregnant?*

"Of course, just tell me where you want them and I'll get it all ready and take a picture and send it to you."

She looks confused and then it dawns on her that I don't want her going up the stairs. "Hell no, McCormick, I'm coming up and supervising and you can't stop me. I want to be a part of this and feel the excitement."

"Have you always been this determined or is it the pregnancy hormones?"

She gives me the evil glare with her eyes but I just laugh it off.

"Fine, you can come but I'm carrying you up the stairs."

"Are you kidding me? I'll break you! I'm so fat now, it will never work."

She's cute when she's frustrated. Vanessa is a tiny thing, pre-pregnancy she probably only weighed about one hundred and ten pounds. "How much weight have you gained?"

Immediately her hands go on her hips. "You're not supposed to ask a woman how much she weighs!" I hope Chad has patience because this woman would try those of a saint.

"Well, it's a good thing I didn't ask you how much you weigh, then. I asked you how much weight you've gained so far."

"Eighteen pounds," she replies with a pout, and that's when I lose my self-control and laugh harder than I have in a long time.

"Woman, I could bench press you in my sleep. I carry you up the stairs or we don't do this, take it or leave it."

"Fine!" I don't miss her being all huffy and puffy. Maybe Chad finds it cute, but it just reminds me of how obnoxious she can really be.

Once we're in the nursery, I put her down gently and help her sit in the rocking chair. Vanessa shows me where she wants the letters but there's a little spot that needs to be touched up first. It's not a big deal, but I don't have any extra clothes with me so I take off my shirt before popping open the paint can in case it splashes. When I hear her gasp, I realize what a huge mistake that just was.

"Vanessa, please don't tell Kate." When I turn around, her eyes are glistening with tears and I know she has to be hormonal because Vanessa is not a crier.

"I knew it," she says softly.

"You knew what?"

She comes up behind me and runs her fingers across the tattoo, and when I turn around she's smiling. "I knew she was the one who was going to fill that spot on your tattoo. From the second I saw the two of you together, I just knew it."

"How?" I really want to know what Vanessa noticed from the outside looking in.

"Well it's kind of hard to explain, but as your ex I'd like to think I know a little bit about you. After all, our relationship wasn't *all* bad, was it?"

"No it wasn't all bad, it just wasn't right," I tell her truthfully. It's something I can admit now even though I couldn't see it when we were dating.

"Not to sound like a stalker, but the night of the wedding wasn't the first time I saw you with Kate. I saw you the day before in front of your house and I was actually sitting on that bench on the beach…you know, the one next door that has a perfect view of your deck?"

She was spying on us. That's sort of demented.

She thumps me on the head to get my attention. "I know what you're thinking and I wasn't spying on you. I was tired and needed to rest. I didn't know you were going to come outside and dance. How could I? You never did that with me."

She's right.

"Anyway, you guys were dancing and I watched you. I've never seen you be so tender and sweet. You had this look of contentment on your face that radiated happiness. I know you were pretty serious about us, but if you had ever looked at me *once* the way you looked at Kate that day…"

"Vanessa, I'm sorry." *God, I feel like such a jerk.* "Really, I didn't realize I had ever been a closed off boyfriend until Kate brought out a side of me that no one has ever seen."

She takes my hand in hers and smiles. "I know, Daniel, and it's really okay. The whole time I was with you, I was trying to sleep with Mike. I was reeling from my breakup with Chad and I never even gave you a fair shot. I just used you and for that I'm truly sorry."

It's nice to hear her admit she wasn't herself back then.

"The point I'm trying to get at is that I've seen you without her and now I've seen her without you. Nothing compares to the spark in the room when you guys are together. It's like everything else fades into the background and all you see is each other. It's magical and I've never seen anything like it. Fight for her, Daniel, and don't give up because I really don't think it's Mike who has her heart. I think it's you."

No one has said that to me at all because no one wants to give me false hope.

"Has she said anything to you to make you think that?" Rapidly, she shakes her head no. *Damn.*

"She earned a place on your skin in the most sacred place, Daniel. You know it, too, or her name wouldn't be there."

"Well, she has a place on Mike's skin, too. His entire sleeve tells their tale."

Vanessa is thinking quietly for a while and finally speaks, "I'm not going to diminish Kate and Mike's story because it's pretty epic, but when something tears you away from your loved ones in such a harsh way, working your way back to perfect isn't always an obtainable goal. I'm not saying it can't happen, I'm just saying my money is on you."

We sit in silence for a few minutes as I touch up the tiny spot on the wall and then I take a seat on the loveseat to wait for it to dry.

"I've got some news to share with you, too," Vanessa says to me nervously.

"Okay, what is your news?" I ask her jokingly.

"Last night, Chad asked me to marry him and I said yes." I quickly glance down at her ring finger to see if I'm completely oblivious and she laughs. "We're waiting on a ring until the swelling goes down. I'm so bloated from the pre-eclampsia, it's easier to wait."

"Not to sound like a jerk, but I thought you guys were waiting so you could get your life together and settle into a role with the whole co-parenting thing." *Was Connor right? Are they just using us for money?*

"We were going to and also to let some time pass since he just got un-engaged. But then we got to talking and we know this is what we want. I've known Chad almost all of my life, and I was miserable without him and he felt the same. We both jumped into new relationships hoping to find something tangible because neither of us were willing to admit we had met our soul mates so young."

Sounds a lot like Kate and Mike. "So what prompted the change of heart?"

"Actually, you did. Kate wasn't the only one who thought you were jealous last week, so did Chad. When your natural dominance reared its ugly head, I guess it got him thinking. Chad said he was only waiting to ask me because he didn't want me to think he was rushing into this, but the reason he broke off his engagement is because he knew the only girl he could ever marry would be me."

"Did you set a date?" Vanessa is getting married and I'm actually really happy for her. Who would have thought?

"Sometime in October, you know how much I love Fall."

"Look at us, growing up into responsible adults."

She laughs at me. "Well, I'm growing for sure, but I think you need to come clean with Kate about the tattoo and about your feelings for her."

"Maybe. The past few weeks I've realized just how hopelessly in love with her I really am," I tell her honestly. Vanessa gets up out of the rocker and starts heading my way when she trips over the box of letters on the floor. She lands on me pretty much belly first but in a really awkward position.

"Ugh, so uncomfortable," she groans and I pull her skirt up a bit to accommodate the position. I'm holding on to her back with my other arm so she doesn't lose her balance and fall. Leaning back a little she tries to get up "ahhh" she starts breathing in and out rapidly.

"Are you okay? Should we get you to the doctor?" She can't really move and she's still at a really awkward angle, so I shift her so at least she's in more of a sitting position in my lap. She takes a few more deeps breaths in and out before responding.

"I think I'm okay, just give me a minute. Distract me, finish what you were saying." She doesn't look good but I'll happily oblige the pregnant woman for a few minutes. "There's not much else to say, she's the one, Vanessa. I love her more than I've ever loved anyone."

"Have you told her yet?" Vanessa asks while exhaling.

"Not yet, I asked her if we could meet tonight but I haven't heard back yet."

"Daniel, you have to tell her before this goes any further. It's not fair. It's better if everything is out in the open. It's the only way we can move on from everything." She says 'we' like it involves her, too. But in a way, I guess it really does; we're all wrapped up in each other's messes right now.

"Ohhh," Vanessa cries out, trying to cover the pain with a laugh.

I'm starting to get worried but I try and play it off. "Careful there, we wouldn't want to hurt Lucas now, would we?" I'm trying not to sound worried but my tone comes out pretty serious.

Her head is pressed against mine hard, each time she tries to lift up she groans in pain. "Careful, just go nice and slow."

After a few more deep, big breaths in and out she tries to move again and fails.

"Okay, Vanessa, I'm going to lift you up and set you on the couch. I'll try and be as gentle as possible. I don't want to hurt you, but we're going to have to get you to the doctor. Okay?"

"Okay, god, I can't believe how clumsy I am. I probably just pulled something." Mike should be here soon but hopefully I'll be able to get her down the stairs alone if not. I'm worried about positioning her right.

"Here, let me try to move your leg over first." Not a good idea.

"Ohhhh, ouch!"

Damn.

Thankfully, Mike walks in but the look on his face isn't good. "What the hell is going on in here?"

I'm sure this doesn't look good. "She tripped over that box and fell. We've been trying to breathe through it and get her standing for about ten or fifteen minutes now, but she's in too much pain. I need you to help me lift her from behind."

Mike jumps into action and leans her back into his arms. Vanessa cries out again when he moves her, but we manage to get her laid out on the couch. Her pains are coming closer together now so we quickly decide to call 911.

Chad pulls up the same time as the ambulance and rides to the hospital with Vanessa. Mike and I hop in his truck and follow behind it. "Do you think she's going into labor?" he asks, gripping the steering wheel tightly.

I shrug my shoulders. "I have no idea, but she didn't look good, did she?"

"No, she didn't and…um…not that you need to hear this right now, but neither did Kate."

What?

"What do you mean neither did Kate? Is she okay? Did something happen to her?" I'm completely freaking out now. *Please, God, don't let there be anything wrong with Kate.*

"Not exactly. Daniel, do you have any idea what it looked and sounded like you guys were doing up there when I walked in?" My phone decides to start going crazy with text alerts but I ignore them.

"I'm guessing it probably looked pretty bad but you know I wouldn't do that. Not with Vanessa and not now with my every happiness hanging in the balance." That might have been the wrong choice of words to share with Mike but I *know* he gets it.

"Well, when I came to the door Kate was running out like a bat out of hell. She looked like she had just seen her worst nightmare come to life. So if you were in that same position when I came up about three minutes before, she saw you and she thinks you were fucking Vanessa."

This is not happening.

"Where did she go? I've got to talk to her and clear this up." Frantically, I pull my phone out of my pocket. "You're probably not going to like this much, but she left in a limo with Marc, Jess, and Connor."

I call her quickly and leave a message "Kate, it's not what you think. Call me, please. Vanessa is in the hospital, she had a minor accident…that's all it was. I would never do that to you. Please call me." I also send her a few text messages asking her to call, letting her know it wasn't what she thought.

Then I realize it's Marc's birthday. She mentioned it a few weeks ago; they were supposed to go out. Suddenly, I've got a sick feeling in the pit of my stomach. Mike's been worried about them hooking up for years. "You don't think she would…" I can't even say the words but Mike knows exactly what I'm getting at.

We pull into the hospital parking lot and continue the discussion on the way inside. Mike is also texting away furiously on his phone; I'm sure they are messages to Kate. "Do I think she would fuck Marc? Unfortunately, yes. It's been a long time coming and I know he'll take any shot he can at finally having his way with her. Sorry, Daniel, but the look on her face…she was devastated."

"Yeah, but she isn't like that, this is stupid to worry about. Right?" Mike avoids making eye contact with me while we take our seats in the waiting room.

"Look, Daniel, the Kate I knew wouldn't but the Kate she is right now, the one who is going through more than anyone should have to, the one who is just a heartbreak way from breaking completely, I'm not so sure. I don't even want to think about what it will do to me if she finally gives into him. But I've been in her shoes before and sometimes you just jump into that high to not have to think about the lows."

It was nothing.

It was so completely innocent.

Just when I get ready to check my messages, Chad comes out with an update. "She's doing well; they gave her something to help with the pain that is safe for the baby. They took some blood and have her hooked up to a fetal monitor. Her doctor is actually the doctor on call tonight so he's here and with her now. They think it's just Braxton Hicks contractions and a pulled abdominal muscle."

Thank God.

"So she's going to be okay?" Mike asks him, and for the first time I notice how worried he is. Of course he is. Why wouldn't he be after Lila Hope?

"Yeah, she's going to be fine, they're keeping her overnight for observation because her blood pressure is higher than they would like. I'm going to stay with her. You guys can go and I'll keep you updated if anything changes."

"Okay, we'll go, take care of her, okay? If you need us, or if anything changes at all make sure to call or text anytime." Mike sounds like a worried father "Will do, man, see you two tomorrow."

"I'm glad she's going to be okay," Mike says as he exhales a deep breath.

"Me, too," I tell him but I'm so distracted, I'm dreading looking at my phone.

"Just read the messages, Daniel. It's not going to get any better until you can fix it and you can't fix it until you read the messages and find out where she is."

Connor:

Why does Kate think you were fucking Vanessa?

Connor:

Daniel seriously you need to call me what the hell happened up there?

Connor:

She's drinking tequila and freaking out. She says you were fucking Vanessa. I know you weren't. You wouldn't.

Connor:

You're not answering me back. You didn't really do it did you?

Connor:

The noises and positions she described sound pretty convincing. You're not answering which makes it more believable. Where are you???

Connor:

They are dancing in a way that should not be legal.

Connor:

Come on man I'm not even getting a chance to cock block them they're too busy grinding all over each other on the dance floor. Why aren't you calling back?

I'm gonna be so sick. Before I can text him back, my phone rings and it's Jess.

"What the hell, McCormick? Where are you? What did you do to my girl? I told you from the beginning if you hurt her, so help me God…"

I don't have time for this crap so I cut her off, "Where are you guys, Jess?"

The tone in my voice tells her I'm not messing around and she answers immediately, "We're at The Scene but you can't get in unless you're on the list."

Oh, I'll get on the list.

"Put Connor on the phone."

"No, I want to know what happened tonight."

Fucking woman!

"Jess, there's not time for this. I didn't do anything with Vanessa, she's actually in the hospital, now put Connor on the phone!" I hear her passing the phone and talking in the background.

"Is Vanessa okay?" Connor asks, concerned.

"Yes, she's fine. They're keeping her for observation. We're on our way now but you need to get me on that list."

"I'll try, man, but they are really tight on security here and there's no hot chicks working the door but I'll see what I can do. Mike's with you?" he asks hesitantly

"Yes, both of us, why?"

"Well, it's just that…shit, I don't want to tell you this but Marc and Kate have kind of been going at it." I can't even hear myself think over the blood rushing in my head.

"What do you mean they're going at it?" When those words come out of my mouth, Mike hits the gas.

"Put that fool on speakerphone."

"Connor, going at it how?" Mike yells at him.

"Aw hell, you two, I can't get in the middle of all this. You just need to come down here and fix it before it's too late."

"We'll be there in five minutes. Do whatever you have to do to keep Kate in your sight and away from Marc."

Mike throws his keys at the Valet when we get there but Connor wasn't kidding—the security here is a nightmare. Tonight the club is closed to the public so you can't get in unless you're on the list. The bouncer is at least sympathetic that we do have friends in the club and lets us stick our heads in really quick to see if we can flag them down.

Mike's calling Connor to get him to come to the door and my eyes are searching for Kate. Out of the corner of my eye I see her on the dance floor with Marc. Connor wasn't kidding; what they're doing should be illegal, but when he leans down and covers her mouth with his my heart breaks. Mike sees it, too.

"Son of a fucking god damned bitch! Look, I don't care who you are, tell them we got past you. My girlfriend is in there making out with some guy."

The bouncer looks conflicted, and when Connor comes to the door to try and get us in, it almost works.

Almost

"Look, man, they're with us, just call Marc or Jack and ask them. They would have been on the list but we didn't think they were coming after all."

"You're here with Marc and Jack?"

Connor nods. "Yes, for Marc's birthday."

Suddenly, this doesn't feel like it's going to go our way. "Who was kissing your girlfriend; do you know the guy?"

Before I can say no because I get the feeling that's the answer we should give him, Mike answers, "Marc was kissing my girlfriend."

The bouncer stiffens up and takes back his professional stance. "Can't let you in then, sorry." The thing is he doesn't look one bit sorry. Mike loses his shit "Why, are you friends with Marc or something?"

The bouncer doesn't answer but a man walks up that Connor greets as Jack. They talk inside for a few minutes and then Connor steps out and pulls us aside. "Well, that just got fucking weird," he says, looking over his shoulder.

"They're not going to let you guys in. I guess it's not public knowledge, and Jack said normally he wouldn't say anything, but they've got some big clients here tonight and he doesn't want a scene. Marc is co-owner of this club. There are no strings I can pull to get you in tonight."

Fuck!

Connor looks down at his phone. "Um, more bad news, guys. Jess can't find Kate anywhere; she's completely disappeared."

A cute drunk girl giggles from behind us, "Sorry, I couldn't help but overhear your conversation. People don't disappear inside The Scene…they go create them."

We all exchange confused glances but Connor pours on the charm. "Really, that's interesting how would that work exactly?" Connor gets close to her and places his hand on her arm and shoots her a panty dropping smile.

"You know The Scene is a sex club, right? Well, not all hard core or anything, but there's almost one hundred hotel rooms in that building and they are all stocked to make your every fantasy come true. But shhh, don't tell anyone I told you. It's supposed to be a secret."

Just as she finishes telling us the big secret, her boyfriend finds her. "Everly, what are you doing out here?" he asks her with a very stern voice. This guy is hard core.

She puts her finger to her mouth in the shhh motion one more time before turning around to greet him. "Hey, baby, these guys got separated from their friend and wanted to know if I could check the bathroom for her."

Perfect timing because right then Jess walks out and any doubt on his face disappears. "Well let's go. It seems as if they've found her now. Have a good evening, you guys."

The Scene is a sex club.

Marc owns a sex club.

Marc is inside with Kate right now in a hotel room in a sex club.

"That's it, you guys, you know that, right? After all of this *bullshit* she picked him!" I'm pissed and my heart is broken.

"Let's go get something to eat," Mike says suddenly.

"What? You want to go eat right now?" I don't understand why he isn't more upset right now. He *hates* Marc and he knows that right now he's probably upstairs banging the hell out of Kate.

"I want to think and I can't think on an empty stomach. I was coming over to have dinner with Vanessa and that was hours ago. Kate's done this dance with Marc for years and hasn't slept with him yet. Maybe there's still hope. This isn't the first time she's kissed him, and until she gets married, it probably won't be the last."

Jess and Connor exchange a look that tells me what they were doing tonight was a whole lot more than just kissing. Hell, from what I saw on the dance floor myself they were fucking right there with their clothes on. He saw it, too. I don't know how he can be so calm.

We all end up piling in his truck and Mike pulls into the first place he sees that looks like it might be serving breakfast. Misty's diner. Could this night get any worse? I try to warn him, "Hey, Mike, you might not want to eat here…"

I don't even get to finish my sentence before he jumps my shit. "Daniel, I don't give a fuck *where* we eat, I just need to eat something." Fuck it, I'm in no mood to fix his shit tonight; he can fix it himself.

Dumb Ass.

And, of course, as soon as we walk in who do we see? Yup. Fucking Misty. Maybe someday Mike will learn to listen before doing what he wants to when he wants to. This night keeps getting better and better. I'm probably enjoying the deer caught in the headlights look Mike has on his face a little more than I should.

"Mike." She says it with reverence as she smoothes out her hair and straightens out her shirt. Interesting. I'm not the only one who thinks so; Jess and Connor are taking it in, too. It's obvious Misty still has feelings for Mike. Isn't that strange, though? They haven't even talked in what…two and a half years?

Stranger still, Mike blushes…flushes? Do guys blush? Fuck if I know, but his face is beet red. Maybe he's just pissed I didn't make him listen to me, but from the look in his eye I would almost say he's happy to see her. Is it a full moon out because this is one strange fucking night.

"Um, hey, Misty, uh…how are you doing?" Holy shit, Mike is at a loss for words, he's actually nervous. If I still thought I had a chance in hell with Kate after tonight I would be happy to see this unfolding right in front of me. It doesn't matter—even if Kate wanted me back, after what I saw, there's no going back.

It's over.

"Oh, you know, working my way through school and taking life one day at a time. It's been a long time, Mike," she tells him sadly, but there's an underlying current with them and I can't put my finger on it. Something's just off.

"It has been a long time," he replies as she walks us to our table "Misty, I'd like to catch up someday soon and maybe apologize properly." Her eyes widen as if she never thought the day would come and then she smiles.

"I'd like that, a lot, actually. I heard you were getting back together with Katherine. Congratulations."

"That's news to me… did I miss out on something?" I know I sound like an asshole but God, I'm pissed tonight.

"Oh, I'm sorry, I didn't know it was a secret…"

Connor interjects, "That's my fault. Sorry, Misty. Kate and I were here a little while back and we told Misty she was working on things. Misty, Daniel and Mike are both in a love triangle kind of situation now with Kate; it's a touchy subject."

"Not after tonight, after tonight it doesn't matter anymore," I snap at them.

"How about I give you a few minutes to look at them menu?" Misty says, retreating.

"Daniel," Jess says reaching out for my hand, "I know you're hurting, but you don't mean that. You don't even know that she's going to go through with it."

But I know, *we all* know.

"After seeing that, I just can't un-see it. Every time I look at her, that's what I'm going to see." I can feel tears burning behind my eyes but there's no way in hell I'm crying in front of them. Over a girl who didn't even give me the benefit of the doubt.

"She didn't trust in us enough to believe I wouldn't do that to her."

There's nothing but silence as we all look at our menus, and after we place our orders, Mike finally speaks.

"Daniel, I could sit here and let you wallow all night and whine about Kate. Don't you fucking think I want to crawl out of my skin right now with the thoughts of Marc fucking her senseless in the back of my mind?"

Nodding, I agree with him because I feel the exact same way. My skin is crawling thinking about his hands on her, caressing her in all the places I know turn her on. Touching her in all the places I've claimed as mine, making her scream his name as she comes over and over again. Are they using a condom? Or is she letting him ride her bare back like she lets me and only me? Is he tasting her essence right now? Licking her come from his lips and going back for more? Or is he fucking her so hard that her pussy clenches him tightly as she screams out from her earth-shattering orgasm.

Maybe he'll get whiskey dick.

Now I get why girls want details when men cheat. What I can picture in my mind has unlimited possibilities. At least if I found out the truth, my imagination could stop running wild and she *would* tell me the truth.

Wouldn't she?

"Look, Daniel, I'm not happy right now, either. This is my worst nightmare coming true and there's *nothing* I can do to stop it. Kate's hurt, she's reeling, and she's seeking comfort in someone else. She thinks that will make everything better but it's only going to make things worse. Kate isn't built to fuck away her sorrows. You're not the only one who is hurting—we're all hurting—but none of us will be hurting as much as she will tomorrow. Trust me on that."

"So what, you think she's going to take the same downward spiral you did?"

"Hell no, she won't because even if she tried, I wouldn't let her. I don't want to even think about Kate with Marc, but after the past four years, what kind of hypocrite would I be if I didn't forgive her for one night of indiscretions?"

Mike looks at me with a gleam in his eyes but it's not a friendly one. "Look, Daniel, if you can't get past this, it's cool. It actually works out better for me. I can forgive Kate and we can continue to fall back into our old life. This is the way it's supposed to be, anyway. You were never supposed to be a part of her story, and the sooner you get that into your head, the better."

Dick,

"So you're enjoying my pain? You're such a fucking condescending prick. Tell me again why we're friends?"

"Hey," Connor intervenes. "Stop it, you two. Nothing is going to get resolved tonight. We're just going to have to wait and see what happens. But if you both need a reminder why we're friends, it's because we're *all* condescending pricks."

Fucking Connor. He's probably the only one who could get me to laugh. Misty brings the food and slips Mike her number, telling him she would like to catch up sometime. She seems really nervous, but then again, so does he.

It seems like every sixty seconds Jess is checking her cell phone, hoping to get a text that is never going to come. I'm just ready to go home; I need to get drunk.

"What do you think about all this, Jess?" Maybe if someone can give me insight on Kate it will be her best friend.

She looks at me sadly. "Honestly. Daniel. I don't know what's going on with Kate lately. She's not the girl I know and love. This has been really hard on her and I know she's retreated into a dark place inside to try and work through it all. She's been different since that weird night when you all were at Vanessa's. If I had to pinpoint the shift. it would be that night."

That's the night she cut me off and stopped really talking to me. Maybe she's just already picked Mike and this is just her way of trying to let me down easy.

"No, Jess, she was acting different before that night. It started when she found out these asshats are friends," Connor argues with her but Jess isn't having it.

"Her weirdness *started* that night, but back when she decided to date them both she was actually sort of happy. Who knows? Maybe the reality of dating two men actually just crashed down on her that night? It's not like you guys are giving her an easy choice, seriously. 'Hey Kate, do you choose, fuckability number one or fuckability number 2? Remember, they *are* best friends *and* brother's, but there are no wrong answers here' Yeah right, I'd be a freaking mess, too."

I'm so over this. I just want to go and drink. "Well, she chose fuckability number three tonight, which I guess really makes him fuckability number one. Can we go now? I've got a date with a bottle of Jack Daniel's."

Mike drives us all back to Kate's house in silence. The house is dark, of course, and so is Vanessa's. Connor and Jess decide to spend the night here and wait for Kate. Mike and I go home in separate trucks. On the way home, I stop off at the nearest liquor store and spend over five hundred dollars on whiskey, tequila, and vodka. I've made the store owner's night and I've got enough alcohol to get us all through this god awful weekend.

When I walk inside with my box of booze, Mike laughs and points to his own box of booze. It's almost comical that one woman can drive someone to want to drink like this but it's not funny because she's one exceptional woman.

Silently, we sit, taking shot after shot, each of us texting every few minutes. I bet if we exchanged phones we would either laugh or beat each other's asses at what we're texting her.

"So, you'd really take her back knowing she's letting Marc fuck her brains out right now?" My words are slurred and things are about to get deep because we're so drunk.

Mike looks thoughtful and then answers with slurred words of his own. "Who am I to judge her? All I'm trying to do is earn her forgiveness, so if I can't give it why should I get it? Fuck, Daniel! I hate Marc…like so much…so much that if I knew…" Then he whispers very loudly, "If I knew I could get away with killing him and never get caught, man, I would do it in a hot minute."

Me, too.

"I didn't like the way he jumped between you two that night he was here. We should have taken him out then."

He nods frantically at me. "Fuck yeah. He's a cocky SOB, that's for fucking sure."

"Mike?"

"Yeah, buddy?"

"Why don't you like him? Did he do something horrible or something?"

Mike hangs his head for a minute and then pours us both another shot of whiskey. "I've never told anyone this and you can't tell anyone either, Daniel."

"Okay."

"No, dude, I mean it…this can never leave this yard, if you remember it tomorrow. Kate can *never* find out."

Damn, it must be serious because he's so super serious. "I've never liked Marc, and when we were about twelve, I heard him tell some of his friends he was going to 'tap that ass' one day when Kate walked by. That really started my dislike of him. Progressively, it got worse and he got possessive of their time together. Like she was his girlfriend or something, you know?"

"Oh, hell no," I tell him, passing him another drink.

"Exactly, hell fucking no. So one day, I ran into Marc at my gym. He was dropping off some girl and making some crude remark to her about her coming back to his house so she could taste the cream inside his chocolate cock this time. She laughed and said something alluding to how big his black dick was and how she needed time to recover because she was already walking funny."

"Man, I seriously did not need to know he's well hung. I was hoping for a steroid dick on that fucker." I tell him dejectedly.

"Don't worry about that. I know a girl who's been with him that I hooked up with about a year ago. She said we're about the same and that it's nothing she would go back for. I don't know if she's telling the truth, but it's comforting. And, uh, since I've seen you fuck and I know what your dick looks like I don't think you have anything to worry about, either."

The level of uncomfortable when he says that is so funny! That is one thing we've never talked about is how our dicks compare in size. I don't think most guys ever have that discussion. "Okay, but none of that really explains why you hate Marc." I'm impatient. I want to know where the hatred comes from. I want something else to hate him for.

"I'm getting there. So anyway, after I finished my workout I went to the locker room to shower and change. There was no one in the changing area but I could hear people fucking in the shower. Marc was fucking this chick, the one that had just told him she was sore a little while before."

"Okay…" I say, encouraging him to get on with it.

"So when this chick came, which by the way sounded so fucking hot, she called out his name over and over. When Marc came, he cried out 'Katherine, oh yeah, Katie Grace. Fuck me, baby girl.'"

"What the fuck? Why the hell would he do that?"

"I almost threw up right then and there. He never saw me and never knew I heard anything."

"Guys don't do that shit. He had to know you were there; he *had* to be fucking with you." He's shaking his head vehemently.

"He didn't know and I overheard this girl a week or so later talking to her friend at the gym. She told her she'd been hooking up with this guy who could fuck her into submission anytime but that she was going to have to call it off because she couldn't take him calling out someone else's name when they fucked. Man, we were only seventeen at the time. He's been plotting this for a long time."

"Well, hell…" That's all I can say.

"Kate has no clue. I know they have their sexual tension and everything, but this would really freak her out if she knew. Who knows, maybe he doesn't do it anymore—maybe it was a phase—but he's been in love with her a very long time."

"So now that they're fucking do you think she'll pick him?"

"Nope, and maybe that's why I'm not letting it bother me as much as I should be. She doesn't love him like that; she's just using him for an escape. She loves us like that. Maybe one of us more than the other," he replies thoughtfully.

"You think so? I don't know. She's super pissed at me right now and she's lashing out. Sorry you're paying for it, too." When he laughs, I laugh, too.

"Daniel, I'm paying for it anyway. She's letting me back in but her heart hasn't opened completely to me. Not *yet* anyway. Can you really do it, though? Let her go because of one mistake?

You do realize that tomorrow she will consider this a mistake, don't you?"

"It's not like she accidentally fell on his dick."

"Oh, you mean the way Vanessa fell on yours tonight?"

"You're an ass, did you know that?"

"Absofuckinglutely and I like it that way. Stop being a bitch, Daniel, and get over this shit. You're dating her but she's not your girlfriend, you're not exclusive. She can fuck whoever she wants to and so can you." What is with the change in his attitude suddenly?

"Look," he says, finally slamming his glass down and wobbily getting to his feet, "I lost her once because I didn't believe in her enough. Don't make that mistake, you'll regret it."

"You sound like you're giving up." Would he just give her to me?

"No, I'll never give up on Kate, not ever. As long as my heart is beating she'll own it completely, but I admitted to myself a while ago that this is her choice not mine. All I can do is love her and earn her forgiveness. Everything else is up to her. Night, man."

"Goodnight."

I'm not sure how long I sit outside thinking about our conversation before finally stumbling upstairs to my room. Before passing out, I call Kate one last time.

"Kate, we all know what you did tonight and I wanted to say I'm sorry for whatever small part I played in it. But, Kate, here's the thing; you didn't believe in *us*, you gave up. You let all those outside influences get in the way of our love. I can never un-see what I saw tonight. The way you were with him, how you opened your perfect little mouth and let him in to taste you. You let him touch you, love you, God, Kate, you let him *claim* you. And how could you not? Because as an outsider looking in that was one of the most erotic scenes I've ever seen play out in front of my eyes. That scene was starring *you* without me, Kate. *You Without Me.* If it would

have been Mike, I could have at least understood, but it *wasn't* me and it *wasn't* Mike and I don't. I don't understand Kate, and maybe that makes me an asshole but I just can't do this anymore. I have to love you enough to let you go now. No, that's a lie Kate. I have to love *myself* enough to let you go. I wish you well, Katie Grace, *always*.

~~~***~~~

When I wake up in the morning, my head is killing me and then I realize it isn't morning but about two in the afternoon.

Fuck.

My body is protesting my movements but I have to get up; I need to call Ben. I'm not surprised I have no messages on my phone. I'm sure Kate is probably passed out in her post coital bliss today.

Fucking Bitch.

That's my hangover talking and I think I need to pacify it with more alcohol. This weekend is going to be spent in one big alcohol induced pity party. Damn, I gotta take a piss before I can call Ben. Why is it when you piss after drinking it takes forever to get it all out? Shit, I think that might have been the longest piss I've ever taken.

Hell, I don't remember bringing the whiskey up, but that's exactly what I'm having for lunch. After taking a shot to calm my nerves, I call Ben.

"Hey, Daniel, what's up?" I can't tell him what I really want; I've got to bullshit him.

"Hey, Ben, are you working tonight?"

"Actually, no, and Callie and the kids went to her parents' for the weekend. What's up?"

I don't like lying to my friends but this one is a necessity. "We're at Connor's and we're going to just have a guys' night tonight. Food, poker, drinking, and maybe a few tattoos. Are you down?"

"Hell yeah. Let me grab my travel kit and I'll be there around five or so."

"Cool, man, see you then."

I'm going to get this tattoo covered up once and for all, completely. Kate was the only person I could have ever imagined filling that spot. If she wasn't who I thought she was, no one will ever be good enough. My stomach is growling. I need some grease if I'm going to keep drinking like this all day.

When I get downstairs, Mike is sitting at the table with a cup of coffee.

"Ben's coming up tonight, want a new tat?" He looks at me suspiciously.

"Actually, yeah I have one I want to get to honor Lila Hope. But what do you need?"

Just then, Connor walks in looking as tired as I feel.

"Jess keep you up all night?" I ask him.

"Kate did."

"Wow, she's really making the rounds this weekend, isn't she? How'd Jess feel about that?"

Okay, I know I'm being an ass and that probably went way too far, but I'm in a shitty mood and I don't care. Instead, I pour myself another shot and forgo the grease for breakfast in lieu of whiskey.

"Look, Daniel, you can be pissed all you want about what happened last night. That's between you and Kate. Well, and Mike and Kate, too, but don't ever fucking talk about my sister like that again to me or we're going to have a major god damned problem. Do you fucking understand me?"

Connor is up in my face and I swear the dude is about to punch me. Mike's just leaning back in his chair enjoying the show. Bastard is enjoying this.

"Sorry, you know I didn't mean it," I say begrudgingly.

Connor takes a seat and Mike asks me again, "What are you having Ben come out to do on you, Daniel?"

"It's pretty obvious that I need a fucking cover up at this point, isn't it?"

"Daniel, don't," they both say at the same time.

"Why not? She obviously doesn't love me the way I love her. Hell, she's dating two out of the three of us and fucking another guy on the side."

Jake picks now to walk in, but at least he's got some food. He pours a bag of burgers onto the table and I immediately grab one.

"I heard you fuckers all had a hell of a night last night. So when are we going to beat Marc's ass? I've got some bats in the car. That fucker is huge; we might need to take him out at the kneecaps first before we can actually beat him down."

Leave it to Jake; he's got me laughing uncontrollably. He's the biggest one of all of us and yet he's still smaller than Marc.

"Nobody is beating anyone," Connor tells him firmly. "Marc isn't a bad guy; he's just what Kate needed last night."

"She said that?" Mike wants to know and I do, too.

"Sort of. Seriously, you guys you need to talk to her. This isn't something I want or need to be in the middle of."

"Ben's coming over, Jake, do you want a new tat?"

"You called Ben? Daniel what the hell are you going to do?"

"A cover up," Connor and Mike reply in unison.

"That's a mistake, a huge one. You need to talk to her before you do that and find out where her head is."

"Oh come on, Jake, really? You're on Mike's side in this whole thing so why should it matter if I get her name covered?"

"Because," he says getting in my space, "you never gave her the chance to choose. Last night fucking sucks but shit, Daniel, she seriously thought you were fucking someone else right in front of her. Give her a minute to come and apologize…or not…maybe she doesn't regret it, but don't take this as an opportunity to make another mistake."

They're all nodding in agreement, even Mike.

"You mean like the mistake I made getting it in the first place? Because right now I agree with you, Jake; it was a huge mistake."

Excusing myself from the table, I grab my whiskey and head out to the garden where I can nurse my wounds in private. A little while later, a hand lands on my shoulder. "Mind if I join you for a bit?" April, I don't know how she knew I needed her but I'm so glad she's here.

"Not at all, come sit with me." When I throw my arm over her shoulder and pull her close, my heart feels a little bit better. We sit in silence for a long time. Sometimes April is less of a speaker and more of a quiet comfort and today seems like one of those days.

"Daniel, I know you don't need anyone telling you what to do and you probably feel like the world is against you right now."

"All very true things, my wise friend."

She looks up at me sadly. "If you really think that then listen to what I'm about to tell you because it's important. Once upon a time, I almost self-destructed and destroyed the only good thing in my life because I listened to everyone around me instead of going to the source of things. There was only one person who could make it better and that was you."

God, I'll never forget that night; she was so down on herself. The other girls were so mean to her just because a beautiful plus size girl managed to steal the captain of the football team's heart.

"Let me help you this time, Daniel. Sober up, leave your tattoo alone, and talk to Kate. The outcome might not be any different, but you'll both feel better once you talk. And this right here," she says, pointing to the bottle of JD, "this isn't making anything better but it sure is making everything worse, including your attitude. JD makes you a mean or an emotional drunk, sometimes both, it always has, McCormick. Don't let your sadness wreck your reality. I get you need the weekend to be sad, that's fine, but call her tomorrow and make time to talk. Until then, keep that tat the way that it is. I haven't seen it but I know you've been waiting a long time to get it. And I know you, Daniel; you wouldn't have done it if it didn't deserve to be where it is."

She gives me a kiss on my stubbly cheek and says one last thing before she walks away. "Jake might be on Mike's side in this, but you've got me, Daniel. *Always*."

Chapter Thirteen – Kate

Shaking. Why am I shaking? "Nooo earthquake stop, *plea*se come back on a day when I'm not hung-over," I groan and hear Jess snickering.

"It's not an earthquake, Kate, but you have to get up."

"Ugh, just go away, Jess. I don't want to hear it right now. Please, I know I messed up last night and I have things to fix but if you don't stop shaking me I'm going to throw up."

Thank God the shaking stops.

"Kate, I'm not here to lecture you, honest. I don't even know if I want to for anything other than you ditching us. You and Marc had that a long time coming. I just hope it was good sex."

"Amazing sex, Jess, absolutely amazing. Even so, my heart still belongs with someone else."

"Well, if that someone else lives at Connor's house, you need to get in the shower and we need to get over there now before something else bad happens."

She's not being dramatic; she's being serious, so I sit up so I can try to pay attention. "Here, I brought you some water and some ibuprofen. You're welcome."

I take them from her gratefully and pray the pounding in my head will lessen soon.

"You said your heart belongs to someone else, do you finally know who?"

"Yeah I do, I think I've always known and just didn't want to admit it because I didn't want to hurt anyone. That worked out well, didn't it? I mean, we all got hurt last night. Mike will never forgive me for sleeping with Marc. *Never.* I'm sure Daniel won't, either."

"Actually, from what I hear, Mike is shockingly okay with everything," she tells me sincerely and my heart leaps in my chest. *There's hope.*

"And Daniel?"

"Daniel is the reason we need to get to Connor's, and the sooner the better. Come on, Kate, this is important and after last night, you owe it to him. You made a huge mistake last night by jumping to conclusions…don't let him make one tonight."

"Tonight? What time is it?"

"It's almost five o'clock, Kate. You've been sleeping all day. I know Connor filled you in on everything this morning before you went to bed, but you should probably get all the messages on your phone out of the way before we leave. You've got an hour, Kate. Be ready."

My stomach is queasy; I decide to shower before checking the messages. I need to be more alert and less likely to climb back into bed from severe depression.

I feel so much better after my shower and once I'm dressed I sit down with my phone. The first few messages are a rotation of voicemails from Connor, Mike, Jess, Daniel, and Chad. Oh God, poor Vanessa. I'm a horrible friend. She was in pain and I thought she was fucking Daniel. It looked and sounded so real. The next message is Marc and it brings me to tears. Absolute, hysterical crying kind of tears.

Kate, I told you I was going to the restroom but really I needed to step into my office for a minute to leave you this message. Tonight has been the best birthday I have ever had and it's about to get a lot better. I need to tell you this before I chicken out, even though on some level I'm sure you already know. I love you, Kate…I'm so in love with you and have been since we were kids. I'm going to do my absolute best to not fall in love with you even more after tonight, but I know it's going to be hard. All my talk of distancing my feelings from the sex was just that…talk. With you, I don't think I'll be able to, and it's okay because I'm sure it's going to be the most mind blowing sex either of us has ever had and will ever have again. Tomorrow, I'm leaving on a two week vacation, and this was planned before I ever knew what was going to happen tonight, so don't freak out. When I get back, we'll talk and maybe by then you'll have made your choice. You know, I can tell who you love, Kate, I have always been able to tell who owns your heart. Baby girl, you need to tell him and let him heal everything that has been broken between you guys. I might not like that you never chose me, but all I want is your happiness. Grab it, Kate, and hold on to it tight, I'm going to try and do the same someday. You make me want to settle, Kate, and if it can't be with you maybe it can be with someone almost as good. I will forever be your soul keeper but now it's time for me to let you cougarize all over my ass. Love you, Kate, now, always and forever. Now, go get your man.

After that message, the tears just keep coming. Why can't I just love Marc the way he loves me? Why do I have to be in love with someone that is going to cause pain to another?

Is it too late to become a sister wife? At least they don't have to break their own heart.

The next message is from Mike and I decide right now that this is a completely make-up free day. His message is short and simple but it's everything I needed to hear from him.

Kate, I knew when I saw you leaving with Marc tonight that you guys were going to finally have sex. The two of you have been a long time coming in that aspect and I don't think a freight train could have stopped it. I know that girls need to explore their sexuality. I know that now more than I ever did when we were together. I hope tonight was special for you and that it was everything you wanted it to be. You know the past few years have changed me, and as much as I thought I would want to murder Marc for this, I know for you... it's just sex. Weird, huh? I never thought you would just have sex for the sake of having sex. I know you love Marc but you're not in love with him. I'm pretty sure I know you well enough to know who you're in love with. I honestly think the only person who doesn't know who you're in love with yet is you. When you figure it out, I can't wait to talk to you about it. The future is bright, Kate, and I'm so glad I get to love you for life. When you're ready to talk, I'm waiting for you with open arms.

Then I get Daniel's last message and it kills me. Last night, I crossed the uncrossable line with him and even if he doesn't love me anymore, I have to make him understand. I can handle him not loving me, but I will never be okay with losing him from my life completely.

"Jess!" I scream and she comes running.

"Kate, oh my God, Kate, what's wrong?" she asks when she sees the tears running down my face and how I'm frantically searching for socks and shoes.

"Where do I start? Marc is head over heels in love with me, so he's taking a breather. Daniel hates me and wants nothing to do with me and Mike…well, Mike is perfect but he always has been, hasn't he?" I ask her with a smile.

"He really has," she replies quietly.

"Let's go, Jess, I'm ready to fix my life. I'm sorry for the hell I've put you through, lately. I love you and I forgive you completely, I just hope you can forgive me."

She hugs onto me for dear life. "Oh, Kate, you're the only person in my life I can't live without. Of course I forgive you, just stop scaring me, okay?"

"Deal."

"Hey, Kate?"

"Yeah, Jess?"

She pauses, trying to decide to say something or not. "Tonight is going to suck but you need to be strong, okay? You're going to finally find out what Daniel's surprise was the night of the wedding and it's going to freak you the fuck out. But he's in a bad spot, too, right now. Just remember that, okay?"

I nod my head affirmatively. "Damn, Jess, I'm such a bitch. I forgot all about that surprise until you just mentioned it."

"Well, you know, it's not like you have an ongoing soap opera in your house or anything. I mean, killers breaking up true loves, true loves becoming siblings, being in the middle of a love triangle you knew nothing about, pregnant ex's showing up out of the blue, all par for the course, right?"

We're both cracking up; I guess my life has become quite exciting lately.

On the way to Connor's we sing Taylor Swift's *Blank Space* and try to keep the mood light but I'm so freaking nervous. I feel like I'm wearing a scarlet letter and I feel even worse when we get there. All we hear is yelling coming from the back of the house so we enter through the gate instead of the front door. When we do, they all stop and stare at me.

Mike is sitting at the table drawing and motions me forward. Connor and Ben pull Daniel inside of the house and April just gives a small wave. I've never felt so uncomfortable in my life. I sit down next to Mike and notice two things. One, he's finally wearing short sleeves and I can see his tats and two, he's drawing a memorial tattoo for Lila Hope.

"That's beautiful, Mike," and it really is. It's a drawing of a fully bloomed gardenia sprinkled with silver. The stem is silver and splits off at the bottom into two parts. Each part forms half a heart and her name is in cursive across the front of the heart. It's breathtaking and all I've ever wanted in a memorial tattoo for her.

"You really like it?" He's like a shy little kid seeking my approval.

I give him a soft kiss and whisper, "I love it."

"Will you get it with me, Kate? I know you said you wanted a certain tattoo. I figured this is the one you were waiting to get." I never thought about getting matching tattoos with Mike before but it makes perfect sense.

"There is nothing in this world that would make me happier, Mike, nothing."

Then I pull his arm out and really look at his tattoos. Each and every one of them has something to do with our past—the moon and stars, the sunken treasure, the catcher's mitt. He takes his shirt off so I can see it all laid out in front of me like a canvas. The script on his chest is his own personal reminder, that even though he was alone, he wasn't lost—just not ready to come back yet. The car with the tombstone as the hood speaks volumes about his life and his thoughts about Grant's death. Lila Hope's tattoo will fit right in next to the catcher's mitt on his forearm, and even though I've never considered a tattoo there before, I want mine in the same spot as his.

"Your arm tells the story of our life, Mike, it's beautiful. I think you should get it here," I say, pointing next to the catcher's mitt. "That's exactly what I was thinking, too."

"It's perfect and I want to match, so I'll get mine in the same spot."

"Kate, you don't have to do that, you wanted it on your hip."

I lace my fingers through his. "I did, but that was before I knew it was an option to do this together. I want them in the same spot. It will mean so much more that way."

Mike pulls me to him and kisses me gently on the lips. His kisses have always been so perfect, even the little ones. I let out a sigh and he pulls me tighter. "I'm going to go get Ben; are you sure about this?"

"I've never been more sure about anything in my life," I tell him truthfully.

When they come back outside, I catch the tail end of their conversation. "Good thinking, Mike. I'll do his tat but after he deals with it first. I won't do it while he's been drinking and he knows that. Hopefully, by the time I'm done with the two of you, he'll be passed out." I'm assuming they're talking about Daniel but I have no idea what tattoo he wants to get now.

Mike goes first and it takes about an hour and a half. I'm a little worried about the pain but he doesn't even flinch. When Ben finishes, it takes my breath away and I can't wait for him to do mine. Ben's an amazing artist; he's done all of Mike and Daniel's tattoos so I'm not the least bit concerned when I hold out my arm for him.

It's uncomfortable and it takes forever to do but it's such an exhilarating feeling knowing that Mike and I are going to be bound forever like this. A huge part of my heart was missing while he was gone and I'm over the moon happy to have it back again. I'm a little sad Daniel has stayed away from me all night and I wonder if I should even go and talk to him.

Once Ben finishes, I can't stop looking at it. All the shading and colors he put into it make it look magical—like something an angel would have created. After he gives me the aftercare instructions and covers it up, I hug him through my tears.

When he sighs, I let him go. "I guess it's time to face the music and go talk to Daniel. Fingers crossed he's passed out already and won't give me hell for not doing his tat tonight."

This is the perfect opportunity for me to go and talk to him. "Wait, Ben, I'll go…we've got a lot to talk about, and if he gets obnoxious I'll show him mine and tell him your hand is tired or you ran out of ink or something."

"Daniel knows I can do a twelve-hour tat without taking a break and this is my road show case and I'd never run out of ink, but it was a nice thought. I will take you up on you talking to him first. In the meantime, I'll have a few beers and then I won't be able to do his tat."

"See, that's an even better idea; just don't let Connor talk you into playing truth," I tell him as I get up "Last time it didn't go over so well." Mike laughs and smacks me on the ass as I walk away.

Ben's voice carries as I walk inside, "I like that one, she's feisty." But it's Mike's response that makes me smile all the way up to Daniel's room. "I'm pretty fond of her myself, have been all my life."

I don't even bother knocking once I reach his room in fear of rejection, so I quietly open the door and peek inside. Daniel is sitting on the edge of the bed with his head in his hands. *Whatever It Takes* by Lifehouse is on his iPod playing softly in the background. It looks like he's crying but I can't tell since his head is down. I try to close the door softly, but he must hear it snap close because he looks up at me. It's one of the most heartbreaking things I have ever seen in my life. There are tears streaming down his cheeks, dark circles under his eyes, and an almost empty bottle of Jack Daniels on the floor next to him, which he promptly picks up and drinks from once he sees me taking in the surrounding situation.

I cross the room without taking my eyes off of him and sit down beside him on the bed. I lean across him, taking the bottle from his grasp and take a big swig of his Jack before setting it on the nightstand. I can tell from his appearance alone that he doesn't need any more, but I sure the hell do if I'm going to have this conversation with him. Taking his hand in mine, I hold on tight as we sit in silence with only the music in the background as our soundtrack. Suddenly, he starts sobbing, grabs me, and hugs me and I'm flooded with emotions. My heart breaks with each and every sob that comes out of him knowing I'm the reason for his pain. "Daniel, I'm so sorry, please forgive me. I didn't mean for this to happen."

"Don't you know I would *never* do that to you, Kate? I know you're all screwed up with dating two guys, but that screws me up, too! The only thing I want is you, Kate—in my bed, in my life, as my wife. But you took that away last night. I saw firsthand how little I actually mean to you. You are my whole world and I am *nothing*." He spits out the last word so bitterly. I know he's angry, but his words break my heart. They also flare up my possessive side.

"Don't you *ever* say you are nothing to me, Daniel. I might be confused, and one of those stupid bitches who just can't make up her mind, but I love you. For three years I was dead inside! Dead, Daniel! And in one night you made me feel *alive* and gave me something I hadn't felt in so long. Daniel, you gave me love, and not just any love, but the purest kind of love."

I'm crying now, too; the both of us make quite the pair. I get off the bed and kneel in front of him, holding his hands. "Daniel, last night was a big miscommunication. I was coming over to ask you to go out with me and when I saw…well, what I thought I saw sent me reeling. So I decided to do what I had said I was going to do all along—loosen up and see where the night took me. Things happened and I don't regret them; it was a long time coming. What I regret is hurting you and losing your trust. I've always been able to keep my distance from Marc, but last night I just didn't think I had any reason to anymore. I knew Mike was sexually promiscuous, even though he's trying to reform, but I never would have expected it from you. I figured if you both were, why couldn't I be?"

The entire time I've been talking he's been rubbing his fingers up and down my arms, careful to avoid my bandage. "Can I see it?' he sounds like a scared little boy.

"Of course you can," I say as I peel the bandage back.

"Wow, Kate, that's perfect."

"It is, I sort of feel like she's finally a part of me now. Like we'll always be together. Mike got one, too."

He nods. "Makes sense; he's been wanting to finish his sleeve. It's kind of the perfect fit."

"I don't know if I can get past this, Kate, and I'm not sure if I even want to try. This pain sucks and if I have to feel it again after you choose…I don't think I'm cut out for that."

"That's understandable, I hate that you feel that way. I hate that I destroyed your faith in me and in us but I totally get it." Pushing up on his knees, I get myself into a standing position. "I'll see myself out."

"Kate, wait!" he calls out as I reach the door. "Baby steps?"

He wants baby steps?

"You want to take baby steps?" Hesitating for only a second, he nods. "I do, but to friendship, Kate. Losing you from my life completely would suck."

My heart falls.

Forcing a smile, I don't feel I reply to his question. "Sure, Daniel, I'd love to take baby steps with you."

Daniel pulls off his shirt and I forget to breathe. I've missed that view.

"That doesn't look like a baby step," I joke, and for the first time tonight, he smiles. That's the smile that pulled me from the dark.

"Actually, I have to show you something. I don't want you to feel bad or freak out, but too many people know and Ben won't fix it until…you know."

What?

In slow motion, he crosses the room and stands directly in front of me. "Remember the surprise I had for you at the wedding?" Biting down on my lip, I nod as he slowly turns around and my world spins on its axis. My fingers reach out on their own accord and trace the lines of my name in his infinity sign.

His forever.

His always.

He thought it was me.

He really wanted me to be his forever; he was in this for the long haul. My tears are falling uncontrollably, my body shakes until I can no longer stand, and for the first time ever I resent Mike coming back into my life. We killed Daniel's love, his grand gesture just another thing wiped out in the catastrophe Mike and I know as love.

"Don't cry, Kate. Please don't cry," he says, kneeling down and pulling me to my feet.

"I've wrecked your life, Daniel, and your beautiful tattoo that was supposed to be reserved for someone special. You're trying to cover it up now, right? That's why Ben came over?"

"Yes."

It's just one word but that one word officially brings down my house of cards and I wail. This isn't just about Daniel or Mike; it's everything that has been locked up since Grant died coming out in a force of nature. Then Daniel, sweet and caring Daniel, in the midst of his pain tries to ease mine. Daniel picks me up and carries me to the bed, removes my shoes, and covers me up. Then he turns off the light and crawls in behind me. Without speaking, he lays with me, my back to his front and wraps his arms around me tight.

My tears are falling and my body is shaking but I've never felt as safe or as loved as I do in this moment. We are all so screwed.

Chapter Fourteen – Mike

"New tattoo?" Misty asks as she pours a refill into my coffee cup.

"Yeah, Kate and I got matching ones last night to honor our daughter."

The look on her face is almost fearful. "You have a child?" her complexion pales as she chokes out the question.

"No, she passed away and I never got to meet her. I didn't even know about her because I was off finding myself." She looks relieved. I've been texting Misty a bit the past few days, kind of getting to know her again, too. I forgot how well we got along in the first place. I can't believe she even forgave me for being such an ass.

Her hand covers mine and she gives it a soft squeeze. "I'm sorry to hear that, Mike, I know that had to have been Kate's worse nightmare come to life. I couldn't even imagine." I think that's one of the things I always loved about Misty is how empathetic she is. It's the thing that made me fall in love with Kate, too, all those years ago. A woman with empathy knows the secrets of the world. Or at least they seem like they do.

"Misty, take your break," her boss says as she walks by.

"Oh, okay," she tells her. "Sorry, Mike, we're down a girl today so I've got to take my breaks when they come."

"Sit with me, have some coffee."

I'd actually really like the company.

"Are you sure?"

"I'm positive."

She flashes me a blinding smile and I remember how much her smile used to make me feel alive. Misty was the only person besides Bev that I ever confided in about Kate. She was such a good friend to me and I treated her like garbage.

As she pours herself a cup of coffee, I take the opportunity to apologize again. "Misty I'm really sorry about what happened before. I was messed up back then, and I know it's not an excuse, but I'm really trying to not be that way anymore."

"Actually, I can tell, Mike. It's weird in a way...before you were hard to crack but now you seem happy and open. It's Kate's influence, right?"

Absolutely.

"It is to an extent, but the longer it takes Kate to get to know me the more I realize I want other people to get to know me, too. Kate spent three years miserable and I spent three years hiding from my feelings. We're both learning how to be new people and it's exhilarating to get to do it together. It'll be easier once Vanessa has the baby."

Her eyebrows scrunch together. "Who's Vanessa?" she demands, probably a little harsher than she meant to by the way her cheeks flush.

"Sorry, I forgot you weren't around for that. Vanessa is Daniel's pregnant ex who drugged me and had sex with me. We don't know if her baby is mine or Daniel's. Odds are that he's mine but I just don't feel it. Maybe it's because I'm still reeling from learning about my daughter, Lila Hope, or maybe it's intuition." I give her a few more details about Vanessa and our rocky history and tell her about how Kate is now supporting her.

She's shocked and it's an adorable look on her. Misty is a pretty girl; she's petite but curvy, blonde and has gorgeous eyes. Did I mention she's smart, too? She works at the diner to put herself through law school. "So you got Kate pregnant and she lost it and you never knew and now you were taken advantage of and might be expecting a baby with a girl you can't stand?"

"That's the gist of it," I reply, thumping a sugar packet before pouring it into my coffee.

"Wow, you must have super sperm or something." She's trying to be funny but her tone comes out uncomfortable.

"Ha! Hardly. Kate was on the pill but we were out of the country and she got sick. They failed to give her the antibiotic warning. Vanessa, well, that was a big fucking slip...since she drugged me, there was no condom. Hence why the baby is likely mine; Daniel bagged it every time he slept with her."

"Well, condoms aren't one hundred percent effective, either. Whenever you have sex you take a risk. That's why I've pretty much sworn off sex with anything that isn't battery operated."

My jaw drops. "You're kidding, right? You've got to have guys lined up at your door. Misty, you're gorgeous."

She blushes and shakes her head. "I'm okay but I've got too much going on to mess up any more than I already have."

"What do you mean already have?"

"Oh, it's nothing I can get into right now but sometime soon, okay? My break is over, anyway, but let's keep talking, Mike. I've really missed you."

"I've missed you, too." And I actually mean it. Misty isn't like other girls, but she also isn't Kate.

I'm on my way back to the house and trying not to dwell on the fact that Kate slept in Daniel's room last night. I know they had a lot to hash out and I'm sure it couldn't have been easy. Between her tattoo, and his, that could have only added fire to the flames.

When I'm about halfway there my phone rings and it's Chad. "Hey, Mike, it's time; the baby is coming today."

"Wait, what? It's too early; I thought Vanessa was okay and it was just a pulled muscle. What's going on?"

"Calm down, it is just a pulled muscle. This is because her blood pressure skyrocketed and it's the only way to get it under control. They're worried about her and the baby with it this high. She's being prepped for a C-section now and they gave her an injection of drugs to help make sure the baby's lungs are ready for the world."

"Alright, I'm on my way. Have you called anyone else?" Holy shit, Vanessa is having the baby. We'll know who the father is by tonight.

"Yeah, I got hold of Kate. She was having breakfast with everyone else and said they were on their way."

"Okay, see you in a few."

After disconnecting the call, I seriously start to lose my shit. I'm not ready to be a dad, not with Vanessa. All the years I wished for a baby with Kate and I'm wishing this one away. It's not that I won't love Lucas…I already do…one way or another, he's family. I'd just rather be his uncle than his dad. Does that make me a horrible person?

For a hot second, I debate about calling my mom but decide against it. There's no need to bring her into this mess unless this baby is actually mine. Kate, I just need Kate right now. Speak of the devil, they just parked three spaces down from me. Everyone is tense as we walk inside; Kate takes my hand in hers and squeezes it. I notice that she and Daniel are keeping their distance. That's interesting.

"How are you holding up?" she asks me sweetly.

"I'm okay," I tell her, placing a kiss on her forehead. We all anxiously pile into the maternity waiting room and the guy Rick has doing the DNA test is already here waiting for us. The only reason I know this is because he greets Daniel by name and announces where he's from.

Forty-five minutes later, Lucas Hunter M… makes his way into the world. Thirty minutes after that, his DNA has been swabbed and is on the way to the lab. So far so good. He's a little tiny, just over five pounds, so they are taking him to the NICU for overnight observation, but he's breathing on his own which is a great sign.

Vanessa is still in recovery. They are having a difficult time getting her blood pressure under control and Chad is with her. Kate promised them she would keep an eye on Lucas and she does. She's glued to the window just staring at him in awe. At first I thought she was trying to figure out who his dad is, but she's not. Kate is literally taking in the wonder of a newborn child. I look down at my new tattoo and let my heart bleed a bit for the loss of my own daughter.

In the meantime, Connor is trying to figure out whose baby it is but he's not having any luck. Lucas is red and tiny and wrinkly. He doesn't look like anyone but himself—his eyes are a blue-grey color but the nurse said all babies have eyes that color. The next eleven hours are going to take forever to pass.

Jess took a trip to Starbucks and brought everyone back some coffee. I've been texting a little bit back and forth with Misty. She's trying to distract me and I still can't get over the fact she is being so nice to me and actually forgave me after the way I treated her.

"Mike, do you want to come and see the baby?" Kate asks sweetly but I decline. Frustrated, she goes to Daniel. "How about you, Daniel, do you want to see the baby?" Daniel declines as well. She's getting even more frustrated. The nurse said someone can go in with Lucas and feed him. Chad won't leave Vanessa's side and Vanessa isn't stable enough yet to even come to the NICU and hold the baby. Neither Daniel nor myself want to get attached until we know how he relates to us and Kate doesn't feel comfortable doing it because she wants his parents to feed him first.

The nurse goes to check one more time to see if Chad wants to feed the baby and comes back with strict orders. She takes Kate by the arm and leads her to the washing and gowning station. "The baby's mother said there is only one person aside from herself she would want to give Lucas his first feeding and that's you, Kate."

Tears are streaming down her face and she's nodding, doing what is asked of her, but I know what a bittersweet moment this is for Kate. Now here were are, Daniel and I, in front of the nursery window watching Kate sit with Lucas trying to feed him from this tiny little bottle. Five minutes ago you couldn't have dragged us to this window and now you can't drag either of us away.

For me, it's a sad moment because I'm wishing this was a memory we had with Lila Hope and the thought that Kate could be feeding my child with another woman right now makes me sick. Daniel watches her with longing. This is what he wanted, a baby and a life with Kate. Now, after her night with Marc, he's barely able to talk to her. They've got a long road ahead if they're ever going to be friends again. I'm glad Kate and I have so much history to build off of to come back from our problems. She and Daniel barely knew each other and that's why they can't just pick up and build off it.

When Kate finishes feeding Lucas and the nurse puts him back in the bassinette, the doctor comes in and checks him out all over again. It's decided to still keep him here as a precaution but he'll be discharged to the main nursery in the morning. Vanessa did well; she brought him into the world happy and healthy. Once Kate takes the gown off, she flees to the restroom. I'd give anything in the world if I could take away her pain.

Daniel is driving me crazy; he won't stop pacing. If he keeps it up, at this rate they might give him his own padded room. Kate tries to talk to him when she comes back but he brushes her off. The pain she's feeling is written all over her face but only time will fix this mess, well, that and possibly a DNA test.

Vanessa is finally brought to a room about seven hours after her delivery and her blood pressure is looking good. She's tired and sore, which is to be expected for sure; she just had major surgery and a baby. Well, I guess it's considered one thing, but fuck that...to me, either one is a major feat. We take turns rotating in to see how she's doing and by now Kate has a full video collage of Lucas on her phone. Vanessa can't see him until they discharge him from the NICU and into the main nursery in the morning. The doctor doesn't want her up and around just yet since they just stabilized her pressure. The man is a stickler for protocol and is flipping out about the DNA results; he wants us to hold off delivering them. Vanessa and I both explained to him that knowing will be much less stressful than not knowing and he finally relented.

Thank God.

For the first time, I really pay attention to how Chad and Vanessa interact together and it reminds me of Kate and me. I'm happy she has someone who loves her like that and who wants to raise the baby with her. I might still think Vanessa is a bitch in the back of my mind but I get the fact that she made a mistake and deserves forgiveness just like the rest of us.

Daniel swaps with me for his visit with Vanessa and I find Kate in the lobby. She's sitting curled up on a couch in the corner. After taking the seat next to her, I pull her into my lap and she rests her head on my shoulder.

"What are you thinking about, Katie Grace?"

She sighs, "I'm just thinking about what blessings babies are and how I wish with all my heart and soul that I could have spent just a day with Lila Hope."

"Me too, Kate, me too."

"What's going through your head, Mike? How are you dealing with all of this?"

"Honestly, I've been thinking how natural you look with Lucas in your arms. You were born to be a mom, Kate. It doesn't surprise me, though; you had one of the best ones ever. I know you don't like to talk about Lila but out of all the bad things that have stuck with me from the day she died only one thing sticks out more."

"What would that be?" she whispers.

"That right before it happened she told you so many times how much she loved you. That was a gift from God, Kate. The last words she ever said and they were professing her love for you. No parent would wish to go out any other way."

She looks surprised. "All these years, Mike, and I've never thought about it that way. Not once. Thank you" she says, placing a kiss on the top of my head. "You've always had a way of making me look at the bright side of things."

"You seem a little more at peace now, is it because Lucas is actually here?" I'm really curious to know what she's thinking.

"No, it's because I realized that night at Vanessa's when Daniel went all Chad crazy how much I already loved Lucas. All the time I spent with Vanessa—rubbing her belly, feeling him kick, getting to talk to him—I guess it was therapeutic in a way. Lucas will change things no matter who he belongs to, there's no doubt about that, but we can all still be happy regardless."

And that's why I love her so much because eventually no matter how bad a situation is she'll find a bright side to it. "So what about Daniel? How did that go last night?"

"He agreed to taking baby steps to try and regain our friendship but he's not interested in a romance. I broke his heart and the tattoo probably just made it break harder." The tone of her voice is so sad; Kate hates the idea of hurting anyone, let alone actually doing it.

"You finally saw it, that's good. It's been a secret for way too long. Besides, I think it was only a secret from you. Everyone else had already seen it and freaked out about it."

"I hate that I've wrecked his idea of the way he wanted to display his love on his skin. It's partially my fault, when he mentioned it I told him I couldn't wait until the day my name was there."

Kate wraps her arms tighter around my neck and I pull her closer to me. "It wasn't your fault, Kate; it was too fast for anyone. The sentiment was nice, but anything could have happened. If it wouldn't have been me, it would have been Vanessa or Marc. The timing for all of us right now is just off. What was that thing your mom used to always say when things started going super crazy all at once and lasted for a while?"

The laughter that peals out of her is a welcome sound. "Oh man, I had almost forgot about that. She would always say 'Mercury must be in retrograde'."

I'm laughing with her, "Yup, that was it. Well, right now that must be happening." Lifting my head to the ceiling, I call out, "Hey, Lila, wanna see if you can pull any strings and fix this Mercury in retrograde situation…thanks, love!"

Kate's crying but at least they are tears of happiness instead of sadness. Daniel shoots us a dirty look, but I don't give a fuck, he can blow me. If he wants to hear Kate laugh he should be talking to her.

"Come on, let's go to the cafeteria and get some dinner." After pulling her to her feet, we walk hand in hand all the way there.

~~~***~~~

Twelve and a half hours.

That's how long it took for the guy from the lab to come back with the DNA test results. By now, Bev and Rick have shown up, too. Bev just couldn't wait any longer; she said she wanted to be here for her boys to see her first grandson. I'm flattered they love me like that, but I still don't want this baby to be mine.

The technician gives the envelope to Vanessa and she nervously opens it. Chad's holding on to her the entire time, and the doctor's standing in the wings, waiting to shout out an 'I told you so' when her blood pressure spikes.

I actually admire Vanessa's strength; instead of being tasteless she actually read through the paperwork and announced her son instead of the father.

"Welcome to the world, Lucas Hunter McCormick."

McCormick not Matthews.

I'm not the father.

Hell yeah! I'm not the father.

There are a myriad of expressions and a host of congratulations flooding the room. I know Vanessa wanted Daniel to be the father; it's a much nicer story to tell your child that you dated his dad and not just drugged him for sex. Besides, they *did* have a relationship that lasted a decent length of time.

Kate gives hugs and congratulations and then quietly leaves the room. Once she is out, though, she flees like a bat out of hell and I'm right behind her. I find her just around the corner on her knees, sobbing hysterically. It's the way I figured she would be but I was hoping I was wrong. After picking her up off the floor, I carry her out to my truck and drive her home. I'm not leaving her alone so I pick her up and carry her upstairs and climb into bed with her.

I stay by her side until she cries herself to sleep and then I pull her close to me and hold on tight for what is sure to be the last time. Because no matter how much I wish she was in love with me, I know she isn't. The first time I really suspected it was that night Daniel seemed jealous of Chad, but what cemented the knowledge was the night she fled from Vanessa's house when she thought she saw them having sex.

That's the real reason I wasn't as upset that she slept with Marc, because by then I already knew for sure she wasn't mine anymore. The crazy thing about it all is that I'm not even mad she didn't choose me. Sad and heartbroken, without a doubt, but she loves one of the best people I've ever met in my life. How can I be angry about that?

Everything happens for a reason; I've always believed that and so has Kate. Once she can finally admit her feelings to me, we can talk strategy. Daniel is one of the most stubborn people I have ever met, and if I'm going to lose Kate because she's in love with him, then he damn well better love her back. I know he does; he's just closing himself off because he's afraid to love her again and then lose her to me. Somehow, I've got to get them on the same page, but it's not going to be easy now that Lucas is here. I haven't quite figured out yet if Lucas is going to be what brings them together or what tears them apart for good. Either way, I'm here for them both.

I pull Kate's body closer to mine and slowly drift off to sleep in the best way possible. With the only person in the world who loves me unconditionally wrapped in my arms. My best friend, and the mother of my daughter, Katherine Grace Moore.

Kate's journey concludes, in Loving Kate, Book Three of The Acceptance Series coming March 2015

Keep reading for an excerpt from D. Kelly's upcoming book,

Just an Illusion coming Spring/Summer 2015

Playlist for Releasing Kate

Keri Hilson – Energy

Taylor Swift – Shake it Off

Sara Bareilles – Gravity

Gavin Rossdale – Love Remains the Same

Blake Shelton – Mine Would be You

Ed Sheeran – Thinking Out Loud

Iggy Azalea & Rita Ora – Black Widow

Chris Brown – New Flame

Jason Derulo – The Other Side

Taylor Swift – Blank Space

Lifehouse – Whatever It Takes

Thank You

I can honestly say that I never thought I would be writing a thank you in *any* book, let alone my *third* book. The only reason I'm even able to write these pages is because you guys are here reading them. I hope with all my heart that if you are reading this page you can feel the heartfelt sincerity in it. Thank you to all the readers who are reading my stories and for being fans. I know it's hard to trust a new author, especially when they write a series. Thank you for believing in me and trusting me to bring you to that HEA we all hope will come in the end.

Thank you to my friends, family, street team, and beta readers for supporting me. Thank you to my fellow authors and bloggers who continue to help out by not only spreading the word about my books, but my giving me such amazing advice on how to navigate my way through this indie world. Thank you for taking the time to read, promote, and review. Your job is far from easy but it is very much appreciated.

Thank you to my amazing editor who has stuck by me through all three books, even with all of my quirks. And a big thank you to my cover designer for the amazing images you create to grace the covers of my books. And a super huge thank you to my PA Ashley for keeping me sane and running things when I can't.

Thank you all for being a part of my story and for taking this journey with me. Hugs and love to you all.

XoXo,

Dee

For those of you who have read my books I know many of you feel strongly about #TeamDaniel and #TeamMike. Your feedback, ratings, and reviews are very important to independent authors. Please leave a rating and consider leaving a review, I'd love to hear your thoughts.

Feel free to visit:

My website ~ http://www.dkellyauthor.com

My Facebook page ~ https://www.facebook.com/dkellyauthor

Google + ~ https://plus.google.com/+DeeKellyAuthor/posts

Twitter ~ https://twitter.com/dkellyauthor

Goodreads ~ https://www.goodreads.com/author/show/7492436.D_Kelly

Pinterest ~ http://www.pinterest.com/deekellyauthor/

Stay up to date on all current news, new releases, and giveaways by joining my mailing list ~

http://www.dkellyauthor.com/mailing-list

Feel free to drop me an email at ~ dkellyauthor@gmail.com

Excerpt from Just an Illusion

Book one of The Illusion Series

Please note all rights are reserved and Copyrighted © by D. Kelly

Prologue

Stories are meant to be told. I firmly believe that or I wouldn't be a writer. And yet, some stories should never be told for a variety of reasons. My story…OUR story…is on the border of both of those thoughts. When I first met them, it was quickly decided I would write their story. And that is a great story—the story I want to tell with all my heart and soul. The only problem is, in order to tell their story I have to tell mine, too, and I'm not sure I'm ready to share my story, yet.

Sighing, I take a look around for a moment and appreciate the silence at the end of the day. It's funny how so many things can change over the course of a few years. I live in the lap of luxury, a beautiful beachfront house with every amenity I could have ever wanted. But at the end of the day, it's just a house, and a house isn't a home until you make it one.

His ultimatum tonight has prompted all of this reflection. He wants to make this a home for us, but he knows my heart may not completely be his.

Is it?

I would like to think so after all this time, but I'm not really sure. The only way to know for sure what I'm feeling is for me to write THE story. His, mine, theirs, and ours—it's the only way.

I fire up my laptop and uncork a bottle of my favorite Pinot Grigio, filling the largest wine glass I own. It's cool and warms me going down. It's soothing and I know that in order to do this, I need something to calm me.

It's just a story, Amelia, you write them all the time. It doesn't have to be published; you're just purging it from your system and getting it on paper. But if anyone ever got their hands on it…

Closing my eyes, I wage the internal battle with myself. He gave me a deadline; I have seventy-two hours to answer his proposal. Three days. I just don't know if three days is long enough for my heart to catch up with my mind. It doesn't matter, he's serious this time. The boys left and went camping, giving me time to do this, to gather myself. It's time to put on my big girl panties and give him an answer. Which leaves me one, and only one option.

It's time to write our story.

Chapter One –

"Amelia! Are you really wearing that to the BAD concert?"

Bastards and Dangerous, otherwise known as BAD, is playing tonight, and from what I hear they are all of the above. I'm not a fan. I've got eclectic tastes in music, but they're just a little too loud for me. And since I'm not a fan, I don't feel the need to wear the 'I'm a groupie' BAD shirt Belle had brought over for me. Instead, I'm wearing my best curve-hugging jeans, my favorite black converse, and a dark blue v-neck sweater. The concert is outdoors at the Greek and it's been fifty degrees out all week which is unusually cold for Southern California. I'm not going to freeze so I can fit in with the crowd.

"Yes, Belle, this is exactly what I'm wearing. Don't like it? I'll happily let you give my ticket to someone else," I reply with a smug smile.

"No, it's fine; you can come just like that. I just hope they're not offended when they meet you and you're not supporting them," she says as she crosses her arms and pouts.

"I don't know why you think we're going to meet them; they are THE biggest band out there right now. And I highly doubt they'll care that one person out of the millions they've met isn't branded in something they make a commission off of."

She rolls her eyes at me, "I've already told you it's inevitable. We've got press seats, thanks to my kick ass job as music editor at Slam magazine, and VIP backstage passes so I can interview them."

I laugh at her, I can't help it. "Belle, I love you, but their manager said if they have time you can interview them. And you know as well as I do that bands don't stick around the venue any longer than they have to. By the time we get backstage, they'll be long gone."

"Nope, that's how it usually works but not tonight. Something big is coming down the pipeline; they're getting ready to announce something. Everyone is talking about it. Slam is the biggest entertainment magazine out there right now and they want us there. They've never sent us backstage passes before. That's why I took them instead of giving them to some rookie reporter. And that's why I want you there, too; since you're an author, you can help me craft an amazing story."

"One book, Belle, I've got one book out. Using the word author is reaching a bit."

"Amelia Greyson! Stop belittling yourself. You may only have one book out, but I know you have at least ten more on your computer you don't think are good enough. Your one book has been number one on the New York Times Bestseller list for the last three weeks! That's huge! That's author status in its finest. You need to be proud of your accomplishment! I tell everyone I can about my best friend, the author. I'm so proud of you, Mel."

Belle is beaming; her smile is as wide as I've ever seen it and I know she's right. It is huge for me, but it could also be a fluke, so I'm not planning on moving out of my crappy one-bedroom apartment anytime soon.

"Alright, we're wasting time being sentimental. Let's get out of here and go meet your BAD boys."

She giggles, "I'm hoping I can get one of them to be bad with me tonight!"

We both burst out in laughter and head down to the limo; Slam sends their staff out to events in style.

Once we're settled in our seats, Belle is bouncing around like an excited teenager, but then again so is almost everyone else here. Thankfully, we're in the press section so it's not too overwhelming with overly excited fans. The people in this section at least pretend to tone it down a bit until the show starts. The opening act was good, but for the life of me I can't remember what they said their name was. Belle is having a blast, just like everyone else. I'm trying to act excited with her, but it's hard to be excited for a band you don't really like.

Music starts blaring and lights begin to flash as the band runs onto the stage one by one.

"How the fuck are you doing tonight, Los Angeles?"

The crowd's response is deafening. Another band member picks up a mic, "I don't think you heard Nick when he asked you, how the fuck are you doing tonight, Los Angeles?"

The crowd screams even louder and I'm wishing I would have brought some earplugs to help take down the decibels a bit. A new band member comes from the side of the stage; he's cute in a tatted down rock star kind of way.

"Alright, we're about to kick this bitch off, but before we do and you all are too drunk and hyped up to remember, Sawyer has some news we want to share with you."

One band member takes his spot on the drums, the other guys are assembling themselves with guitars, and Sawyer takes the mic. He looks a lot like the cute one, just a little more sinful. I think Belle mentioned there were brothers in the band. I can't say for sure from here, but I think he even has dimples. Suddenly, I wish Belle's wish from earlier would come true and we could get them to be bad with us tonight.

"Los Angeles, are you ready to rock?"

More deafening screams. I think a girl in the front row just passed out. Good God, it isn't all that. They're just men. Sexy as sin men, but just men, and self-proclaimed bastards at that.

"First, I want to say thank you all for coming out to see us tonight. There were no California shows on our tour schedule since we're winding down the tour. However, we have some really big news to announce and needed to stop off to give Slam magazine an exclusive interview."

I look at Belle and her eyes are wide as saucers; she had no clue the extent of their generosity when they gave Slam tickets and passes. They really wanted to keep this secret since Slam didn't get a heads up, only an 'if they have time' statement.

"So we figured two birds, one stone. We play for you then do the interview before heading out. And encourage you to pick up Slam magazine in two weeks to read about our exciting news."

More cheers and applause explode as the band kicks off the show. Belle has mellowed somewhat and I know she's wondering how she's going to pull this off in just a few days. I'll definitely have to help her now. Slam just went to print with next week's issue which should be out in a few days. She's got a small window to write and perfect this article before next week's issue goes to print.

Whatever her worries are, she's over them in a flash and she bounces back up to dance and scream the night away. Of course, I'm not a total downer, so I dance along with her, sharing in her happiness. Even though I'm not a fan of the band I'm a huge fan of Belle and this article is going to launch her career even farther. I'm so proud of her.

Before the band comes back onstage for their encore, Belle and I make our way down to the backstage entrance. We're not the only ones with this idea, but we are the only ones with the passes that grant us access to BAD. Thankfully, there are a few bodyguards posted and able to guide us thorough the crowd of crazy bitches. I seriously thought one was going to fight me just to get my pass. Hardcore fans are crazy—throwing underwear, yelling out they want to have their babies. Don't they realize these men are just people? I don't know how they can do this; I don't think I would ever get used to that. How would you ever know someone wanted you just for you and not for all you can do for them?

We're ushered down a hallway where we see the band standing, getting ready to go back onstage. From the looks of it, besides the normal crew and staff, we are literally the only people back here with passes. Interesting…

"We have to go past the band to get to the green room where they'll meet with you later. Please, don't make me get rough with you two. If you have fan girl shit to get out of your system, do it in the green room. Don't say anything to them as we pass, don't freak out and try to grope them. You're here in a professional capacity and I hope you'll continue to act that way."

Belle and I exchange looks and I know she's thinking exactly what I am: this guy is a dick. But he's doing his job and I guess it's got to be a hard one. Belle is a fan but she's professional first. As for me, no worries; I have no need to fan girl over a band I don't even like.

As we pass the band, their PA is giving them a two minute countdown. One of the guys looks up at us as we walk by with an interested look on his face. He's cute, and from the smirk on his face, he knows it. I still feel his eyes on me as we walk by; however, when I cock my head to the side I see it's not him, but the hot one with the dimples who is staring at my ass. These jeans were so worth the price I paid for them they make my ass look great.

Mr. gruff and serious puts us in the green room and lets us know we can help ourselves to anything and he'll be right outside the door.

"Amelia! Pinch me! Can you believe this? BAD gave one and only one exclusive and it's mine! Oh my God! This is going to skyrocket my career as long as I don't screw it up." I can't help but laugh at her. Her work is amazing and she has no need to worry.

"Belle, you've got this. Get your squealing out now, take some deep breaths, and get ready for the story of your life. I'm so proud of you and I'm right here, so I'll help take notes, too."

"Thanks, Mel, I knew I could count on you." After giving me a quick hug, she does indeed get her squealing out of her system while watching the band on the very large TV which is mounted on the wall.

I can't stop thinking about 'dimples' watching me as we passed by. The thought brings heat between my legs. Even if I shouldn't let it, he's not relationship material and I'm nowhere in his league. Besides, all these men have a reputation for one night stands and unemotional flings. Those are two things I can't do. When I'm sleeping with someone, it's because I'm invested in them emotionally.

After the encore, we hear the thunderous applause from the green room. I could swear the walls are shaking from it. Belle starts tapping her foot and picking at her nails because she's getting nervous.

"Belle, you need to breathe. They're just people. You've interviewed tons of musicians before and I've never seen you this nervous."

"I know, Amelia, but this is BAD and they are the holy grail of interviews. I can't help but be nervous, and besides, they're super hot."

I can't argue with her there, they are good looking men.

The voices resonating from the hallway are making their way closer to the room and the door slams open.

"That was fucking awesome! One of the best shows we've done this entire tour. The outdoor venues are so much better, don't you guys think so?" As they talk amongst themselves, I'm drawn in by their excitement.

Watching these men come in on their post-performance high is captivating. Their happiness is almost contagious. Belle and I are taking them in, just watching them in fascination. They've got a posse of people with them. The PA I saw earlier is trying to wrangle them up while I assume a stylist is the one carrying a few extra shirts.

The cute one with the dimples takes one of those shirts, pulls his sweaty shirt off over his head, and I watch, mesmerized, by the way his muscles move. His abs are screaming at me to come and lick them, the beads of sweat he's about to wipe off with the towel are crying out my name. I want to taste his essence on my tongue. But then as fast as the mini porn played out in my head it's over as the shirt goes on. He catches me looking at him and gives me a sexy smirk again. I'm sure the flush I feel spreading over my face is nothing compared to how it looks.

I open my water bottle to try and cool myself down from the sudden heat enveloping my body. He's watching my lips as they touch the rim of the bottle and I wish I was wrapping them around him. I drink slowly, knowing he's watching me and as I glance up, I see him lick his lips. Holy hell, this is foreplay and yet at the same time couldn't be anything further from that.

After about twenty minutes, they dismiss the posse surrounding them and finally sit down across from us. Their manager is an older man with a gentle smile who finally makes all the introductions.

"I'm Warren, BAD's manager, and these are the bastards themselves."

That elicits a laugh from us all and breaks the ice.

"Warren, it's nice to meet you. Thank you for extending this opportunity to Slam magazine. We're honored for the exclusive. I'm Belle Dixson and this is my good friend Amelia Greyson but we all call her Mel."

The cute one snorts out loud and it's kind of a dick sound.

"Amelia and Belle. Look, guys, we've got our own Disney fucking princesses for the night."

"Shut up, Sawyer."

"Dick." It escapes my mouth before I have a chance to even think and Belle looks horrified. Sawyer actually shuts up and a hush falls over the room.

"That was fucking AWESOME! I've never seen anyone call Sawyer out on his shit and I've known him all my life. I'm Nick Weston and I'm very pleased to meet you, Amelia."

I see Belle exhale then flash me a smile. "Nice to meet you, too, Nick."

"I'm with Nick; that was great to see. I'm Darren and the guy at the end of the couch with his head in the book is Wyatt."

Wyatt peeks up from the book in his lap and smiles at us.

"Sorry, I'm behind. I promised my wife I would read this book and I haven't had much time. I wanted to at least try and squeeze in a chapter before we skype on the bus later."

"You're such a pussy, Wyatt. What man is actually reading The O Factor?" Sawyer laughs at Wyatt and my stomach plummets fast as Belle starts laughing. That's my book and this is about to get really uncomfortable.

"One who loves his wife. Why don't you just go find a chick to hook up with already so you'll stop being such an ass."

"What do you think of the book so far, Wyatt?" Belle asks him and I could kill her!

"On or off the record?"

"Off," Belle replies.

"It's interesting. I mean, I've never read a girl's point of view on sex before…it's crazy. It's definitely keeping me reading for sure."

"Well, it has been number one on the New York Times Bestseller list for three weeks so it's got to be good."

Couch, just swallow me up now, please. I close my eyes and take a breath.

"What's wrong, princess Amelia? Are you too prude to talk about a sex book?" Sawyer asks.

Belle laughs so loud and so long tears are starting to pool in her eyes.

"Why do I get the feeling I'm missing something here?" Nick asks.

Belle wipes the corner of her eye and outs me. She's officially off my Christmas list. "Who wrote that book, Wyatt?" Belle asks sweetly.

Wyatt flips the book over and a huge smile breaks out across his face. I don't have a photo on the book, but how many Amelia Greyson's are just out there walking around? My guess is not many.

"I think Sawyer is about to eat his words. This night is getting better and better." Wyatt grabs a pen off the table and brings his book to me. He's going for dramatic. Lovely.

"Miss Amelia Greyson, will you please autograph my book for my wife? And before you say no, just keep in mind she's a huge fan and if I tell her I met you and didn't get your autograph, I won't be getting any O's, either. Her name is Beth."

I can't even bring myself to look at the rest of these guys. Belle is giggling again and I make a note to kill her when we leave here. But Wyatt asked so nicely; how could I not sign his book? I reach out, taking the pen and book from him, and autograph it quickly. I look up when I hand it back to him and all eyes are on me.

"Never judge a book by its cover, Sawyer," Nick says to him smugly but his eyes and smile are focused solely on me.

Nick's beautiful. I know, it's odd to describe a man that way but he is and so is Sawyer because they look practically identical. Their eyes are green as a forest, they each have strong, jutted jaw lines, and both are about six feet tall. Sawyer has dimples where Nick is lacking them, but Nick has personality where Sawyer is just an ass. Nick has coppery brown hair but Sawyer's is black. Sawyer has his lip pierced, Nick his eyebrow. Both have tattoos. I wouldn't kick either out of my bed.

Made in the USA
Monee, IL
20 November 2025